00 2016727 X 8

CW01180297

METROPOLITAN BOROUGH
OF SEFTON
LEISURE DEPT.
3 MAY 2008
WITHDRAWN
FROM STOCK

JUL
03.
09.
07. NOV
28. NOV
27. DEC

SEFTON PU
CROSBY L
CROSBY R
WATERLOO
L22 0LQ
TEL 0151
     0151
FAX 0151

A fine will be charged

2.
02
12
DEC 06
06.
0151 - 928
0151 - 257
0151 934 5770

plus the cost of reminders sent

Command Influence

Command Influence

Jack Ehrlich

ROBERT HALE · LONDON

© Jack Ehrlich 2000
First published in Great Britain 2000

ISBN 0 7090 6593 0

Robert Hale Limited
Clerkenwell House
Clerkenwell Green
London EC1R 0HT

The right of Jack Ehrlich to be identified as
author of this work has been asserted by him
in accordance with the Copyright, Designs and
Patents Act 1988.

2 4 6 8 10 9 7 5 3

Typeset by
Derek Doyle & Associates, Liverpool.
Printed in Great Britain by
St Edmundsbury Press, Bury St Edmunds, Suffolk.

Prologue

Waiting for the jury to come in is always the antsiest part of any trial. Not having tried a case in almost five years, I'd almost forgotten that feeling in the gut as one waited. And as I sat on the top floor of the county office building trying to do all the things that required my attention, it occurred to me that taking on this case personally was not because of outrage over the crime nor because I do not have assistants capable. Nor was it because of the amount of publicity.

Knute Helbig had been goaded into trying this case. It is September, a warm beautiful one, but also an election year and for the first time ever, I am being challenged. Challenged by a hot-shot prosecutor from the Manhattan district attorney's office, the city's chief prosecutor who had moved into my county and immediately won his party's nomination to take me on.

'He's a feather merchant, a pencil pusher and, at best, a civil servant mentality who's lost his touch.' That was the accusation. Perhaps my opponent was right: I ran my office, I picked my assistants, I judged what pleas to take or reject. I was adviser to my assistants, attended meetings which varied from budget battles to feely-touchy discussions. But in almost five years, I had not done what district attorneys do – try cases.

They do not call Norwegians square-heads for nothing. They mean thick as shit. Guilty, Knute Helbig.

So this square-head was goaded into trying the most brutal first-degree murder case in the county in eleven years. Only cop killers in New York face first-degree charges that could lead to the death chamber. And this felony involved cop killing. I did not take this case because he'd been a cop. Nor because of all the publicity. Knute Helbig has been district attorney for the county so long, I do not need name recognition. I am not a feather merchant. I am not a pencil pusher. I do not have a civil servant mind.

But as district attorney, after three terms unopposed, I became an administrator. And now Knute Helbig as well as Tyrone Jackson was on trial. If this defendant was acquitted of killing and brutalizing a cop, he'd be free and I guess I could be out of office. However, that would not be the worst thing in the world for me either, because my wife Mary would love to return to England. But Tyrone Jackson would be free to kill another cop.

Perhaps, I reflected, it had not been goading at all. Perhaps it was boredom. Being a trial lawyer is an exciting job. It upsets the stomach, makes the adrenalin pump. It's combat, and a far cry from being an administrator. My assistants had the fun while I worried about justifying the office budget to the legislature.

The buzzer on my intercom took me out of my musings.

'Yes, Jenny?' I said.

'No,' my secretary said laughingly, 'nothing yet from the jury. Jim Walsh wants five minutes.' Jim Walsh was my chief assistant.

'Send him in, Jenny, if you please.'

Jim Walsh had been orphaned at the age of ten when his parents took a vacation flight to Mexico that got as far as Iowa. He was raised by a series of relatives and orphanages, joined the Marine Corps at age seventeen and from there directly to the New York City Police Department. It took him twelve years to get his bachelor and law degrees, working straight nights so he could cram as many courses as possible each term. I had hired him straight out of law school, even before he passed the bar exam at a time when I was still an assistant district attorney, chief of the investigations bureau. He's been with me ever since.

I always think of Jim Walsh when I hear sob stories about how a tough childhood had caused a man to go wrong. Jim had a bad childhood and had always gone right.

'Hey boss,' he said coming in and slouching into the chair in front of my desk. 'No word yet?'

'Nothing.'

'How long they been out now?'

'They were sequestered after the judge's charge last night. They've been at it since ten this morning.'

'That's almost four hours. What do you think?'

'I would have liked them to say they didn't need to retire from the jury box because the defendant was guilty as shit, so let's get on with it.'

'Yeah, Knute, so would I. But I'll be god damned if I can ever figure out why you had to try this one. It was a dirty bastard crime and all but all of the evidence was so circumstantial. I mean horrible as the killing was, all of our evidence was so damn dicey.'

'Just before you came in, I was wondering myself if I took it on because my unnameable opponent called me a feather merchant, etcetera. At first I thought he goaded me into it. But only small county DAs try cases. Big county DAs have to administer the office. I don't think Henry Morgenthau (New York County District Attorney) ever tried a case in his life, and he is the most respected DA in the country.

'No, Jim, I think I was just bored with all the bullshit of running an office. I think I just got the hankering to get my hands dirty again, to get into the pit and slug it out. You know, when Ken Jason Jones said he'd take the case *pro bono*, maybe that was it. I guess I don't really know.'

'Yeah, well. A black kills a white cop. A black defense lawyer comes in *pro bono* to defend. This trial had all the trappings of the OJ Simpson case. You sure didn't pick yourself a sure bet, boss.'

'Well, I could have been one of those Republican Congressmen who tried to sink Clinton in the Senate. Clinton will go after them like a duck on a June bug. None of them better buy green bananas,' I said.

'You think that thing was on the level, boss?'

'Everybody knew before any evidence was advanced that the vote would be for him. It was politics, not justice, and it violated the Constitution.'

'Yeah. If that dumb bastard Jablonski hadn't admitted he hadn't read him his rights, the confession could have come in.'

'Jablonski is as dumb a son of a bitch as I ever met. But he is honest, even if it kills us all.'

'Well, anyway, I got a bunch of things you got to decide, boss. I got a list. First being a sexual abuse charge one of our girl dicks is bringing against Flanders. . . .'

The intercom buzzed. 'Yes, Jenny?'

'The jury has returned, boss.'

'Thanks, Jenny.'

'This the toughest case ever, boss?'

I smiled. 'No, Jim, many years back, when I met Mary, I tried a bitch of a case. It was the only time in my life that I was a defense attorney. I knew I had an innocent man at my side, my former brother-in-law. I also knew about a thing called command influence. The thing I feel in my gut right now, I felt then. It was something. That's when I met Mary.

'I remember it all started on a Sunday when I was watching a big time football game. A Giants game, I think. . . .'

1
Football

The telephone call came on Sunday afternoon just before half-time in the Giants–Bears playoff game. A lousy time for the telephone to ring.

'Jesus, Knute, don't answer the goddam thing,' one of my guests, Ricci, yelled.

'For God's sake, let it ring,' my other guest Vizzi said.

I shrugged helplessly, got off my seedy couch and went to the small front hall a few steps away, to answer the phone. They both knew I had to answer the telephone. If I was not at home I had to have the car receiver on, or when I was not in the car, the omnipresent beeper. Neither Ricci nor Vizzi gave a particular damn, of course, if I was called out. But since they were with me, they'd have to go also. Except for the times they had night or weekend duty, they were not on call. But they knew since they were right here, I'd take them rather than hunting down the duty detectives. The duty detectives were invariably on a call at the other end of the county.

'Hello,' I grunted, watching the Giants trying to get close enough for a field goal in the final minutes of the half. The game was tied.

'Is this Knute Helbig?'

'Yeah.'

'The attorney?'

'What's this, twenty questions?'

'Oh, I'm sorry. This is Lieutenant Day, Judge Advocate General. I'm calling from RAF Singlebury. That's in England ... outside London.'

'What can I do for you, Lieutenant?'

My guests had been straining to hear what our fate might be this football afternoon. When they heard me say 'Lieutenant' they groaned loudly in unison.

I covered the mouthpiece. 'Relax, It's a soldier calling from England.' They turned their full attention back to the game. Soldiers from England were no threat to the second half.

'You are Paul Kelly's brother-in-law?' The line was so clear the call could have originated next door. Except for the accent. Nobody on Long Island sounded like the voice I was hearing.

'I *was*. Lieutenant, would you hold on a minute? I want to take the call in another room.' I put down the phone, went into the bedroom just off the tiny hall, picked that phone up and put it on the bed, returned and hung up the hall telephone and then closed the bedroom door and picked up my bedside phone. To most people, it would seem wasteful to have two telephones ten feet apart, but not in my line of work. Also, the county paid for the telephones which was fine, except that every month I had to go through the printout to check and pay for my private calls.

'OK, Lieutenant, all set,' I said, lighting a cigarette. 'I was married to Paul's sister. Matter of fact, he lived with us on and off for about five years after his father died and Momma went to work. Until he joined the Air Force. I take it he's in trouble ... again.'

'Real bad trouble, Mr Helbig. I've been appointed as his counsel. But I don't think I can do much for him.'

'You'll have to explain that, Lieutenant.'

'I intend to. That's why I'm bothering you on a Sunday. It's the only way I can use the office tie-line without everyone hearing me. I'm alone here now, so I can talk. Our base commander is going to convene a court martial. Every member of the board will be hand picked. The officer-in-charge of our office, Lieutenant Colonel Kuss, will prosecute. I work for the boss in the same office. The base commander has sent officers who displease him to Greenland.

'I'm in my second year of a three-year commitment. Right out of law school. I'm way over my head here. Also, I have a wife and baby here and I don't fancy leaving them and going to Greenland for the rest of my tour.'

'Lieutenant,' I said, crushing the Marlboro and taking a swig of my Budweiser, 'I respect your honesty. I know something about military fiefdoms. I also know Paul and I know he is not on the straight road to sainthood. It does not surprise me that with seventeen years in the service, and three to go for a fifty-per-cent retirement, he'd screw himself up. But that's Paul. He's a charmer. He can charm the birds out of the trees. He's also a minor-grade fuck-up. Undoubtedly, he's guilty as charged.

'I suggest you work out the best deal you can and plead him guilty.'

'The Code won't allow that. And, inexperienced as I am, I don't believe he's guilty.'

'I just said he's a charmer.'

'Mr Helbig, I'm very short on hands-on experience, I admit that. But I did graduate with honors from Michigan State Law. I may be raw, but I am not stupid. I know the base commander, Colonel J.J. Smith has his name up before Congress ... to become a brigadier general. I know this case can cause him some grief in that regard. It's going to be a kangaroo court. I can't be part of that. But I can't do anything about it.'

'I just said, plead him.' I was getting annoyed now, knowing the half was over and not knowing if the teams went into their locker rooms tied or if the Giants got their field goal. Somehow, at that moment, it seemed more important than the time and trials of Paul R. Kelly.

'And I said the Code ... the Code of Military Justice ... won't allow that, and I don't think he's guilty.'

Obviously, Lieutenant Day did not know Paul Kelly as I did. Paul was thrust into my life after I returned from the war that nobody wanted and married the girl of my dreams, to coin a real original phrase. I was serving out my time at Langley Air Force Base in lovely Tidewater, Virginia. After the wedding, we moved, Helen and I, into a brand new off-base housing project. My duties were minimal. I had time to come home for lunch and a roll in the sack every day. I had fought for all that was great in the American way of life. And now, with a lovely young wife, was enjoying the fruits. Wallowing in the fruits. I'd saved money overseas because you couldn't spend it. So now, I had a new car and a lovely new house, except for the roaches, and a gorgeous new wife.

Langley Air Force Base, headquarters for the Tactical Air Command, was plush. The officers' club overlooked part of Norfolk Bay. It had a humongous pool and inexpensive steaks and what we now call happy hour.

Soft, wonderful living for the returning hero. And then Paul Kelly showed up on a Greyhound Bus at the Newport News bus station. He was tall for his age and scrawny and he looked dirty, his brown hair full of kid grease. His father had died the month before. His mother, a career woman in the first instance, returned to work. Somebody had to take Paul in. Helen and I were elected.

Paul had been brought up in the best part of White Plains, when it was still a wholly white suburb of New York City. But Daddy died of rheumatic fever, a disease he had had since childhood. There was no insurance, so I got Paul.

By the time we got Paul, my bride and I, he had been in juvenile court three times. The first time he had stolen a bike and rode it into one of the few beat cops White Plains put on the street: The other two related to being a runner for the numbers his candy-store boss operated on the side. We sent him off to private schools, with some financial help from Mother. He kept getting kicked out, the last time for setting up a very successful still. That was a last resort school in Kentucky. So, he stayed with us, quitting high school and working in a car wash and stealing tapes from the car radios.

When I was allowed to leave active duty, I became a New York City cop and I started law school. I received the condensed version of the World War II GI bill. We made ends meet. Paul was eighteen years of age and back in court. If he joined the military he wouldn't go to jail. I personally took Paul to the recruiting office and, with a great sigh of relief, saw him off to Sampson Air Force Base for recruit training.

After that, I saw little of Paul. He apparently mastered aerial radar. He also, while stationed in Tampa, Florida, stabbed a colored cohort. That was the last time I got a call about him. He skated free on that. He also married with no notice to any part of the family. Some five years and two kids later, his lovely, gorgeous sister, Helen, met a man. She had been working in a bank. This man was apparently a high roller. The bank loved him. So did Helen.

The nice thing was, it didn't cost me a dime. If you are very lucky, divorce is like that.

'Lieutenant Day, I appreciate your call. I appreciate your problem. Now, what would you like of me?'

'He ... Paul ... as is his right' – the voice of the Midwest was now very low despite the great connection – 'has requested outside counsel. I agree with him, since everything I told you means I am not capable of his defense. He has asked for you to defend him.'

'Aw, shit.'

2
Football

'What did our boy do this time, Lieutenant?'
'He's charged with premeditated murder. A death-sentence crime, though it usually ends up commuted to life.'

I stood there holding the telephone and staring out a window, in need of cleaning, at the choppy water of the wide canal just a few feet from my bedroom. The wind was whipping the water into white caps and my little Penn Yan was bouncing against her lines and then against the bumpers that kept her from destroying herself against the dock. It was a lousy, cold, damp and sullen December day. Ugly grey clouds that looked nine months pregnant with snow diffused the thin daylight.

'Lieutenant, Paul is no Boy Scout. He once – down at McDill – stabbed a gentleman of color with his pocket knife. Didn't do much harm and was apparently provoked sufficiently to get himself off. I can envision Paul, shit-faced and pissed, bashing in somebody's skull. But not premeditated murder. That's not his style.'

'Paul admits being AWOL. He says he got very drunk, probably because he takes some sort of pain pills. He says he went off the deep end because he still hasn't been able to get housing for his family over here and he's been separated from his wife and kids for nine months. He says he deserves to lose a stripe for being AWOL. He says that will put him down even further on the housing list and it was stupid to go AWOL. But he said he didn't hurt anybody . . . and I believe him.'

Bobby Ricci came into my small bedroom, handed me a cold Bud and helped himself to a cigarette from my pack. Ricci smoked more than I do, but I've never seen him smoke anything but other people's. If he ever sneaked off and paid for a pack it would have to be when there were no OP's anywhere in walking distance.

'Bears are up three at the half,' he grunted, and slouched back to the living-room couch.

'Lieutenant, what am I supposed to do? Drop everything and jump over there to pull his chestnuts out of the fire? I got a job for Christ's sake.'

'Mr Helbig, there isn't much point in hollering at me. I'm the messenger.'

He was right, of course. I was instantly pissed off because here once again, Paul R. Kelly was dropping into my life just as it was getting back into some semblance of order. I have said that I was lucky my divorce didn't cost me a dime. But it devastated me in every other way. When you have thirty-five detectives and six prosecutors working for you and you can't even keep your home together, you start to look funny at yourself and become convinced they do, too. When you try to think of yourself as a macho defender of the defenseless and get hit over the head with the fact that while you are out chasing bad guys your little woman is out giving head, it hurts. No, not hurts, it destroys.

'Mr Helbig, are you still there?'

'Yeah. I'm still here. I don't mean to raise my voice to you, but that bastard hasn't sent me a Christmas card in eight years. I didn't even know he had kids.

'And now he expects me to drop my whole god damn life to try and save his useless butt. I don't think so.'

'As I said, sir, I'm just the messenger. He obviously can't afford to hire outside counsel. He doesn't have the money for that. If you don't feel you can help him, we'll just go through the motions here and perhaps after he's convicted, we can somehow get him a life sentence without parole to Leavenworth. That's better than an execution, I suppose, even if Paul has to spend the rest of his natural life in a maximum security penitentiary for a crime he didn't commit.

'One of my problems, I guess, Mr Helbig, is that we Midwesterners don't understand you sophisticated Easterners. If we did, we'd ... I'd ... understand that inconveniencing your lifestyle for a month or so is much worse than letting a nobody spend his life behind bars and letting his kids grow up with a convict father. I guess we surely did go to different law schools and, just to set the record straight, my name is Day. D-A-Y.'

Lieutenant Day managed beautifully to slam down his telephone. The sound of the slamdown jarred me. 'You little, Midwestern, wet-behind-the-ears cock-sucker,' I said into the dead telephone. 'You sanctimonious little prick.' I slammed the telephone receiver down just as hard. That didn't do a thing for me. I knew standing there, looking out over the canal and the big bay beyond the canal, that Paul R. Kelly had re-entered my life no matter what I did.

3

Helen

Bears beat the Giants by ten. It may have been a good game, but my mind was everywhere but on the game. I always particularly liked the Giants-Bears game. When my kids were little they had a Yogi Bear record on which Yogi left Jellystone Park and Ranger Smith because he had heard on the radio that the Bears were going to battle the Giants. Yogi went to Chicago to help his brothers.

'What's wrong, grump? Beer all stale?' Ricci asked me.

'It was the phone call, Bobby. Some lieutenant recalled Knute to active duty,' Vizzi said.

'Is that right?' Ricci asked in mock shock.

'Like that,' I agreed. 'The lieutenant wants me to go to England to defend my ex-brother-in-law. He's charged with murder.'

'Holy shit,' Vizzi said, 'you never defended anybody in your life.'

'Yeah, but what a blast. You get to wear a robe which you'll never do here, and a curly toupee,' Ricci said.

'It's a court martial; he's in the Air Force.'

'Oh.' Then, after bumming another cigarette, 'They must have legal aid guys in the service. Sure, judge advocate. They do that shit.'

'I did some summary court martial just before I got out of the Air Force. Before I went to law school. It's a regular kangaroo court. The base commander appoints the jury, the judge advocate prosecutes and one of his junior officers defends. If the commander wants the guy there aren't too many acquittals and apparently the top honcho wants my ex-brother-in-law's ass.' I slid further down on the couch, used the remote to kill the locker-room chatter coming from the television and lighted a smoke.

'You're not seriously thinking about going?' Ricci asked.

'Bobby, I don't know what I think.'

'Jees, Knut . . . your *ex*-brother-in-law. What are you, out of your fucking mind?'

'If I go?'

'Hey, buddy,' Ricci said, grabbing my shoulder and sliding down next to me. 'Don't even think about it. That's your ex-wife's brother you're talking about. I lived with you through all that, remember? You don't owe her shit, my man.'

'That's exactly what I owe her.'

'You got that right, old buddy. So, let's forget it and go down to Codfish Bob's for a couple of tap brews. I'm getting bloated on this canned stuff,' Ricci said.

'Yeah . . . you guys go ahead. I want to start the stew and wait 'til it's hot and then put it on simmer. I'll be right along. And don't let me forget we need a loaf of Jewish rye from the deli.'

'Fuck the Jewish rye, kiddo. You have the rare pleasure of serving your Mulligan stew to a couple of Ginzos. We demand a loaf of Italian,' he said, making it sound like 'Eye-talion'.

'Nah, Ricci,' Vizzi said. 'Italian bread was delivered Friday or Saturday. This is Sunday. It would make a better billy than a sandwich.'

The telephone rang again.

'We're gone,' Ricci said, jumping up from the sagging couch with amazing agility. 'Don't touch that fucking machine 'til I'm out the door.' He leaped for the front door with Vizzi lumbering after him. They both grabbed their weapons and jackets and slammed the door so it rattled its poorly fitted glass panes.

'Yeah,' I said into the hall telephone.

'You've just got to go.'

Oh, great. It was the beautiful Helen, sister of Paul R. Kelly. I had neither seen or talked with her since the day, about three years ago, when we sold the house. I wondered briefly how she got my unlisted telephone number, which I shouldn't have bothered wondering about. Helen knew all of my friends.

'Who is this?' I said, just to be a prick.

'You know perfectly well who this is, Knute.' Like all the phoney intellectuals who all were full-up with European culture, she pronounced my name as she was convinced 'real' Norwegians pronounce it. They all say K-newt.

'So? Should I ask how you and the high roller are faring?'

'Don't be cute, Knute.'

'That rhymes real nice.'

'You know why I'm calling. I spoke to that nice Lieutenant Day and they let me speak to Paul. He's just obsessed that you are the only one who can help him. I mean, it's all ridiculous, but he is charged with murder. And murder is a serious charge.'

'Yep.'

'Knute, why are you being like this? We have a family crisis here. Paul needs you. Anthony offered to hire the best legal talent there is, but for some obscure reason, Paul wants you. I told him you don't defend people, you only persecute them. . . .' She giggled a little at that cute-ism.

'It's not *my* family crisis.'

'Don't be difficult, Knute. You've been Paul's hero since he was a little boy. You raised him. You were a father to him. Frankly, I can think of thousands of lawyers I'd prefer to represent me. Any lawyer, for that matter. There are American lawyers in Europe, Anthony learned, that do nothing else but defend court-martial cases. Paul doesn't want any of them: he wants you.'

'He's not as smart as you, Helen.'

'Well, of course not. My God, he didn't even finish high school. But that's neither here nor there. Paul wants *you*. So, we all want you, and Anthony will pay your expenses.'

'How the hell do you know all that?'

'Your "Merry Men" as you call them, have wives. Some of them are still my friends. I know what's going on in your life, don't kid yourself. I even know about the ex-wife of that homicide detective you've been shacking up with. I think her name is Helen, like mine.'

I reverted to type. I said, 'Aw shit.' Then I did a fair imitation of the slamdown Lieutenant Day had done to me.

4
William William

District Attorney William William was not a really bad guy, but God, he was pompous. I think he must have been born that way but I didn't know him until he was an adult, a graduate of the VMI (the finest institution of higher learning in the South, so he said). He had also served as a reserve officer for several years in the navy (the last real gentleman's club left in the world). 'We use marines, sea-going bellhops, instead of Negroes to run our errands, ho, ho, ho.'

We sat this Monday morning of December in his sixth floor office in the H. Lee Dennison building in Hauppauge, New York. It was cold outside, so much so that the swirling snow was too cold to land. It just blew around in angry gusts, tiny snowflakes of no substance. It was an office with a wall of windows looking at a parking-lot and some woods. Wood-paneled, it was filled with a huge desk for the boss, some comfortable chairs, leather not fake, some sideboards, and a couch. There were also several television sets and some other stuff I did not understand and which I know William William didn't understand. It made things look very official and warlike, as though we were in touch with Interpol at all times.

The walls, the good wood walls, were filled with William William. He had now been the DA ten years. There had to be one hundred plaques: wood plaques, metal plaques, fancy, not fancy. And pictures with important people, with caches of dope and guns and so on and so forth. But right as you came in was a picture of the boss, stripped to the waist as we all were, on the fishing boat *Venture 11* out of Montauk. In it were my guys Vizzi and Ricci and a guy who owns an Italian restaurant named Pauli (him, not the restaurant) and a guy named Goldie who was now a squad dick, but who had once saved my life. We had caught blue fish that day, and striped bass and a lot of sunburn. It had been a grand day. I had to love a guy who displayed a picture of himself, gut bulging out, with his guys, in a place of honor among all the awards from Temple Beth-El.

'Well,' I said to the grand man playing with a ball point pen behind his massive desk. 'Well, I don't know. I never defended anybody. I got things to do here. I don't owe. But, I like the rotten son-of-a-bitch. He's a fuck-up, he's a jerk. But he is not a cold-blooded killer. And I know what a court martial can be like overseas. I worked a couple of them. Guilty before the trial starts. He ain't much good. But Jesus, Willy, I never railroaded anybody. You never did either. And as much as you wanted to be DA, I know you wouldn't have done it over some poor guy's body.'

'Your Colonel Smith, I gather, would do so. I say bully. Go. Do it. You must do it, old chap. And it should be fun. And how often have I told you to go to the British Isles? It will be an eye-opener for you, laddie. You have so much time on the books. You can only accumulate one hundred and twenty days. If you don't take some time, you'll lose forty-five days. I respect commitment, old boy. But this is ridiculous. You have the chance to get away, all paid for. You have the chance to appreciate Great Britain. By all means go. Your job is here when you return. You've got fine deputies. Nothing to stop you, old sod.

'You are covered here, Knute. But one thing I insist: your Guinea friend will pay for travel. Well, you must go British Airways. That is my only demand.'

'Jesus, Willy, you are full of it.'

'Perhaps. But that is the condition on which you desert me to defend a murderer. And an Irish murderer, of whom I think the worst. You must fly British Airways. I have stock in it.'

5
British Airways

It was 15 January. A heavy rain whipped by a wicked wind made driving damn near impossible so that Ricci and I got to the British Airways departure doors with less than a half-hour until departure. Earlier I had called the airline, convinced that if I could hardly drive, airplanes couldn't fly. But thanks to William William, who had been totally serious, I was booked on the airline with the stiff upper lip.

As usual, the Port Authority cops let us leave the car in front of the entrance. Port Authority cops always went way out of their way for all cops. Departure time was 2 a.m. We arrived a quarter before the hour in an almost totally deserted airport. All the shops and even the bar were closed and the huge terminal was bright but creepy. I shook hands with Ricci, got my passport stamped and was waved through to the gate. I could have been carrying ten kilos of high grade coke but Customs doesn't give a damn what you take out of the country.

Two stewardesses, or whatever they are now called, checked my ticket and helped me stow my old leather briefcase in an overhead locker where I also stuffed my equally old raincoat. A male stewardess with a pencil-line blond mustache hiding his youth told me, 'Sit anywhere, old chap, we've very few passengers.' William William would have loved him. He would also, and more dangerously have loved the female stewardesses. The uniforms would have made a marine proud.

Although I had been a flier eons ago, I didn't and still do not know anything about airplanes that carry more than two people. I knew that the gooney bird in civilian parlance was a DC3, but except for commuter routes over the Himalayas, that grand old bird was in the dustbin of aviation history. These big mothers had about as much charm as the men's room in Penn Station. Two window seats on each side, four seats squeezed together in the middle, with exit signs all over the place to give the place a secure feeling. Like the terminal, the aircraft was deserted. Toward the back I could see and hear a woman with two small children. Near the front and across from the entrance door was an old guy wearing a homburg hat. He looked like a character out of *Punch*, reading a newspaper and picking at a red, bulbous nose.

I had borrowed a yellowed, beat-up book in a red cover called *Manual for Court Martial United States, 1951*. There were undoubtedly manuals of more recent vintage, but I hadn't run across one. I was sure that Lieutenant Day would have the up-to-date version. Therefore, I reasoned, I might as well forget about reading and stretch out in one of the four-across center seats, as far as possible from the lady with the babies. It's not that I don't like kids when they are in a good mood, but from experience, I knew that kids who are dragged through the rain and plopped into strange surroundings when they should be asleep are never in a good mood.

It was possible to raise the arm rests between the seats but not to avoid the lumps and ridges between the seats. Or maybe it was the elevator music, or the wind-whipped rain pelting the windows or portholes or whatever. I'd been up since 6 a.m. so I knew I needed sleep, but it didn't come. Probably I couldn't sleep because I still didn't know what in hell I was doing, going off to a place called RAF Singlebury to defend a man I hadn't known or seen in years who had never even bothered to send me a Christmas card. The only person I had ever defended in my life was myself, first on the streets of Bay Ridge, Brooklyn, New York, and later in a boxing ring.

'Would you like a blanket and pillow?' It was a female voice.

'Thank you, but no. I'm wide awake.' I sat up and looked at the stewardess. I'd seen pictures of women, no, lasses would be better, in old English hunting paintings. Those paintings were always of hounds and rotund and bewhiskered hunters in red coats and black hats. I recalled a painting where the fearless huntsmen had stopped at a country inn. The huntsmen sat in their saddles, their mounts frothing white, chewing their bits, the hounds lying about with huge red tongues lolling from their mouths. But best of all, were the serving wenches. They were all barefoot and wore long, rough-sewn skirts and white peasant blouses off their shoulders and just covering full, jutting jugs. The serving wenches were displayed in various poses, mostly on tiptoe handing tankards of beer to the gentlemen of the chase.

Why those gentlemen of the hunt with their round bellies and red coats would rather chase after a mangy fox when these serving wenches were available to serve their every wish had always escaped me. Even as a twelve year old being guided around the library by Miss Hutchinson, I had hankered after those earthy beauties in the peasant blouses with their small waists and their serious hips and asses. In the paintings they were either smiling or letting their tongues, little red tongues, slide over small even teeth.

'Have I amused you, Yank?'

'No, not amused. You just remind me of a painting I saw once or twice in a public library. I was in Miss Hutchinson's sixth grade class then. Miss Hutchinson was very proper and very English. She would have been shocked if she knew why I liked the paintings.'

'What sort of painting?'

'A painting of serving wenches handing up stirrup cups to a fox hunt.'

'So . . . I remind you of the serving wenches . . . or the hounds, or the horses, or the gentlemen on horseback? No matter which, it is not, decidedly not, a compliment.' She said it severely, but the humor in the blue eyes betrayed the tone.

'I could never understand why those gentlemen a'horseback

wanted to chase a fox over field and fence when they could have spent the time chasing after those lovely wenches.'

'You Americans are all alike,' she said sitting down on the end of the seat next to me with a flash of very sheer nylon.

'Well,' I said, holding out my hand, 'I'm Knute Helbig.'

She took and held my hand in hers, which was not stylishly slender but firm and blunt, and although I am much too old for such things, I felt a sort of current in the touch. Second childhood. Early senility.

'Well, hello, Knute. I'm Mary . . . Mary Buttons.

'Are you coming over to vacation?'

'No. And if this damn machine doesn't get off the ground I'll never get to your British Isles and I'll never get the drink I both deserve and need.'

'I'll tell you what,' she said wrinkling her brow, 'we can't serve until we're airborn. Except first class. Golly, there's no one in first class and the boarding gate is closed. There will not be anybody in first class.' She reached down and grabbed my hand and gave it a tug. 'Come on, in first class there's champagne even before the flight takes off. Let's drink some champagne in first class.'

She held my hand as I came to my feet and inched out of the seat and continued to hold it as she led me up the narrow aisle and through the magical curtains to first class, where there was no center row of seats and the aisle was wide and the window seats were magnificent. She plopped me into a window seat and then retreated to the magic curtain where she whispered with the other stewardess. Then she came back to my seat with a bottle of Moët and two glasses. She pulled out one of the serving trays and went toward the golden curtain, bringing an ice bucket, cigarettes, Players without filters, an ashtray. She stood to uncork the wine as the plane, at last, began to move.

'Don't worry, Yank. The lads at the controls are true pros. I've been with them for years. Between them, the captain, first officer and flight engineer, they've got one hundred and fifty years in the air.'

'I used to fly. And mostly as a passenger. I washed out of flying school. I became a rear seater, so I know how to be a passenger. Just open the bottle, please.'

She did. And then with another flourish of nylon, which I am certain was well practiced, she sat in the inside seat and we clinked glasses, and thank God, I got some alcohol flowing into this up-tight body. I drank down the first frosty glass and she poured me a second as the plane began to taxi more quickly. I felt the huge machine stop, then turn, then rev up the engines. I knew what that was all about. Mary Buttons poured my third glass of bubbly and we both lighted cigarettes, me a Marlboro and she a Players. Through the smoke I could see the little red light that said: 'Fasten seat belts. No smoking.'

She then kicked off her heels and curled her legs up in her seat and put her left arm through my right arm like we were going roller-skating. She then bent us both out of shape refilling the glasses which we had to hold as the aircraft became airborn and lifted at what felt like a ninety-degree rise.

When the airplane finally began to level off and roar less, I unbuttoned her arm. 'Serving wench, the bottle is dry and you are becoming altogether too familiar.' She grinned, uncurled and went aft for another bottle. I watched her. It was a lovely sight, and although she was wearing nylons, she was barefoot. My painting had come alive. Also my sex organ. She came back to me with the new cold bottle. She had shed her uniform jacket and although her grey blouse went up to her collar and was not of the peasant variety, it was filled much the same.

She came back, she sat down, she grinned at me.

For the first time in more years than I wish to remember, I was acutely embarrassed. Not really since Mrs O'Brien's English class did I have to cover myself so my hard-on was not seen. Mrs O'Brien liked low cut blouses and she had magnificent jugs.

'It's all right,' she said, patting the top of my head. 'Your Mae West had a grand line about that. But we are going to talk, just talk. Ellery ... the other hostess and Slim Jim, the boy steward, will handle things. We take turns on slow flights like this. So, we've got hours and hours and buckets of good things to eat and drink. Talk to me.'

'I'm embarrassed. Christ, this hasn't happened to me since I was a kid.'

'Miss Hutchinson in sixth grade?' She grinned.

'No, Mrs O'Brien in eleventh.'

'And now Miss Buttons in post-grad. You're lucky it still works the same way.'

6

Knute Helbig

I had never talked very much about myself and actually hadn't thought all that much about the trials and tribulations of Knute Helbig. It seemed to me that my life was pretty much like that of all the other guys of my age. Not the early years, maybe, because they had been so different, so un-American.

Yet, here I was sitting in a snug first-class cabin with a lovely young woman curled up in the next seat, being coaxed to let her know something about one of the innumerable Yanks who went back and forth in her aircraft.

'I think you picked a poor example, Miss Buttons. I'm not a typical American.'

'Oh? Why do you say that?'

'I was born here... Brooklyn to be precise, but until I was about twelve I didn't really live in the United States. Oh, hell, I don't mean it that way. I never left a small few blocks of Brooklyn until I was twelve. But those blocks were not part of the rest of the country. People always say that America is a melting pot. Maybe so, but that pot is full of ice and the flame under it is very small.

'My grandfather was a ship's pilot. A rather master pilot from what I gather. Do you know what that is?'

She shook her head and refilled my glass once more and I drank once more.

'Ship's pilots guide large ships through harbors or fiords in my grandfather's case. They run the ship... take over from the ship's regular captain in confined waters. There are a lot of them in New York Harbor. They are aboard almost every large vessel leaving the harbor, steering to the open sea. Then they salute the captain, return his ship to him and jump on a tugboat to go home. When a ship arrives, the tug with the pilot is there to bring her in.

'My grandfather had worked in Southampton and Brest, but mostly in his native Norway. New York was apparently short of pilots in the 1930s. It was depression time all over the world, so he not only came to work, he brought his son, my father, who was apprentice to him, and my mother, his bride, and my grandmother. They didn't come through Ellis Island like most immigrants or refugees. Unlike that unwanted riffraff, Gramps was wanted and had a good, paying job. He was welcomed with his family and, of course, Norwegians who were already here, most of them worked on or near the water, were there to greet him. There was a furnished apartment ready for him and his family.

'The fact is, my father, my mother, my grandmother didn't need to know the language. They had been moved into an apartment in Bay Ridge, Brooklyn, overlooking the entrance to New York Harbor. The area around 51st Avenue in Bay Ridge, Brooklyn, was not part of the United States. It was a Norwegian colony.'

'It must have been marvellous,' she said, squeezing my arm.

'I spoke Norwegian before I spoke English.

'Until I started kindergarten, it was a grand life. It was noisy and rambunctious, particularly every seven days, and there was always plenty to eat. But when I started going to school . . . well, that was not Norwegian. It was very American . . . all women teachers whose forebears must all have come over on the *Mayflower*, spinster ladies who believed fervently in the melting-pot view of the country. They were strict, they were good, but they made me feel like I didn't know where I belonged.

'I can remember one day that . . . around fourth grade . . . the teacher, Mrs Flanders was teaching me not to think in Norwegian. She told me to bring in my birth certificate to make the point that I was an American, not a Norwegian. My ma had given birth to me at home. I didn't have a birth certificate. I remember my pa coming to school in his only suit to explain things to Mrs Flanders. That lady was something else. She arranged to get me a birth certificate, and she did. The problem was, nobody remembered when I was born. They knew the year, they knew it was in early April, but not what day.

'They went to the doctor who helped deliver me. His office had burned down and his records destroyed. So, to this day, I don't know exactly when I was born. They decided on 6 April because that had been a Sunday, and very lucky according to Norsman tales.

'When I was twelve, Gramps bought a house. Forty miles east in a place called West Islip, Long Island, New York. I forgot to mention that my pa, having sired four, had decided to join the free Norwegians in England. He told me the day he left, and I was still very little, that Norway was occupied by the Nazis, but unlike any other country that was overrun, Norway was occupied but not conquered. He was parachuted back into Norway and we never heard of him again. After the war, the king sent Ma a medal.

'That's really most of the story.

'The rest is pretty dull, There was a war or police action or whatever. I was called up, I went to flight school in Texas. I was flunked out, probably because the war was shutting down. I went to navigator and radar school, got my second-class wings, served a tour, part of it was FO ... forward observer on the ground in front of the First Marine brigade. I caught a very lucky piece of shrapnel under my left nipple, got sent home with a couple of medals, and the GI Bill.

'When I got back, the family was struggling. So I joined New York's finest. Oh, OK, the cops in the city. Regular money, not much but steady. I could help out. After a while, I went on the lobster shift full time ... midnight to eight. That way I could go to law school full time, with a part scholarship and the GI Bill. That was a thing that gave veterans money to help them educate themselves. When I finished, I went back to West Islip.

'First, I was made a cop ... an investigator for the district attorney. Then, I became an assistant district attorney. I'm now in charge of an investigations bureau. Me and my merry men investigate, then my assistant district attorneys try the cases, take guilty pleas, or whatever. The nasty cases I try.'

'That's not all, Knute?'

'Pretty much. And I don't know what in hell I'm doing going to your land to defend an ex-brother-in-law. I never defended anybody, although I don't believe this boy did what they say he did.'

'But you were married?'

'Yes, part of the iced melting pot. I married a lace-curtain Irish lass. Do you know what that means?'

She shook her head, and I realized that she held her champagne better than I.

'We have the shanty Irish and the lace-curtain. The shanty are the working people, the lace-curtain try to be aristocrats. I wish I had married a shanty. I didn't. Anyway, it didn't work out. It's been over a long time. Water over the dam and all that.'

Then, finally, I passed out.

7
RAF Singlebury

The airliner's wheels going down and clunking into lock awakened me. I was all alone in first class with a tongue that felt the size of a football, a mouth that tasted like a gorilla's armpit and a head that felt as though a burly blacksmith was using it as an anvil. Christ, I thought to myself, I knew how bad a champagne hangover could be. I'd been to enough weddings to know better. It didn't help the head when I remembered that I had spent damn near the entire flight going on and on and on about me, me, me.

'Hello, sleepy head,' Mary Buttons said, peeking her head through the heavy curtain that separates first class from the common folks. 'How you feeling, love?'

'Uh. . . .'

She wrinkled the pert, upturned nose and grinned. She looked like she'd had a nap, a shower and was ready for a night on the town. 'Can't keep up with the big boys and girls?'

'I can't keep up with the thirteen year olds.'

'I've got to go. Things to do, don't you know.'

Mary Buttons did not help this still half-drunk, half-sleepy, totally hungover idiot through the trials and rigors of Heathrow Airport. It is all still a blur to this day, a cacophony of sound in several foreign languages, including the Queen's English. Getting my luggage was quick since there was not much luggage aboard. Ditto for Customs since there were not many passengers.

'Business or pleasure, sir?' the Customs guy asked as he stamped my passport.

'I'm going to an American airbase to represent a defendant, a military defendant on a military base. I guess you'd call it business.'

'There are no American airbases in the British Isles, sir. There are American personnel stationed on British air bases. Bad business,' he said. He gave me a baleful look from glassy blue eyes. He was all beef running to fat. 'I suppose another of your superheroes raped some poor twelve-year-old English lass and you came to get him off, as it were.'

I was not in the mood for this. 'She was seven, and after he raped her he butchered her with a large carving knife and ate her liver.'

After another baleful stare, he slid my passport back to me. The baggage was not opened. Apparently, Customs didn't think I was man enough to smuggle in plastic for the IRA. I took an elevator, painfully aware of how heavy my bags were at this particular moment, and then I was in an even louder hall. It was my thought to take a taxi to the nearest motel, sleep and sober up and then a car the next day.

But that was not to be. 'Would you be Knute Helbig, sir? From New York?' I was halfway to the taxi stand. He was scrawny and tall with hair like black Brillo and sky-blue eyes, wearing blue jeans and an Air Force parka. Also, he sounded as though this was his first visit from the Emerald Isle.

'I would.'

'Quirk McQuirk at your service, sir. I'm a friend of Paul, a fellow NCO. I've come to fetch you, sir.'

He took both my bags and nudged me toward a parking area. At this point, my stomach was beginning to groan and heave and from many past experiences, I knew I was going to be up-chucking two bottles of champagneor, thereabouts, plus peanuts, truffles and liver on crackers with a fancy name. I followed behind the lanky frame, stumbling along as best as I could, breathing deep and swallowing constantly in the hope that I could keep my guts from spilling all that expensive food and drink. My escort tossed my bags into a huge Chevy station wagon, turned and grinned.

'They call these Yank Tanks over here. The Brits don't like them. Nor that we gas them on base at US prices. But then, we wee Irish lads love every fucking thing the Brits hate.'

I got behind the 'Yank Tank' and threw up. I threw up like a man wanting to display all his wares at Saturday's flea market. My new friend put his arms around me to keep me from falling into my own stench. For such a scrawny-looking guy, he was very strong. I am not a light weight.

'Well, lad,' he said when the convulsions of my stomach began to slow down, 'British food is notorious, don't you know. You should have flown Aer Lingus. Best of food and drink, beautiful lasses to serve.'

'Not the food.' I gagged. 'I must have drunk ten bottles of champagne.'

He clapped a surprisingly large hand over my shoulder, opened the station wagon front passenger seat door and boosted me in.

'Now, sir, perhaps in your temporary shape, you should close your eyes. Over here, the Brits, as Paul always says, drive on the wrong side of the road. Driving a Yank Tank with left-hand controls on the wrong side of the street gets a mate a might nervous. But not to worry, I'm well used to it. Just lie back a bit and we'll get you fixed up in no time at all.'

I did lie back, opening my eyes occasionally. It seemed like traffic circles were the in thing in the British Isles.

Quirk McQuirk, if that was his name, was absolutely right about keeping my eyes off the road. In my self-induced but nevertheless very real agony, watching car after car apparently commandeered by kamikaze drivers zooming along on the wrong side of the road were more than a mite nerve-racking. My stomach felt like a storm-swept sea and I was certain that I had not retched up all the poison I had ingested. I did notice that my feet and legs were beginning to feel as cold as a witch's tit. I did not have the strength to stamp any circulation into them. I also noticed that Quirk McQuirk was a terrible driver, zooming ahead, abusing the brake, speeding up, slowing down to a crawl. But I refused to look at the road.

I awoke with a start. 'There she is in all her glory. Colonel J.J. Smith's house of ill-repute.' Quirk McQuirk grinned a lopsided grin, at me. 'I don't suggest we go in, sir. Not 'til you've had a chance to straighten out a bit.' Just ahead of us was an entry gate between high wire fences. Two air policemen stepped in and out of the small gatehouse as cars and trucks came in and out. Above the entry gate mounted high over the roadway, the sign said: RAF Singlebury.

'I'd better sleep for a few hours.'

'Right you are, sir. There's a wee hotel just down the road. Mostly for locals, but we've got you a room there 'til tomorrow, sir. Has a small bar, too. For the hair of the dog, you know. Brit rules, the bars are closed now, except for guests. So we booked you a room, sir. Primitive but clean.'

He stripped gears and roared off and my stomach began to churn again. Fortunately, it was a short ride to what looked like a rundown old family house. Which is what it was. It had apparently become a hotel by the addition of a small bar near a fireplace in what had been the living-room and the substitution of several small, old tables for one large dining-room table. My driver, guide and new friend dropped my suitcases inside the front door and put an arm over my shoulder to guide me to the bar-room and a small table by the fire. I aimed my feet toward the fire and in no time, my toes began to tingle. They had not fallen off after all. Although I have read that 'phantom pain' can be excruciating in extremities lost years earlier.

Quirk McQuirk had disappeared into the kitchen and now emerged with two pewter tankards. He took them behind the bar to the beer tap and brought them to the table, setting them down as though wanting to smash them.

'Hair of the dog, sir. Drink up and don't ask what's in them.' The tankard smelled like beer and it had foam like beer, but the foam was bright red. The bloody mess in the tankard apparently changed my coloration as it knotted my stomach because Quirk McQuirk laughed, patted my shoulder and said, 'Hold your nose and drink up, mate. I would not steer you wrong.'

I did just that, also closing my eyes. For a long moment I was certain that everything was going to spew all over the scarred table top, then very suddenly, the seas of my stomach became calm. Not as in calm before the storm. I looked into the tankard in which the beer suds had parted sufficiently to allow me to see what appeared to be sudsy tomato juice. After staring long enough to be pretty certain no creatures were about to crawl out, I took another long pull. Nothing bad happened. In point of fact, I began to feel better than I had ever imagined could happen again in this lifetime. I was also very thirsty and drained the tankard.

'Thank you, Sergeant. You have saved my life. One more of those and I'll be a new man . . . although I don't know if they take American Express here.'

Quirk McQuirk rose with the empty tankards in his large, bony hands. 'Our pleasure, sir,' he grinned. 'And no, they don't take Yankee wampum. It's a locals' place. There's just a few of us from the base ever come here. Yanks are not overly welcome, you see. Just a few of us . . . we have sort of an arrangement, as they say.' He left me to ponder that as he disappeared again into the kitchen.

'Well, sir, here's to your complete recovery,' he said, sitting down. We clinked tankards and drank. 'It's some bitter herbs, a goodly shot of vodka, salt, tabasco, tomato juice and light beer. Light as they make it here. Works every time.'

'I'm glad you didn't tell me before the first mouthful.'

'I wouldn't do that, sir. We're all on your side.'

'We?'

'The noncoms, sir. We're a fraternity. Mostly a very loose fraternity. Love bashing each other. But when something like this thing with Pauli comes down, we all get very tight. Even the AP NCOs; they're NCOs first and policemen second.'

'What came down with Paul?'

'He'll tell you. But you got to understand something, mate. I know you were in the Air Force. But that was wartime. The peacetime thing is different. Every overseas base commander has a fiefdom, like merry old England of long ago. I don't know how it is in the States, I've never served in the States. But overseas, every base commander is lord of all he surveys. Here, it's Colonel J.J. Smith, a tried and true son-of-a-bitch. He never liked Pauli. You see, Pauli holds a very responsible slot. He's the only man on this god-forsaken base who knows the route and destination of every aircraft. Even the base commander doesn't. All hush-hush security shit. But Pauli runs the flight simulator where the pilots practice their runs to target. He's guardian of every tape for every flight that leaves here if the balloon goes up.

'Smith doesn't like Pauli, never did. You know Pauli, maybe a little careless with the 'yes, sir, no, sir' shit, or the shiny boots. Smith tried to transfer Pauli but he's got a very scarce APSC ... I think they called it a 'MOS' in your time. A scarce specialty. So, he fucked Pauli. No housing for Pauli's family, no leave long enough for a visit Stateside. So, Pauli gets into what could be a small AWOL, and Smith decides Pauli killed a bird. That's horseshit. But Smith, who's got his papers in for one star, just waiting for the rubber stamp from Congress, now he's solved the crime of the century, took the fucking Brits off the hook because they couldn't find an Irishman in Derry, and he got a replacement for Pauli.

'Nice, neat package.'

'What time is it here now?' I said, trying to stifle a yawn.

'Seventeen hundred, and beddy time, lad. Can you eat something before I take you to your poor excuse for a room?'

'Believe it or not, I'm starved.'

'Mrs Quinn makes a fine steak and kidney pie. Will you try one?'

I nodded, not knowing if my newly calmed and friendly stomach would welcome a pie. But I felt sleepy and fine. The bloody drinks had settled me down.

My stomach rejoiced at Mrs Quinn's steak and kidney pie and the 'black and tan' that went with it. It was now opening time and surly-looking, unshaven men in huge rubber boots and dirty scarves and sheepskin coats tramped into the small rooms. It did not take me long to know why the men from the base did not frequent this establishment. This was a 'locals' bar, and the foreigners who lived in their self-contained unit called RAF Singlebury were not the saviors of World War II movies. But I wolfed down a second pie and a second brew, ignoring the hostility that flashed like summer lightning around the small two rooms.

8
Colonel J.J. Smith

At precisely 1000 hours, as I had indicated to the receptionist, at the office of the base commander, I reported in.

Colonel J.J. Smith was not ready for me. Not at 1000 hours, nor at 1100 hours. I sat in one of the three fake leather lounging chairs in the great man's waiting-room. There were no dog eared magazines that make doctors' offices so inviting. The base/wing commander's headquarters were located in the lower part of the control tower. The building had been thrown up during the Second World War, around 1942. It was a square, squat building made of concrete block which now sweated despite the cold, peeling the thin light-yellow paint. Much of the outer offices' sweating, pale-yellow walls were covered with pictures of B-47 bombers.

There were also some scrolls and awards honoring the 345th Light Bomber Wing for various acts of training bravery. After admiring each and every scroll, award and photograph of B-47s doing their various training and refueling missions, there was nothing else to look at. An aging credenza held a Joe Dimaggio-type coffee maker with cups and sugar cubes and a powdered creamer, and the secretary's desk, a WW II relic of battleship grey with no front between the drawers and typewriter stand. That gave me a view of long, shapely, nylon-clad legs. The legs belonged to the secretary; 'Miss Terry' the sign on her desk stated.

Miss Terry was kept very busy. She answered the telephone consol, she made outgoing calls, she accepted messages delivered every few moments, some of which she signed for. Several times, she disappeared behind the plain wooden door on which hung a removable wooden sign which read: 'Col. J.J. Smith, Commander, 345th Light Bomb Wing'. She also typed a great deal. I judged Miss Terry to be about forty, with some silver in her blonde hair. She wore a knobby sort of tweed suit of which the jacket was now on the chair behind her. Her clingy purple-silk blouse was pleasant to look at. There wasn't much else to do so I varied watching the ever-shifting long legs and then the rise and fall and twists of the purple blouse with its awesome hidden treasure.

At 1135 hours, Miss; Terry said, 'You may go right in.'

Which I did. I almost saluted. This office overlooked the runways through windows that sparkled despite the overcast. Everything was in place . . . the stars and stripes, the Air Force flag, the 345th Wing banner. The walls were not peeling or sweating in here. They were a soft green, subdued. The lighting from various lamps were also subdued. The massive wooden desk backed on to the large windows overlooking the runways. On both side walls were huge blow-ups. One was the colonel standing while all his crew kneeled before a B-47. They wore the leather and sheepskin flying gear the Air Force had made famous. On the opposite wall, was a B-47 in a power dive, like a WW II Avenger dive bomber. B-47s do not do Stuka runs, so this had to be a picture of an airplane in trouble.

'Colonel Smith. I'm Knute Helbig. I've been asked to defend Paul Kelly. I asked to see you to pay my respects. There are some minor requests also, Colonel. . . .' It was as far as I got. There had been none of that come-around-the-desk and friendly handshake. The officer behind the desk was small and delicate, perhaps five foot five inches and 130 pounds. The head was large for the body, full head of dark hair, with an aquiline, straight nose, square jaw with small cleft and very dark eyes.

'Let me spare the niceties, Helbig. Kelly is a deserting murderer. I mean to see him convicted. And no Jew-boy New York City shyster is going to change that. Where that excuse-for-a-sergeant in this man's Air Force got the money to hire a New York City shyster, I do not know. Doesn't matter. I've got nothing else to say to you, Helbig. I don't want to see you again, is that clear? You go ahead and try to screw up the record for appeal. By that time, it won't concern me anymore.'

I've dealt with a lot of shitheads in my short, happy life. Been insulted by experts. But I don't believe I've ever heard the likes of this and I was very proud of myself. Proud because I didn't leap across the desk and toss that scrawny sack out of one of his huge windows.

When I spoke, it sounded as though butter wouldn't melt in my mouth. I was totally calm, like seething ice. 'Colonel, our government says that every man charged with a crime is entitled to an attorney of his choosing. My job is to try to clear him of these charges. And yes, if errors are made on trial, I'll appeal those errors. I'm also aware, Colonel, that your name is before the Congress for promotion to general rank. I don't want to upset that. I just want a fair trial.'

'He'll get it.'

'Colonel, I'd like access to everything the accused is entitled to. I plan to stay at the BOQ and do most of my business there. I want all the time I need to spend with Paul. In short, for a fair trial, I want all the help I request, including a driver and car. Someone who knows his way around.'

'Negative, Mr Helbig. No BOQ, no drivers. I don't coddle murderers, nor their counsel. You can come and go on this base. You can see and talk to Kelly, but there will be no privileges. None. You are the enemy, Helbig. I show no quarter to the enemy. Do I make myself clear?' The black eyes were snapping.

'Colonel, I'm an Air Force reserve captain.'

'That and three English pounds will get you a taxi to London.

'No favors. No BOQ, no officers' club mess privileges. No golf course, no tennis, no Post Exchange.

'You get the picture, son?'

'Oh, yes, sir. I got the whole picture. And in a hurry.'

'Well, that's just fine, boy. Now you get out of my office, and get out of my sight. Do I make myself clear, boy?'

'Colonel, you have made yourself perfectly clear,' I said.

I stood outside Base Ops shivering in the thin January light. The air felt damp and heavy and the grey clouds looked loaded with wet snow. I understood Colonel J.J. Smith. His academy counterparts had had four rough years, he had had twenty-some. But still, he should have taken Class 103 in Civilian Ass-Kissing. I had come here inclined to plead out Paul Kelly to some lesser offense. That wouldn't entirely remove the colonel's blot, but it would neatly sweep it under the rug and there would be no appeal for the officers and gentlemen who dine at Andrews Air Force Base to discuss. Colonel Smith had made it apparently clear that there could be no plea.

9
The Sunbury

When I got back to the 'Yank Tank' Quirk McQuirk had made available to me, there was a tech sergeant lounging against its side.

'Conyers, sir,' he said half-saluting and drawing himself up to ramshackle but impressive height. 'I'll be driving you for awhile, sir. First to the pub to get your gear and then to the Sunbury.'

'Sergeant, I don't understand this.'

'Well, sir, since you can't stay at the BOQ and you'll be wanting to stay close to the base, we got you a place at the Sunbury. It's close and convenientL. Not the Waldorf, of course, but not too bad for a motel, and there's a restaurant right there, too.'

'You don't think I can find my way?'

'Oh, it's not that, sir. The APs have been alerted. Seems the big man wants you. Drunk or reckless driving, or something like that. Anything to let him bar you from base. We figured you'd be better off with a driver, sir. We've got lots of us and only one of you, if you get my drift.'

I had to grin. 'Sergeant Conyers, you seem to be very well briefed.'

'Oh, yes sir. The APs, mostly. They may be APs, but they are sergeants first. We all wet our whistle in the same club, if you get my, drift.'

'I get your drift, Sergeant.' I walked around the station wagon, got in and handed Conyers the keys.

For a big, laconic man, the sergeant drove very carefully, stopping fully for the Stop signs and keeping his speed under the thirty-mile limit. 'I expect you'll be wanting to see Paul. He knows you're here. I'm available 'til 2300 hours. After that, you get Sergeant Young if you need him tonight. By the by, it's good if you plan ahead when you need transport. No phone in your room.'

'I'd like to see Lieutenant Day or Knight, whatever, first. See what the charges are.'

'Yes, sir. We figured that. He'll be coming to see you after work. Around 1730 hours. He thought it might be better not to meet at his office. Big ears, if you get my drift. He don't much want you around his home – on base housing. He's not a bad little man, really, but scared to death. Scared of going to Greenland or such as that, what with his wife and little baby and another in the oven.'

'Sergeant, I'm beginning to feel like Al Capone . . . without his muscle.'

The sergeant grinned at me and nodded at the AP on the Singlebury gate. 'You got lots of muscle, Captain. You got more than four hundred NCOs in your corner and none of us a'scared of going to Greenland. I'd say you got better muscle than old Al Capone. None of us, if you get my drift, would ever sell out to the other side.'

'I get your drift,' I said.

The Sunbury was decidedly not the Waldorf. Nor, I found, a Day's Inn. It sat back from the highway across about fifty yards of bluestone, a one-storey, flat-roofed, stucco building about one football field in length. Its yellow-painted stucco walls were punctuated every few feet by a metal door painted a bright red with white numerals, and a small, bathroom sized window with blinds. The blinds were all closed and the whole affair looked like a row of one-eyed, blind monsters next to a yawing mouth containing one white tooth.

While I stood next to the Yank Tank admiring my new digs, Sergeant Conyers dug my gear out of the rear of the car, unlocked the monster-mouth door to room 11 and banged my things into the darkness. I stood for a moment surveying the scene around me. I'd seen motels like this, only made of clapboard along highways in the deep South: 'For colored'. The highway behind me was bleak and little traveled, a strip of concrete dividing flat, scrub country. Off aways on the far side of the highway, I could see the top of the gate to Singlebury, dark blue and bright yellow against the swollen grey clouds.

Sergeant Conyer's assurances did not weigh very heavily at the moment.

'Come on in, Captain. Ain't near bad as she looks,' Conyers shouted. He was wrong. It was as bad as it looked. There was a very short hall straight ahead into the small motel room. The bath was off to the right, where I had seen the blind eye of a closed bathroom window. The bed was narrow and hard, the blankets felt as though they came from the tropics ... years ago ... and the only heat was a small electric unit with a fifteen-minute timer on it. It had to be punched on every fifteen minutes to give off its tiny, matchlike portion of heat. There was also a rickety chair and a bar across the far corner of the room to hang clothes. In the bathroom there was, in fact, a tub, but no shower. The wash basin had a cold water tap. Incongruously, there was a towel warmer with no fifteen–minute switch-off. I turned it on. It would scorch no towels for eternity but gave off about as much warmth as the heater. Also, incongruously, the tub filled with boiling hot water. I let it fill to give the room some steamy warmth. There seemed no end to the hot, the boiling-hot water.

'Real nice,' I said coming into my main living quarter. Conyers had been unpacking for me, hanging my wrinkled suits on the bar and such.

'You've had worse, Captain. Much worse.'

'Sure. I was a kid then.' I sat down on the bed and studied my host.

'Just how in hell do you know if I had worse, Sergeant? And for Christ's sake, stop calling me Captain. I'm in the inactive reserve and not likely to be called back. Knute will do.'

The big man sprawled across the bed from me, grinning from ear to ear. 'I'm Chuck to my friends. The US Air Force screwed me once. Just once, but bad. I intend to stay with it 'til I screw it back enough to feel all is square, if you get my drift.' It was the first time I had heard the inflection of a southern drawl. Just a word or two.

'As to your question, Captain, I figure I told you, sort of indirect who runs this service. We do. The NCOs. I figure you knew that, being a lawyer and all and having done your time. By the way, the CO can't keep you out of the NCO Club. The sergeant major got you a card. You're entitled.' He took a plastic-coated card from the pocket of his fatigues and laid it on the bed in front of me.

'As to what we know about you. . . .' The crooked grin reappeared, this time not just around his mouth but also in the deep-blue eyes. 'I figure maybe we know more about you than you do. We got us a copy of everything from that there depository of files for reserve officers they have in Denver.'

'That's all classified, Sergeant. That can even resist the Freedom of Information lawsuits.'

'Yes, sir. Sure is.' By now, his eyes were twinkling with good humor.

'But you got it?'

'Yes, sir. Somehow, through all that there classified, secret or top-secret clearance, we also got a file on our colonel and all the members he appointed to the court martial. Figured you'd like to see all that, if you get my drift.'

'Sergeant.'

'Captain?'

'Chuck?'

'Noot?'

'Back in the States from which I came, it is not just before twelve, high noon. It is either five or six in the evening, depending on what time they are on back there.'

'Yes, sir.'

'In my home country, between five and six in the evening is cocktail time.'

'Somewhere in the world, Noot, it is always cocktail time. However, we have taken the privilege of reserving a semi-private room at the NCO Club so that some of your gun-bearers and runners could get to know you a bit. Above and beyond the paperwork we already have. Would you do me the honor, sir?'

10
NCOs and the NCO Club

Lunch at the Non-commissioned Officers Club was less expensive but as good as at any officers' club in which I had ever lunched. On this day, the special was corned beef and cabbage with new potatoes, one of my favorite meals. The bar area had the usual assortment of pinball machines and other games demanding skill and concentration and the sounds and bells of a small arcade. As on many airbases where ground personnel and air crews worked shifts around the clock, a snack bar boasting a variety of goodies from hard-boiled eggs to jello and the long polished bar never closed. Adding to the din was a juke-box in top voice. It looked to be a World War II vintage Wurlitzer stacked with 45 r.p.m. records. With squadron and group decals and banners interspersed with photographs of flyers and an assortment of old ancient and modern warplanes, the memory of old war movies flashed to mind. 'Never in the field of human conflict was so much owed by so many to so few' and 'Live today, for tomorrow we die' flashed through my mind.

It was a different service from some years ago – my time. The men and women for the most part wore jungle fatigues and paratroop boots. Few were dressed in Air Force blue, and this, too, had become fancier. In my time the Air Force was still being de-glamorized in the lingering jealousies of the other services and everyone of us had looked like Greyhound bus drivers. That was now apparently a thing of the past, at least here in a combat wing that was constantly trained for first strike or first retaliation missions – armed with nuclear weapons.

Just past twelve noon of a working day, the place was jumping and vital. Sergeant Conyers gave me a very brief tour before leading me past an orchestra shell, across a small dance floor on which a bingo game was set up and to a round corner table, set off from the main room by a three-foot high wooden partition, topped with some sort of ivy in painted buckets. Conyers guided me to the seat which backed into the corner. From there I had a panoramic view of the room which I finally realized was nothing more than a corrugated Quonset hut of old. A fake roof had been added and the walls, in spots, were straightened with wood paneling. The windows held curtains that looked suspiciously like parachute silk or nylon and the overall feeling was that this was where the respectable wives of the noncoms dined and danced and played bingo and had kaffee katsch and more-or-less high teas.

'Nice.'

'You said that about the Sunbury. I take it you don't approve.'

'That "nice" was sarcastic; this "nice" is for real. I really dig the bar.'

'Well, this is sort of home away from home for most of us. Shifts we work, what with kids in school and all, we can't really socialize much to home. Three hundred hours is no time to party with a houseful of kids, if you get my drift. Me, I live off-base out in the boonies with a lady friend. Sort of like a bigger Sunbury but with no electric heat. But it suits me and my lady friend. Being non-essential myself, I can live where I please. Most of the lads can't do that and there's precious little on-base housing for married family men. So it's the rotten barracks for most and this then is really home.'

This had been the sergeant's longest soliloquy, interrupted only to ask a waitress for two shots of Canadian and two mugs of tan.

After the beer and whiskey arrived and was set down, Conyers grabbed the waitress's hand.

'This is Captain Helbig, Cindy, come from New York to help Pauli.'

'Pleased to meet you, I'm sure,' she said with a sort of curtsy, a plain, plump, acned young girl with a nice smile.

'My pleasure,' I mumbled.

'I surely pray you can sort this all out about Pauli. Always joking and kidding and cutting up, Pauli wouldn't hurt a fly. A really sweet man, that's what he is. And he wouldn't have had to... you know... force himself with Maggie. She liked him a lot. It's the constable if you ask me. That nasty old man. Well,' she said shrugging her shoulders coquettishly, 'nobody asks me. And I'm sure you'll know what to do, sir. My pleasure, I'm sure,' she said, with another shrug and turned away.

'She's right there. Maggie and Pauli had a little thing, if you get my drift. Nothing serious, just a fun in the sun sort of thing. She worked here so Pauli saw a lot of her. Then, of course, we all did. But she did take a shine to Pauli. But then I figure most all of us,' he said, sweeping his arm around the room in that slow laconic way he had, 'all of us took a shine to Pauli. Well, you got to know better than me, being his brother-in-law and all.'

'I *was* his brother-in-law, Chuck. Haven't seen him or had a call or a postcard in seven years. Didn't know he married and had kids. His present brother-in-law at his sister's push and shove paid for my ticket to get here. When Paul was a kid and lived with us he was a pain in my ass. Now he's a pain in my ass again.'

I must have sounded more bitter than I had intended. The sergeant emptied his shot glass, gulped some beer and set down the mug with obvious force before he turned to stare at me. There was no laughter in the eyes now.

'Wal,' he said with the hint of the South again in his voice, 'If you don't love the lad and believe he's being railroaded, what the fuck you doing here, boy?'

'Sergeant Conyers, the reason that I am here happens to be none of your fucking business. Suffice it to say that I will do my very best for Paul Kelly, guilty or innocent. That's my job. That's my oath. I've prosecuted people I would rather have been friends with. I will do all I can for Paul, within the law. And that is all you have to know.'

We looked at each other without pleasure and then we looked away from each other and sat in silence until the waitress came back and the sergeant ordered refills and the corned beef special. It never seemed to occur to him that my choice of food or drink might just not happen to coincide with his.

After a long silence he said, 'Sorry, Captain, I was out of line.' I did not respond. Our little rotund waitress brought our meal. We avoided looking at each other. And that was when, timed as in a play, the rest of the senior NCOs came to look me over.

First came Master Sergeant Victor T. Hamilton, Wing Sergeant Major and thereby the most important man on any military post. The sergeant major stood about six feet six and looked to weigh about 200 well-conditioned pounds. His uniform with its hashmarks and stripes was immaculate: his chest covered by rows of ribbons above which he wore his combat infantryman's badge, the red badge of courage. His face was deeply lined under a bushy blond mustache and closed cropped blond hair.

'People call me Ham,' he said in a gravelly Southern voice, holding out a hand that could also be called a ham. 'I know who you are and welcome.'

'Thank you.' We sat down, the little waitress took his order, the same as mine and scampered off.

'You got a fine record in the military . . . from an enlisted man's point of view,' he said, chuckling at his great sense of humor. But I had to grin also. 'You must have really fried some high-ranking butts to get taken out of a combat aircraft and stuck in the trenches as an FO with the Marines.' The sergeant major was enjoying himself, undoubtedly helped by the double Canadian he gulped.

'You were a mud-slogger, huh? Hell, you could have been an enlisted man,' Conyers said, the ultimate compliment to an officer.

'You do see what I mean, Captain?' The sergeant major beamed. He dug into his corned beef and cabbage as though he were attacking the enemy. His portion was obviously a special for the man who ran everything, twice the size of my own generous $1.25 portion. I also noticed later that our table did not get a check, proving once again RHIP (rank has its privileges). Before we all left the table, everyone anteed up one buck for the waitress. Brits may no longer love Americans, but that lack of feeling did not extend to the Yankee dollar.

Within minutes, Sgts Halderman, Russo, Phillippi and Jansen joined us, were introduced by name, rank and occupational specialty, ordered shots and beer and the daily special and spent some time needling each other. Sergeant Russo was from Brooklyn and it soon turned out he was from the Italian neighborhood which adjoined my Norwegian one. They were all master sergeants except Conyers, one rank down.

As soon as the sergeant major finished off his gargantuan portion of corned beef and cabbage and the last of his beer, he wiped a paper napkin across his mouth and thumped once, gently, on the table.

There was immediate silence.

'Captain, we here among and between us, can supply you with anything you will need. McQuirk, that crazy Irish bastard and Conyers here will be available to drive you in Pauli's car, or an armored personnel carrier if you prefer, twenty-four hours a day. Also available to you are world-wide communications, any files or records or background information that you may need. Sergeant Phillippi runs the APs. Any investigations you need, he'll gladly do. If you need cash for information or witnesses, you've got it.

'In so many words, whatever you need, you've got. And don't hesitate to ask.'

'Ham's got that right,' Sergeant Jansen said softly. 'If you want birds, as the Brits call them, ask Conyers. That pimping ... is his specialty and why Ham keeps him around.' This was greeted with general agreement and much merriment.

The sergeant major cleared his throat and again, there was immediate silence.

'Captain, Paul is a tech sergeant. He should be master by now, but we all know he got busted several times. We also all know he put a shiv in a guy when he was shit-faced. I think I can safely say that none of us would take Paul Kelly around the country as a recruiter. This is all a political thing. A nice girl is killed. She worked here. Paul knew her, been fucking her. The Brits need a killer quick so this does not become a big, Scotland Yard thing: Paul's in the keep. Nice, neat, easy. And our base commander has never liked Paul. He does like all the Limey letters extolling his excellence to the Congress. Bingo. Paul is the killer.'

'You all believe he's innocent.' The table was silent as each man nodded gravely.

'Captain,' Sergeant Russo said, 'the girl was crazy about Paul.'

There was silence around our table so that the noise from the bar, and even the music from the juke-box were loud and distinct.

'That little shit will never get his star,' the sergeant major said softly. 'He don't know that, but it's taken care of.'

There were sighs of relief around the table. This startling statement was accepted as gospel.

11
Lieutenant Day

Lieutenant Clarence Darrow Day, Judge Advocate General's office did not look as he had sounded on the telephone. He was big and athletic-looking with a blond crew cut, an unlined face and a prominent square jaw divided by a deep cleft. In point of fact he didn't look much like any lawyer I'd known, more like a lumberjack.

We shook hands and I guided him and a large file to sit on the bed and I drew up the solitary straight-back chair. After a couple of after-lunch drinks at the NCO Club bar, McQuirk had come to collect me. He had a carton of cigarettes (my brand) a bottle of Canadian whiskey and a six pack of American beer for me and refused payment. He said the 'defense fund' paid for such things. Then I had slept until just a few minutes before the lieutenant knocked on the door of my castle.

'Can I get you a whiskey or a beer, Lieutenant?'

'Beer would be fine, thank you.' He was shuffling papers into neat little individual piles around him on the bed.

I opened the window that looked out the back of the room and popped two cans from the plastic holding together the six-pack, which I perched precipitously on the small window sill. I closed the window and hit the electric heater's 'on' button for its fifteen minutes of sparse warmth. The room had grown cold and damp while I slept. After a few days of freezing my ass off and leaping in and out of bed all night to hit the heater 'on' button, I learned that while room heat was barely possible, the hot-water system produced an endless flow of almost boiling water. It was, therefore, possible to fill and refill the tub and get an endless supply of steam heat. Dewy but warm. The British, I learned, did a lot of that sort of thing. There was, for instance, an electric towel warmer in the bathroom, something the Helmsley and Pierre don't boast.

I put the lieutenant's beer and my own on the floor in front of him and sat down, holding my glass of whiskey and water, no ice. Ice machines had apparently not yet invaded the Empire.

The lieutenant stopped shuffling papers and looked at me. It was a totally honest, open and innocent gaze as though he could not perceive that nothing is on the level on a round world.

'I'd like to say, on behalf of Paul and myself, how grateful we are that you came. And if I said anything offensive to you ... please forgive me. I guess I was overwhelmed by the responsibility they thrust on me and I needed you to bail me out.'

'Don't apologize, Lieutenant. When you called, the Giants–Bears game was the most important event of the month. I wasn't exactly Miss Manners myself. So, let's forget all that and get started.'

The nice, innocent grin. 'OK, but first, Sally, my wife, would like you to join us for dinner tomorrow. She'd like to know your favorite meal. She's quite a good cook. And please call me CD, everyone does.'

'CD?'

'Clarence Darrow. You can see my father has rather exaggerated expectations.'

'Lawyer?'

'Yes, he and my grandfather both.'

'I'm sure you won't disappoint them, CD'

He blushed like a teenage girl. 'I'll try very hard not to.'

'Now, Paul Kelly. Where are we at in the proceedings? When are we scheduled to kick off? Have you a list of prosecution witnesses, that's probably most important? And does your code allow them to bring in last-minute ringers? Other than character witnesses, do you have defense witnesses?'

CD Day looked perplexed. Nice young man, I thought. He'll be a great and thorough and honest and decent drawer and executor of wills and a dandy and careful real estate specialist and estate planner. But Clarence Darrow he would never be. If the old Clarence had been filled with Christian charity and decency, William Jennings Bryant might still be alive.

'What we have gone through are all the preliminaries. The investigative officer's report and exhibits are here,' he said, laying a hand on a pile of papers. 'The Article 32 proceedings. We've also been through the Article 39 A session.'

'Meaning?'

'Like a felony hearing, I suppose. Are the charges sufficient that we should hold a trial, that sort of thing. That's this pile over here. This pile is all the paperwork convening the court, the special orders naming the members of the court and so forth.

'We haven't had the RCM 802 yet but I just got word on who will be law officer; Major Mills. He's from Wiesbaden, not under our colonel. I don't know a thing about him.'

'In Enlish please, CD.'

'Oh ... the RCM 802, Rules of Court Martial, that's under Article 32 of the Uniform Code of Military Justice. Our bible, so to speak. It's like a pre-trial conference with the law officer or military judge. Sort of to settle on how the trial is going to go along. Major Mills will hold that. Just before the trial begins. Oh, also he wants to know when you think you'll be ready to proceed. He won't come over until then.'

I went to my disarray of luggage and dug out pencil and a yellow pad. 'Can you spell out all of Major Mills's name, serial number and such?'

'Certainly,' he said, and dug out as much information as he had on the major. Not much. 'May I ask why?'

'Yeah. I want to know all about him.'

'I don't think that's going to be possible, Mr Helbig.'

'It's Knute, if you please. And I'll know how many cavities the major has by tomorrow at this time.'

The perplexed look crossed that innocent face again. 'I don't know . . . I do have the name of the court-martial board, if that will help.'

'I don't need that, I've got their 201 files.'

'You what?'

'I have their 201 files; you know, their personnel files.'

'How could you possibly? They are not even available under the Freedom of Information Act.'

'Yeah, I know. How about the list of prosecution witnesses?'

He patted the fourth little pile on the bed, gazing at me in that sweet, innocent way. It was pretty easy to see why he had been appointed to represent Paul, why Paul had wanted me and why the NCOs were leaning over backwards for me. I had never been an enlisted man, but they already knew that I liked to play the game the way they do, not like an officer and a gentleman. They knew me better than I knew myself, I thought. It occurred to me that I had been a cop before I was a lawyer. Cops are very much like NCOs. The motto was to get the job done and protect their own. Honesty, decency and strict adherence to every rule were much admired in rabbis, priests and preachers; it wasn't expected of teachers or doctors – and you don't shovel shit with a hay fork.

He patted the list of prosecution witnesses again, looking uncomfortable and bewildered. He finished his beer in large gulps, ready to escape from this wild character sitting before him guzzling booze and destroying all the great ideals drummed into him in a fine law school in Michigan where professors and deans all lived in never-never land.

'I'll go over the witness list tonight, CD. Tomorrow in the morning, I'll see Paul and figure out how long it will take me to talk to all the witnesses. I'd like you along taking notes with Paul and the witnesses. Might be fun for you. You won't have to say a word.

Before quitting time, we should be able to tell Major Mills when we can kick off this kangaroo court.'

'Yes, sir. I'll be in the office when you want me.' He stood up and grabbed his go-to-hell cap with its shiny new bar.

12
Paul Kelly

The prisoner's conference room was a single storey, draughty wooden addition to the concrete block stockade which housed several air police offices and half-a-dozen cells. It contained a battered conference table with half-a-dozen equally aged straight chairs. The unpainted plasterboard siding reached the wooden floor jaggedly and I could see daylight where wall allegedly met floor. At the far end of the narrow room, across from where room met concrete block building, was a Franklin wood stove, a stove pipe around which there was also skylight where it went through the roof. A cardboard box held a small supply of chunks of coal. There was also a long fluorescent fixture dangling from wires and several small, permanently closed and barred windows.

Paul came into the room alone, wearing a two-piece fatigue outfit which had large 'Ps' lettered front and back on trousers and jacket. He stood with his back to the door and grinned his lopsided contagious grin at me. He looked well in his bean-pole way, his hair cut and his face clean shaven. The grin did not belong on the face of a man facing a firing squad or whatever our government now used to exterminate the really unwanted. But the grin was Paul, never hurry never worry Paul. 'It was only a little burglary, Judge.'

He sauntered to a seat across from me and draped himself into it, lighting a cigarette and pulling a tin ashtray – *the* tin ashtray – toward him. He did not offer to shake hands and he did not stop grinning. 'Sis says you are as pissed off at me as you always used to be. Or more so.'

'Sis is right.'

'But here you are anyway. Good old reliable Knute. Ready to do or die for old Alpha Phi.'

'Alpha Phi is a sorority.'

'*Gsmacht nichts.*'

'Why me, Paul? You know I don't defend cases.'

'Hell, you *are* a trial lawyer. And I know you're the best. I've read some of the clippings. Sis still sends them. Probably to piss off her second. You investigate and then try criminal cases. Well, old buddy, this one needs investigating and trying. That's why you, among other things. Such as if I got myself some sharp New York City type, the gentlemen of the court wouldn't even look at him. There's also a handful of mouthpieces floating around Europe and the Isles who couldn't make it back in the States. They do court martials. The military believes that if you shake hands with them you better count your fingers.

'So here is Knute, an officer and gentleman like themselves, Air Force at that. And a guy with both the infantry badge and a flying cross. A prosecutor who stands for law and order and putting the bad guys away, taking leave from upholding apple pie and motherhood to defend his poor, wrongly charged little brother-in-law. Jesus, old buddy, it's like a movie script. That's why it's you, you, you,' he said, singing the last words and still grinning.

'Why do you think I won't sell you out, you unmitigated bastard?' I asked, seriously considering wiping the grin off his face.

'A bastard, I'm not. My sainted mother wanted three children. That was tradition. So she did the act three times in her life. First for Sis, then me and last time for ever and ever, Bobby. Bastard, no way. But,' he said, still grinning and starting a fresh cigarette, 'son of a bitch, oh yes. Liar, cheat, burglar, pick-pocket, seducer, card-shark, goof-off, bully, knife-fighter, pot-smoker, booze-hound, whore-master. Guilty, all counts.'

He ground out the fresh cigarette. The smile disappeared and his eyes met and held mine. 'AWOL, yes; murder, no. And this time, old buddy, I'm in deep shit. Between the proverbial rock and a very hard place. That little fuck, Smith, wants my ass and he's got the horsepower. He's the king here.

'I told the lieutenant here,' he said, jerking a thumb at the silent and unmoving figure of CD Day, 'I liked that girl. I had fun with her. I fucked her. She filled in a little for not having a wife and kids for more than a year. She knew that, too. We were friends. I do not hurt my friends, drunk or sober. I guess the lieutenant gave you the whole scenario.'

He shrugged and now there was a sag in the jaunty shoulders and his hands shook when he held a match to the new cigarette.

'Why you? Because you know I never lied to you. Little fuck-up that I was, I never bit the hand that fed me. I won't bring out the violins, don't worry. But I figured that once you stopped cussing me out for the shit-bird I am, you'd come. It ain't blood between us exactly, but we both had to live with Momma and Sis.'

'I didn't ask the lieutenant for the scenario. I wanted to hear it directly from the horse's ass.'

The grin was back and even stone-face CD had to chuckle. I reached across and took one of Paul's cigarettes and lit it with his matches, although I had my own lighter and smokes. In one of those power courses the county required me to take from time to time, they taught not only about red ties but also that my gesture was one of friendship.

'I can't get unlimited supplies of those,' Paul said. I took out my own pack, same brand, and slid it across the table.

'Sorry, wasn't thinking. Just trying to get back one of the thousands you owe me.' We both grinned and the ice between was gone. It was like the old days. Paul in trouble, me trying to set it right. Things never really change, I suppose. I could feel CD relax slightly. He was not all lumberjack.

'From the top, Paul.'

'From the top, OK, for about the fifth time.'

'Fifth time?'

'About. First the air police. Then the CID guys. Then the investigating officer. The shrink, and then the lieutenant here. I should have recorded it the first time.'

'I don't see the shrink on your list, CD. Just a name here I didn't fit in, Captain Shaw. Was that the shrink, Paul?'

'I think so, although he didn't look much like George Bernard. More like Nehru before he started to shave.'

'CD?'

'I didn't give it much thought. I assumed he was going to swear Paul wasn't on morning report or something trivial like that.'

'The way I learned it, CD ... assume ... makes an ass of U and me. Check it out. Name rank and serial number and if he's stationed here.'

'Naw ... they took me to see him at Alconbury in cuffs.'

'CD, you've heard Paul's story before. Check him out now, right now. And when you know who he is, go over to Training and give the information to Sergeant Conyers.'

'Just give it to him?'

'Just give it to him,' I agreed.

'Yes, sir.' He stood up. 'And then come back here?'

'And then come back here,' I agreed again. He left, dumbfounded but willing.

After the door to the brick stockade closed behind him, Paul looked at me and grinned. 'Wouldn't he make a great husband for your daughter?'

'Great.'

'OK, from the top. On that Thursday, whatever the date, the lieutenant has all that. On that Thursday I found, I finally found a farmhouse near here where I could rent a sort of loft over a barn. Crude as shit, but I could have made it liveable and Joannie and the kids would have made do. Close enough to base for the kids to get to school.

'I went for an OK to Wing. I was happy as hell. It's been more than a year I seen Joannie and the kids. Sergeant major OK'd it, so did the Exec. Colonel Smith would have none of it. Disapproved.

I'm vital. I have to live on base, twenty-four hour call and all that shit.'

'What do you do on base, Paul?'

'I run the combat simulator.'

'Meaning?'

'Every B-47 on this base carries the bomb. Every one has a set target if the flag goes up. Every aircraft has to fly its pre-set route to target every month on the simulator. The U-2s update every route all the time. If some poor peasant gets a TV antenna, it shows up on the spy-plane films and they update the exact route. Every pilot knows every bridge, every house, every radio station on his bomb run. Every pilot knows where he is to drop the bomb.

'I'm the only one on this base who knows where every one of thirty-seven bomb-carrying aircraft are targeted. Colonel Smith only knows his own bomb run. I know them all. That's why he says he wouldn't let me live off base. If the flag goes up they don't need me. They all have their assignments, so that's bullshit. He says it's not secure for a guy who knows what I know to live off base. I could be kidnapped. Now that's all bullshit because what good would it do for the Russkies to know. They got to know if they kick it off, every city over there's going to be rubble.

'But, I'm a staff sergeant, he's a bird colonel. No living off-base. No housing on base. That Thursday, I had two crews to run through, a.m. amd p.m. Just some clean up and maintenance. So, I go to the club and have a couple of shooters. I'm feeling real low. I also hurt. Remember when I fell off that wing and busted my back? You said I should go for a medical discharge. I got Tylenol and codeine instead. I popped a couple and had a few more shooters and now I'm mad at the world, and half in the bag. You ain't supposed to mix them pills with booze. I know, but by now I could give a shit less.

'Finally, Maggie comes to work, and I told you, we're friends. So I tell her my problems and she kids around awhile and then she says that if I go AWOL, she'll go AWOL from the club. She says meet me at the Huntington Arms. That's a hotel about fifteen miles from here. On the M42. It's at a crossroads like. So, I go. How in hell I drove there in one piece, I don't know. I got there. The bar is closed. They got funny laws here. Bars open and close and open again and like that. But if you register for a room, you can drink when the bar is closed. So, I registered for a room, best as I recollect.

'No Maggie. Well, I knew she lived nearby. Probably went to change. Told the 'keep to tell her what room I had, took another pint, remember taking another pain pill. Sometimes I don't take a pill for a week, others ten a day when I'm really hurting. Comes and goes like that with a spine. Waited for my bird. She arrives, we eat and drink. Couple of NCOs drop in. After that, nothing.

'Later, bright lights in my eyes, I'm being shaken. I'm seeing double and my head feels like a busted watermelon. And I'm seeing two Maggies on the floor by the bed, right next to me. Legs up, no panties, her bush showing, her blouse ripped and titties sticking straight up. My double vision came back real quick to a single, pounding sight. Her face was so awful, eyes and mouth open. Just about no blood though. Maggie dead as a doornail.

'I'm charged with rape and murder. A hanging offense, I'm told. Maggie asked me to come play so I'd feel better. That, counselor, is the story.'

'Who was the first person you saw in the room?'

'Innkeeper and the constable.'

'I keep hearing constable. Is that his name? Who is he?'

'It's not his name. He's the local fuzz.'

'Uniform?'

'Oh, sure. Very impressive uniform. Sort of local god. The boonies cop. I suppose the innkeeper said he heard noise and called him.'

'You're assuming that, Paul, and you know what I think of assumptions.'

The grin came again, slow and easy. 'Yeah, old buddy, I surely do. You being pretty hard on Lieutenant Day, ain't you? He ain't a bad guy.'

'Anything more?'

'I don't think so. If I think of something I'll let you know.'

'Is this the same story you told six times before, Paul?'

'I don't know. First couple of times around I'd probably have admitted the Lindbergh kidnapping. I was out of it. When's the trial?'

'Don't know yet. I've got witnesses to interview, and your colonel pushing to get you hanged in a hurry. Paul, you said you never lied to me as a kid, I believe that. You were a kid then and you were not facing a death penalty. I've put an awful lot of guys away because they lied to their lawyers.'

'Knute, if I'd done Maggie, I'd have hanged myself in my cell. They let me keep my belt. I don't claim I loved her. We were friends and she was all that kept me sane over here. If I believed that in my drug and drunk stupor that I hurt her, I couldn't keep going. She was the only good thing that's happened to me since I got sent here. And she knew how much I missed Joannie and the kids. She always said she was just keeping me from the foggy foggy dew, whatever that means. I cared for her. I'd like you to find out who killed her as much as I'd want you to get me back on active duty.'

'This isn't the *Perry Mason* show, Paul.'

'I told you, Sis sends me clippings. They say you go around to other police departments to give talks about how you and your men do things. They say you have an almost perfect conviction rate because of how you guys work. They say you are the best in the country. Jesus, I do need that.'

That 'best in the country' hit me about the same as 'boy'. I was not used to build-ups nor professional put-downs. I knew I was not best anything. My boss, William William had allowed me to put together a team of eager young lawyers and seasoned and cynical investigators so that I headed one fine bureau. And yes, I had given some lectures around on all-expense paid visits. Paid for by the recipients. And yes, I'd convicted some really bad dudes.

I stood up. 'Paul, you'll get a run for your money. And if they do hang you, you can always say you had a lousy, thieving lawyer. Your sis would agree.'

'I'll take my chances, Counselor.'

13

Prosecution Witnesses

CD and I spent the rest of the day interviewing the prosecution's bread-and-butter witnesses. Dullsville. The noncom who makes out morning reports showing Paul absent without official leave, the investigating officer whose report did not vary from his response to my questions, the air police called to the hotel who interviewed Paul and took him into custody. CD and I split for lunch, he home and I to the NCO Club for liver with bacon and onions, another favorite, with some small talk with several of the resident NCOs. I also got a preliminary report on the military judge, Major Mills.

Major Henry DeWitt Mills had left Harvard Law School to enter flight training and to fly combat missions in Korea. He then returned to finish his education and took his law degree back into the Air Force where he was granted a regular commission. Although he served as a JAG officer, and against all regulations, he was on flight status and remained there by flying the required number of hours monthly and thereby drawing flight pay. He had been stationed at the Pentagon before coming to Wiesbaden with his wife and four children. There were no negative notations accompanying his file.

I read this information off to CD as he drove us to meet Captain Shaw, the shrink stationed at RAF Alconbury. Alconbury, Singlebury, Sunbury . . . ah, the imaginative Brits.

'You don't think his being on flying status would be grounds for a reversal, do you?' CD asked me studiously.

'Naw, I think that's great. Besides, I've already got grounds for a reversal. *If* we lose. But a reversal just means another trial in another place way down the road somewhere while Paul hangs out in the stockade. Our best shot is not to look for a reversal; it's to win.'

'What do you mean you already got grounds for a reversal?'

'My interview with Colonel Smith.'

'He'd never admit anything negative. . . .'

'He doesn't have to do anything. I wore a Nigra during that short, pleasant chat.'

'A what?'

'A Nigra. Borrowed it from my office. Very small, very concealable recording device. Best made.'

'You mean you secretly taped your interview with the colonel?' CD almost drove the little English Morris off the road and into the ditch running alongside the narrow highway. He turned several times to glance at me, not believing. I nodded and patted his arm.

'You really like to win, don't you?' CD said after a long silence.

'Vince Lombardi said it better than I can, CD.'

'Who?'

Jesus, I thought, kids.

'Vince Lombardi is oft quoted as saying "winning isn't everything . . . it's the only thing".'

'You think I'm a total and complete asshole, don't you?' he said at last.

'I'm sorry, CD. And no, I don't think you're a total asshole.'

'Just a plain old asshole, huh?' The almost beatific smile was back on his face. Incredible. We were friends again.

'Colonel Smith flies in a couple . . . two . . . whores every couple of weeks from Wiesbaden,' I said, to unhinge the flow of warmth and good fellowship. 'Every time his wife goes to London or Paris to shop or whatever, he sends an old gooney-bird that's somehow still in the Air Force to fetch them. Pretty high-class stuff, according to the crew chief. Want to see his notes?'

'Lordy, Captain, nothing you do or say will ever surprise me again. I guess if you tell me the sun is going to rise in the west tomorrow, I'll likely believe you.

'Thing is, I didn't know there were still gooney-birds on active duty.'

Law-school and recent law-school graduates came into the military with a first lieutenant's commission, something an academy graduate has to wait eighteen months for after coming on active duty as a second lieutenant, if then. Doctors come in with captain's bars, railroad tracks in the vernacular. Both professions are issued a booklet on how to be an officer and a gentleman and where to buy their uniforms. Captain I.A. Shaw had signed up for five years to repay the money the government had spent on his medical and psychiatric education. He wore a non-regulation brown cardigan instead of his uniform jacket. He ushered us into his ground-floor office in a wing of the base hospital. The bare, cement block office was sprayed in the same pale yellow as I had been seeing everywhere. Probably made from WW II powdered eggs, surplus. Not to be wasted as food in Ethiopia. There were no pictures on the wall, nothing but a GI standard blotter on the desk. The lone metal file cabinet was closed. The lone window had no curtains.

The captain motioned us into the two chairs facing his GI issue desk, and sat down behind it gingerly. Paul was right, he looked like a young but arrogant Nehru. Or maybe self-conscious. Or maybe the smug surface was hiding a huge inferiority complex. I had read his psychiatric evaluation. That was smug also. I had a copy of his file and quite a bit more. I realized as I sat here in the bare office looking out at another day of dull grey that I already hated Captain I.A. Shaw. But then, I hated all psychiatrists. I had to use them a lot because every time the defense brought one in to say one thing, I had to hire one to say the opposite. They made their dough destroying families and ruining lives and testifying against each other. I could hire a shrink to say Adolph Hitler was a humanitarian worthy of the Nobel Prize, second only in goodliness to Heinrich Himmler.

'What can I do for you, gentlemen?' The British accented tone said: 'Please waste as little of my time as you boobs can manage.'

'OK, Doctor, we are not going to be friends. And after this little talk, you are going to dread the day you take the stand. It's going to keep you awake nights between now and then. You may end up as an emergency-room doctor in Calcutta instead of a shrink on Park Avenue when I finish with you.

'We're defense counsel for Paul Kelly, as my associate told you on the phone yesterday. You are going to be a witness in his trial, and we have the legal right to interview you. We also have the right to call you to testify if the prosecution doesn't. I hope that's clear. You will be a witness come what may. If you get sick or called on emergency, the court will wait for your appearance. Unless you die, you will come to court.

'My name is Helbig,' I spelled it, very slowly. 'Norwegian. His is Day, English–Irish. Yours isn't Shaw, you are decidedly not Irish. And why the initials I.A.? Why not your true Indian name?'

I.A. Shaw looked at me as though I had slapped him. So did CD.

'Why aren't you in uniform,' he said finally, the British intonations fading rapidly.

'Because I'm a civilian. Now, answer my question. Why the phoney name and the initials? Ashamed of being Indian?'

He put his delicate hands on the desk blotter, clenched. Perhaps he was going to leap across the desk to belt me. I'd have loved that, but it is not in the manual for shrinks.

'Did you come here to insult me or interview me?' he said very softly.

'Right. You interviewed Paul Kelly December 13 according to your report. I note the time as 0945 hours to 1015 hours, is that correct?'

'It is.'

'So, is it fair to say that in one half-hour you concluded that Paul Kelly had not been under sedation at the time of the death, that he was not mentally incompetent under the McNaughten rule at the time of the murder, and that he is now competent to stand trial. Is that correct, Doctor?'

'It is.'

'And you will so testify?'

'Yes.'

'Thank you, Doctor. Thank you very much....' I let him breathe deeply. He knew he had out-gunned me. 'One thing, Doctor: when you come to court, and we have a stand-by subpoena here which we are now serving on you in the event the prosecution elects not to call you, you will save yourself some wear and tear and the court's time, if you bring all of your background records with you. I mean everything from your Indian birth certificate to the record of your analysis in California. Everything.

'I even want your divorce papers, you know, the allegations of mental cruelty and all that.'

He and CD sat and stared at me in total disbelief. Neither knew if I was bluffing, or had every intelligence agency in the world at my service. It was totally silent in the little bare office.

'You want to put me on the stand to destroy me, and my career.'

'Absolutely.'

'For God's sake, why?' The first sign of emotion. I was getting there.

'Because you took thirty minutes of your precious time to condemn a man to the gallows.'

We stared at each other in the silent cubicle while CD took copious notes of God knows what. 'Could we talk alone for a few minutes,' he said, nodding to a suddenly alert CD.

'No way. We are co-counsel,' I said. CD started to get up to indicate that he was more than willing to go. A shake of my head sat him down.

'You think I was hasty, Counselor?' At this point, I activated the Nigra that CD disapproved of so heartily. 'Perhaps I was hasty. They brought him on a day I had a full schedule.'

'Doctor Shaw, we are talking about the interview you had with Paul Kelly in regard to his being charged with murdering a young girl. You had one, only one, interview which lasted all of thirty minutes. Is that correct, Doctor?'

'Yes, of course, that's what we are talking about, Paul Kelly. Perhaps I should have spent more time with him, more sessions. You want me to soften my observations at the trial, is that it?'

'I want you to tell the truth, Dr Shaw. Nothing more, nothing less.'

'Well, of course. Perhaps I should have analyzed his blood tests. Perhaps I should have spent more time with him. Perhaps that could have led me to a different conclusion. It's just the stress of the job here. I'm interviewing flying personnel ten hours a day. The flight surgeon sends them over in droves. Such problems. . . .'

'They all bananas, Dr Shaw?'

'Bananas? Yes, or worse. Most of them should be in a padded room quilting blankets. It's horrible.'

'Tell me about the blood tests, Doctor.' There had been no indication of any blood tests in any of the reams of reports I had read.

'I didn't study them, I'm afraid. Too much job pressure.'

'I want them, or a copy, Doctor.'

'Of course, surely.' He got up and went to his filing cabinet where the Paul Kelly file had been pulled and lay on top of the neatly hung jackets. He leafed through briefly, found two pieces of paper stapled together and extracted them. 'I'll have them copied, all right?'

I nodded and the good doctor disappeared like Houdini. CD turned and looked at me. 'You taped him. I know you did. The way you identified him and Paul. You taped him, you son-of-a-gun. Didn't you?'

'You are learning.'

The beautiful grin covered his face and looked at me in wonderment. It was the first time he had seen scummy-soap water turn into beautiful, multi-covered bubbles floating in the air with the stroke of an ordinary little circular tool.

'Captain, you're too much. Why did you lean on him like that?'

'Because he is now ready to admit his mother is the whore of

Calcutta. He's an arrogant fuck. Do you know what his testimony, left unchallenged would do? He'd sink Paul. I don't like fuckers, willing to do that because they are busy.'

'Point taken, sir. So it's win at all costs, but only if you believe.'

'The name is Knute. You've spent too much time with the NCOs. Please don't call me "sir" or "captain". I'm Knute. I know it's a tongue twister, but that's my name. OK?'

'Yes, sir,' he said and then he grinned his innocent grin at me.

I can't say I was happy, but all in all, it had been a good day. I still felt the so-called jet-lag and I was tired. There was a restaurant at the Sunbury which I was told served grog and food. It didn't have to be good food or good grog. I was hungry and tired and it was well past three in the afternoon of this overcast day when CD wheeled into the parking lot of the Sunbury Motel and Restaurant. I just wanted to sleep and then eat and then sleep some more.

'Thanks, CD. See you tomorow p.m. for the constable. This time I'll pick you up.'

14
Anthony Lane

As I got out of the small car and faced door number 11 of the Sunbury Motel, I saw a man sitting on some sort of contraption, reading a sports magazine. As I approached, he stood up and folded a small round seat up along what appeared to be the staff of a walking stick, hung the cane over his arm and folded the magazine into a pocket of his mackinaw. He was of medium height with pepper-and-salt hair cut short, a clipped mustache over a firm mouth. His face was nicely weathered and the blue eyes were amused.

'Barrister Helbig, I presume,' he said, holding out his right hand. When he arose, so did a dog lying at his feet. The dog looked something like a large collie in build and size. 'Mary asked me to give you a shout, some of our well-known British hospitality, I suppose. I'm Anthony Lane, Mary's mother's brother. Lord, man, Mary Buttons from the airplane. I gather you made rather more of an impression than she did.'

'I'm sorry; Mary Buttons made quite an impression, I just didn't connect her with anything up here.'

'Understandable. Well, now that you're over the shock of it all, do you suppose we might talk inside? I've been out here in the raw and it's getting into my old bones.'

'Sorry. Of course, come in,' I said unlocking the door, 'although the room is not all that warm either.' Anthony Lane and dog came in and I turned on both lamps, hit the electric heater for its rationed dose of warmth.

'I have some Canadian whiskey.'

'Straight please. That should take the chill from the old bones.' He looked around the room with that amused crinkle at his eyes and took off his coat, first leaning the cane-gadget against the bed. I went into the bathroom for plastic glasses and the bottle and we sat down. I poured two stiff shots and we both sipped. Then we both lighted cigarettes, each to his own, and looked at each other.

'Not exactly Buckingham Palace, I'd say. Thought you'd be staying at the air station.'

'The commander wouldn't have me.'

'Oh, it's like that is it? You're the spanner in the works, eh? I live stone's throw from here. Read the local papers about that Irish fellow you're here for. Nice and neat package and along comes a spanner.'

'I don't know how much of a spanner I'm going to be.'

'Mary seems to think you'll be quite a spanner. Girl is full of surprises. Hardly ever gives me a ring so that was the first shock. Then, she seems taken a bit by an American of all people. She's not much taken by anybody, but I never heard a kind word about Yanks escape from her before. Made me very curious, indeed, you see. So I said I'd be glad to look in on you.

'All very interesting,' he said, finishing his drink. I poured him another. The dog had crawled near the electric heater and stretched out.

'You're a policeman, aren't you?'

He looked up quickly, the small lines around his eyes laughing. 'Retired,' he said after a pause. 'Pensioned off to the sheep meadow. Churchill and I,' he said, indicating the dog with his foot, 'run a few sheep. Keeps us occupied a bit.' The dog raised his head when he heard his name, stared at his master and then laid his head down again.

'Quite a coincidence, Mary calling I mean. Fact is, I followed the murder case as closely as one can by reading the scandal sheets. Also, I've a few acquaintances at the air station. That's how I learned you were here. And, of course, I've been around here a bit.

Strikes me the lad, your client, has no motive. From what little I've gathered, that is. I never liked arresting a chap for a crime he had no reason to commit. And this was rather an ugly and vicious one at that. But then, I'm sure you've had all the reports.'

'Yes. Skimmed them. They're right here. Mr Lane, let me understand what's happening here. Maybe I've still got jet-lag, but I'm confused. I happen to meet a very attractive English stewardess to whom I have the bad grace to talk too much about myself. She happens to have an uncle who's a retired cop living hard by Singlebury, who happens to have a strange interest for a retiree in a local homicide.'

He smiled broadly at me, showing teeth to envy, the eyes dancing merrily. 'You don't believe a word of it. Good lad. I'd have doubts about Mary's judgement if you swallowed the whole thing, hook, line and sinker. It's not jet-lag, Barrister, it's good thinking. Copper thinking. . . .' He chuckled.

'I'm a cop, Mr Lane, in addition to being a lawyer. I was a cop, what we call a beat cop, before becoming a lawyer. To us, it's not a dirty word. Our detractors have other names for us. Pigs used to be very big, along with fuzz, motherfucker, asshole, cocksucker and so forth. And no, I don't believe a word of it.' I was now also grinning because whatever Anthony Lane's game was, he played it very well. Challengingly. I jumped up to restart the electric heater. The dog didn't budge when I stepped over him. When I got back to my hard-backed chair, Mr Lane held out his empty plastic glass.

I refilled our glasses and we knocked them together, toasting I know not what. We sat grinning at each other, the Canadian whiskey undoubtedly adding warmth to our new acquaintanceship.

'Well, laddie, nor should you. But after you've checked everything out, you'll find it nothing more than the old war horse out to pasture, hearing the bugle and wanting to once more gallop into the fray. When Mary called her old uncle you see, she didn't do so to pull me back into harness; I do verily believe she just wanted me to check you out so that when time allows, she could make a quick trip up here. I'm not suggesting that our Mary is quick off the mark, but like her mother she is a very determined sort. By our country-folk standards, she's well on her way to becoming an old maid – not for lack of asking, mind you. Choosy, like her mother, who'd settle for no one less than a top sergeant. Dreary, boring sort of chap, but successful enough. The mother's the strong one there.

'Are you married, lad?'

'Not for the last seven years.'

'Ah, sorry. I'm a widower myself.'

'I'm divorced.'

'Ah, even more sorry. Lots more cost than a simple funeral.'

I let that drift around awhile because I didn't have an answer. But I knew now that Anthony Lane was what he claimed he was. He was also one very slick article. I would have loved to bring him into my bureau.

'Mr Lane, you can take all of the files and review them. See what you think. All but this one,' I said separating out the various dossiers. 'This one is Constable O'Brien. Finder of the body. I'm to see him tomorrow.'

'Ah, laddie,' he smiled, full of merriment. 'More and more I see why little Mary has taken a shine. Now, if you'll be so good as to add a wee drop into my cup, we'll talk.'

'We've been talking.'

'No we've been throwing small talk about. Feeling each other out, I'd think you would say. I'm feeling rather comfortable with you about now. So is Churchill,' he said, pointing a booted foot toward the dog. Churchill raised and lowered his head again as before. 'Churchill trusts you. He doesn't many. Most chaps step over him the way you did would lose a fair part of their calf. He's part Collie, you see, Collies fight best on their backs.'

I stepped over Churchill again, refilled our plastic glasses and lighted a cigarette. 'You are a piece of work, Mr Lane.'

'Ah, lad, no mister, please. Anthony, even Tony is a bit too formal for me. Friends call me Ruff.

'Now, since you've already zeroed in on Constable O'Brien, let me give you fair warning: he's a mean sort, not just to soft little birds. Spent four years in Northern Ireland and I'm told he loved it. He's now a policeman here where we have no war, but he's still a mean sort.'

'Meaning?'

'Oh, I do verily believe that he wanted little Maggie. Been chasing her with no luck, I've heard, Resented her working at the air station, I've heard. Not exactly high on Yanks, I've heard. And, oh yes, he's had lots of experience bashing in skulls.'

'You think Constable O'Brien killed that girl?'

'Without a doubt.'

I let that one hang also. We sat and looked at each other and Churchill farted. 'Sorry, outdoor dog.'

'We'll let the gas pass. How are you to prove it?'

He set his empty glass on the linoleum and grinned at me.

'Ah, lad. That's the whole point of this don't you see? Retired Copper Lane couldn't do sod all about this. And suddenly,' he said, waving expansively for the first time, his face now glowing cherry red, 'out of the blue comes Sir Galahad from America.

'My little niece finds you and sends you to me. I can't catch the bugger, but you can.'

'I'm here to defend Paul Kelly, not to indict Constable O'Brien.'

'Ah, but one will lead to the other, surely as God made little green apples.'

'Ruff, I'm hungry and tired. There is a restaurant at the far end of this blockhouse. What say we go there and eat something?'

'Splendid. We'll give the heater one more punch for Churchill and bring some back for him.'

15
Constable O'Brien

At first glance, Constable John J. O'Brien looked like every Irish cop I've ever seen. Burly, red-faced, lumbering walk.

At first glance. That overblown first impression can be deceiving. The constable had more broken blood vessels in his face than his mid-years dictated. Below a walrus mustache, a nondescript sandy color, was a small, pinched mouth and his excuse for a chin receded into his neck. The eyes were very light blue, set close together like bookends to a bulbous nose. He sat behind a battered wooden desk in a messy little office with dirty windows letting in some grey light on another overcast day. The office was part of some sort of municipal building and the whole affair looked run down and neglected. I had never thought of anything to do with the British Government as being anything but coldly efficient and spotless. Too many British films, I suppose.

'Well, gents, what will it be, eh?' he said, after waving us, CD and me, into chairs across the desk from him.

'The Kellogg homicide, Constable,' I said.

'Well, I've ruddy well been over that often enough with you chaps.'

'Yes, sir, but that was with the prosecution and its police. We're the defense. For the defendant, the accused.'

'Well, you'll ruddy well get no help from me, boys. I want to see that bloody Yank rapist hang high. By the testes would suit me.'

'The autopsy doesn't indicate recent penetration, semen, no bruising in the genital area.'

'Don't mean that's not what he was after. Believe me, sonny.'

'I see ... well, sir, tell me, you were the first at the scene, the crime scene, is that right?'

'Right.'

'The scene, the crime scene, was in one of the upstairs rooms in the Huntington Arms, is that correct?'

'It's all in the reports, sonny. You're like a dog coming back to eat its own vomit.'

'Sir, if I'm not permitted to question you then you will not be permitted to testify. Since there's no confession, you are the key to the prosecution case. The judge advocate general, his staff and all your local higher-ups would not want that to happen, if you get my drift,' I said, thinking of the laconic Sergeant Conyers.

'Oh, you'd ruddy well like that, wouldn't you? In a rented room upstairs in the Huntington Arms, yes.'

'The report said you were downstairs near the reception desk when you heard a rumpus. Just what does "rumpus" mean?'

'Noise ... like fighting, things crashing about.'

'Screams? Woman's screams?'

The eyes narrowed in sudden anger. The question had not been asked 'in all the reports'. The interviewers had accepted 'rumpus' and gone no further. Constable O'Brien now had to think fast which I gathered happily was not his forte. But I could see what Anthony Lane said about a mean sort.

'Well, it doesn't matter, really, sir. The innkeeper, Mr Rudman, was at the reception desk with you when you heard the rumpus. Perhaps he'll recall.' I had let the constable off the hook. He knew now, remembered now that his statement said he told the innkeeper he thought he heard a rumpus upstairs. No screams.

'I don't need Mr Rudman to refresh my memory. There were no screams. He shut her up forever with the first blow.'

'You were there to see the first blow?'

'It was bloody well all over when I got there, and I mean bloody, all right.'

'Blood all over the place?'

'Right.'

'On Paul Kelly?'

'Right.'

'On the truncheon you found partly under the bed?'

'Right.'

'What is a truncheon, actually?'

'Like a small baseball bat, somewhat. Go look at it for yourself, you've got the right to see the physical evidence before trial.'

This time it sank in. I almost missed it the first time when he told me 'I don't need Mr Rudman to refresh my memory'. That's a phrase in one variation or another I'd heard in hundreds of trials. Always coming from cops or expert witnesses. It usually went: 'May I use my notes to refresh my memory?' Never: 'I'm not sure, can I look at my notes?' or 'Gee, I can't recall, is it OK if I look in my day book?' Invariably, the witness had to 'refresh my memory'. Just as in police parlance, nobody, but nobody, ever gets out of a car. 'They' or 'he' or 'I' always 'exited the vehicle'.

When I put together the constable's legal phrase with his knowing I had a right to examine every item the prosecution wished to introduce into evidence, I knew I had a cute one here, fast thinker or no. Constable O'Brien knew the rules of discovery, similar on both sides of the ocean.

'Oh, right you are, sir. Thank you.

'Just one or two more questions please, sir. The reports don't mention how long you were up there before you called down to Mr Rudman to get an ambulance.'

'As I said in the reports, I entered the room, saw the lass on the floor covered with blood, the killer next to her. I gave him a wallop to stretch him out and checked to see if she was still breathing, poor dear. She wasn't. I went to the top of the stairs, didn't want to go down and maybe lose the Yank, you see, and hollered for Mr Rudman.'

'You gave Kelly one wallop, sir?'

'That's all it takes me,' he said. He was beginning to enjoy himself now. The pig eyes were no longer mean.

'When you first heard the rumpus and rushed upstairs, the rumpus was still going on so you knew which room it was coming from?'

'Right.'

'Was the door open or locked, the door behind which the crime took place?'

'I wouldn't know, sonny. I heard the rumpus, I stood back and kicked it in. One kick was what it took. For me.'

'So it would be fair to say that Paul Kelly must have struck the last blow just as you burst into the room, or moments before that.' I had to guide him a bit here. 'He was still causing a rumpus so as to lead you to the right room?'

'Right.'

'Thank you, Constable O'Brien, you've been a great help.'

'I'm plain shocked,' CD said, as soon as we got back into his car. 'After what you did to that doctor, I thought you'd eat this guy up and chew out little pieces. I couldn't believe all that "sir" this and "sir" that. Like you were interviewing the pope, for heaven's sake.'

'One minute, CD.' I pulled out the Nigra and spoke into it. I gave the date, time of interview and the fact that Lieutenant Day took notes to corroborate that there were no erasures on the tape.

'The shrink,' I said, 'I want wound up tight as a drum; the constable I want relaxed.'

'Why, for heaven's sake?'

'*Peritis nec crede.* Put not thy trust in experts. CD, expert witnesses have to be made afraid. They have to come to court scared shitless that all their palaver is going to be seen through as so much oxen shit. Experts give you oxen shit. That's why I had a computer dig out that piece of Latin. When you quote something said thousands of years ago it puts things back into perspective for a jury. Our Captain Shrink now knows that I've read the books. He knows I'm going to make him look like the asshole he is. He's going to come into that courtroom agreeing with everything I say so as not to be embarrassed. He'll agree that yellow is actually green.

'If we let his testimony stand, as he meant to give it, we're dead. But now, he's going to call one of his forensic shrink societies back in the States. And they are going to tell him that I have made mashed potatoes out of some of their best. So, one of our toughest witnesses ain't going to be tough anymore.'

'How long does it take to become so jaundiced?'

'When did I become jaundiced? When my wife introduced me to her boyfriend? When the boss told me C.G. Edwards and Company never tried to cheat anybody? When I found six knives under the body of some poor black guy that a cop shot, thinking the dude was armed. Six cops, each on his own, must have ransacked his cars to find the right knives so that that poor, unarmed dude got shot because he posed a threat.'

16
RCM 802

Major Henry Dewitt Mills looked like a poster of an airline pilot to whom you would gladly entrust your life to fly the friendly skies. He was tall, tanned, with a lithe, muscular body, short blond hair, a firm, square jaw and deep-blue eyes. There was just a touch of grey at the temples, hard to distinguish from the blond. His smile showed even white teeth and lighted up his whole face. Sincere. Honest. What you see is what you get. His immaculate uniform showed senior pilot wings and several rows of decorations including an Air Medal, some unit citations, Bronze Star and Purple Heart. Not the usual fruit salad of a military lawyer.

'Gentlemen, please make yourselves as comfortable as circumstances permit,' he said in a slight western twang. We were in a square office in the squat, cement block building, also square, which served as legal office and courthouse. Everything was painted the same peeling yellow as all the other old buildings. This one was undoubtedly a World War II model, built to withstand all but direct bomb hits.

'I'm Major Mills, Hank to most of my associates. Do you all know each other?'

'I'm Knute Helbig, I have not met the prosecutor.' Major John J. Sully was introduced JAG for this base, having recently replaced Lt Col Kuss as top dog. We shook hands all around and reseated ourselves. Major Sully was of medium height and build with a pleasant, nondescript face. He would not stand out in a crowd but seemed amiable and relaxed.

'Did you fly in today, Major?' I asked the military judge.

He grinned. 'Commercial to Gatwick and staff car here. Last night. Too expensive for the Air Force to let me fly in here directly. Did you know that the British charge us for every landing and take-off we make from their bases?

'Matter of fact I thought I'd meet you last night at the BOQ so we could get acquainted.'

'The BOQ is off limits to me, Major. Ditto the Officers' Club ... by order of the commander.'

'Well, that's rather uncivilized. This is a trial, not a war.'

Major Sully cleared his throat and chuckled good-naturedly. 'Major Mills, this is a court martial to you, to me, and to Civilian Counsel here, who, I understand, is normally a prosecutor, a district attorney and a good one, but it's war for Colonel Smith. The accused, Paul Kelly is in actuality Ho Chi Minh and Counsel here is Lucifer in disguise come to save him from the clutches of all that is right and good in the world.' He chuckled again and pulled cellophane off a cigar.

'I realize that this is a capital case, quite out of the ordinary, and that the good people of Huntington hereabouts are incensed that one of their lovely young daughters was brutally murdered by a foreigner ... an American foreigner at that. I can see the wing commander acting the part of the shocked and outraged for the locals, but to disallow Counsel common courtesy....'

'Frankly, Major Mills—'

'In chambers, Hank, please.'

'Fine, Hank. My friends call me Jack. Anyway, frankly, Colonel Smith couldn't give a flying fuck for what the locals think. His name is before Congress for a star. The accused has the highest security clearance on the base. When he went AWOL, our colonel went ape shit. The accused has it in his power to destroy the function this wing has. Trained now for years. Scandal like that and you can kiss your star on the ass as it turns its back on you for eternity.

'The colonel called in the CID, Scotland Yard, CIA . . . name it. Then they found the accused less than ten miles from base. No desertion, no Russians. Just a drunk who bashed in a girl's skull. He wants Paul Kelly's ass with a passion. And I aim to give it to him.'

'Guilty or not?' I asked very softly.

Major Sully turned light-blue eyes and just looked at me. 'I play golf with the colonel. Not because I like him, but he's wing commander and writes up my ERs. I never beat him yet. He don't like losing. Round here, the boss says shit, you squat. He says jump through that window, all you hear is the sound of breaking glass.

'Like it? No. Put up with it? You better bet your ass. I got a lot of years to put in and five mouths plus my own to feed. So, yeah, Counselor, I aim to give the boss Paul Kelly on a platter.'

'If you can,' I said.

He grinned at me and chuckled, then cleared his throat. 'Frankly, I put in a call to some friends from my West Hampton Beach days. They tell me you are the biggest gun in the prosecution arsenal out there. They tell me you make Tom Dewey look like a first-year law student. I'll tell you, Counselor, frankly, I asked my friends to put together all the newspaper stories about you, from all the papers. You know why?'

I shook my head.

'Because I want the colonel to see them. See what came over here to take on a run-of-the-mill military lawyer. I want an excuse, frankly, if I can't hand him Paul Kelly's ass. But you better believe I'm going to do my goddamnedest to win this case.'

'I've often heard that on some of these outlying air bases, it was more a wing commander's fiefdom than an American military establishment. But surely, Major Sully, as a JAG officer, your responsibility is to ensure justice, not win one for the Gipper?' There was toughness now in Major Mill's voice, the western twang very pronounced.

'My responsibility, sir, is to carry out my commander's orders.' There was now steel in Major Sully's tone.

'Look, Major,' Sully continued, now sounding remorseful. 'I haven't got a ranch with oil wells to retire to when I stop playing soldier. I'm a poor kid from the southside of Chicago who got into college and law school by hook or crook. I can't afford *noblesse oblige*. I ain't exactly proud of it, but if I can feed my kids I'll have done more than my old man did for his.'

'Well, this all shapes up to becoming more interesting than I had anticipated. When I had to cancel a trip to Spain to come here I must admit I was disappointed and annoyed. But now, I'm glad I got this assignment.

'Now, Captain Helbig, I've heard Trial Counsel's view of the case. I'd like yours.'

'It's half-baked. And you won't believe it. It'll sound like the *Perry Mason* show.'

'Try me, Counselor.'

'When I agreed to come over here to defend my ex-brother-in-law, I thought he and I would talk and I'd get him the best plea possible. I even thought that I had enough clout to do a lot better for him than CD here or any JAG could do.

'That's what I thought. But I now know that Paul, who is no angel, did not kill Maggie Kellogg.'

'Frankly, Counselor, that's the way the defense is supposed to talk, whether they believe it or not. But if your boy didn't do her in, as the English say, then who the hell did?' Major Sully made sense. Open and shut. I looked at the prosecutor puffing his cigar and lighted a Marlboro. It was very quiet in the little office.

'For Christ's sake, man, the air policeman, no, correction, the Brit constable found him beating her to death. I'm willing to try to talk plea here, the colonel be damned. *Try*, I say. But, frankly, it's open and shut.'

'I've had a private investigator working for me the last few days. A retired policeman, British of course. Lives here, knows his way around,' I said.

Next to me, I heard CD draw his breath in loudly. Thinking no doubt that I was lying through my teeth again. Major Mills folded his fingers together, put his elbows on the desk and rested his chin on his fingers.

'Go on,' he said.

'I know who killed Maggie Kellogg, and it was not Paul.'

'But who, for Christ's sake? The constable?' Major Sully was upset, half out of his chair, the cigar glowing bright red.

'You got it right, Major. The constable.'

Major Sully rose. 'That's the most ridiculous thing I've ever heard. It's . . . it's criminal to even suggest. . . . We are talking cover-up here . . . we are talking scandal here. We are impugning the British system of justice. Counselor, I've heard you fight hard, but this is monstrous, monstrous.'

'And you are prepared to prove this?' Major Mills asked.

'No, sir. That's not my job. I'm here for the defense. This is also the wrong jurisdiction to prove it. That's up to the Brits. I only intend to do what I have to do. Establish a reasonable doubt. I hope you'll give me the leeway to do that.'

'Within the rules of evidence, of course.'

'You might have to bend them a little, Major Mills.'

'I do not do that. But, perhaps my intransigence will give you grounds for appeal.'

'I neither want nor need grounds for appeal, Major. I already have grounds.'

'Oh, Lord,' CD Sighed.

'Well now, that's interesting, Counselor. The trial has not started.'

'But the good colonel has. I've got him on tape, Major Mills. His prejudice alone is enough to sink him and his star and his trial. I want neither to sink the star nor appeal the trial. I'm not an appeals lawyer. I want things decided in the courtroom.'

'Holy Mary, Mother of God,' Major Sully said.

'Well said,' Major Mills said.

'On that tape, I am referred to as a "Jew-boy New York City shyster". It goes, on in that vein. And no, Major Sully, that tape is not in my quarters here; it's on its way to a very safe place in the deep vaults of the Office of the District Attorney of Suffolk County. But there are plenty of copies around if you want to hear those immortal words.'

'It appears to me that we had better call this whole thing off for the time. Review your evidence with the British authorities. I do certainly hope you are dead serious.' Major Mills's twang had deepened. He was very upset. Major Sully appeared dazed. CD stared at me, open-mouthed. Even the farm boy would not have carried discovery this far. He was in for more shocks.

'There will be none of that, Judge. We ain't going to put fudge on any cake. I came here to defend a man accused of a death-penalty offense. That's what we are going to do. And we are going to let the chips fall where they may. I'm ready for trial, Judge.'

'Or?' Major Mills was now very pissed off.

'Or, Judge, I am going to take my evidence to all the American newspaper and TV people over here. You can't write me off a kook. Or a Kunstler. My reputation is pretty solid. The pinko, liberal, long-haired Jew-boy shyster from New York won't play, Major.

'I'll make you this deal, Mr Military Judge. I don't want the colonel's star, he probably earned it, but I want a fair trial. And if that trial ruffles feathers, so be it. That's not my concern. It should not concern anybody in this room. Criminal trials are supposed to establish guilt beyond a reasonable doubt, or an acquittal. I want nothing more, nothing less.'

'And if you lose, you've got your appeal,' Major Sully said.

'That, Counselor, will not hurt your efficiency report.'

'Frankly, that's true. I'll have done my job.'

'Let me try to understand this. You both want to proceed when there is now a serious question of whether or not the right man is on trial?'

'Hank, frankly, at this point, all we've got is a slick, and admittedly sharp lawyer telling us that the butler did it. That's no reason to get all whacked out. Defense counselors grasp at straws. He comes in here and says he's going to prove the butler did it. Fine. Let him do his damnedest. I say his boy went AWOL and killed a

girl in cold blood. I'll do my damnedest to prove that, that's all.'
Major Sully chuckled and started a new cigar. 'The butler did it,' he chuckled. 'Big deal.'

'And you agree with him, Mr Helbig?'

'My client, my brother-in-law, ex as he may be, is sitting in the can, the stockade. You want to leave him there while you straighten out the legal niceties, keep everybody who fucked this thing up off the hot seat. No way, Major Henry DeWitt Mills. The United States of America, not Colonel Smith, has charged Paul Kelly with rape and murder. The charge reads: 'The United States vs Paul R. Kelly'. It doesn't say some lowlife looking for a star dreamed this up. It says the United States of America is accusing one of its native born of a heinous crime.

'If what happened here is what I think happened here, if my government intends to do in one of its own for better relations with the British Empire, then it has gotten me fucking A-well pissed. I do not care about international relations. The majesty that is the law, at the instigation of some little schmuck named Smith, has decreed to charge a little nothing sergeant with a capital crime. It has brought the full weight of the Government of the United States and its agencies down on him.

'You think I'm going to sit still for that, Major Henry Dewitt Mills, you better think again.'

Major Mills rose, his face red as the proverbial beet. 'This meeting is adjourned for the afternoon. 0900 hours tomorrow. We'll go to trial immediately after.'

Most people I've seen, can't stalk. Major Henry DeWitt Mills stalked.

17
Skull Bashing

It had started out such a grand evening. Anthony 'Ruff' Lane and I, had a fine number of Canadian or Irish or whatever with tan chasers and some steak and kidney pie. The pie was not what Mrs Quinn had served on my first night in the Great British Empire in the place they didn't much like Yanks, but, although a bit salty, it was good. And we had a bread pudding afterwards with a custard better than I'd ever tasted.

'Well, lad, if you laid all your cards on the table, you may be in for a spot of trouble.'

'I wouldn't think so. It was all in camera . . . just the military judge and counsel. That's how it's supposed to be.'

Those wonderful blue eyes smiled at me. 'Ah, laddie, you are reputed, your NCO friends tell me, to be among the best. And yet, so naïve, so naïve. I cannot believe that you say that the world is round and so nothing is on the level, yet you yourself think it is indeed, on the level. W. Somerset Maugham, whom I much admire, fairy or no, wrote in his book *Summing Up* that nothing in the world is certain. And of that, he wrote, he was certain.

'So it goes, laddie.'

'Whatever,' I said borrowing Archie Bunker's best line.

'Speaking of "whatever", Knute, I must confess a little indiscretion. In my own, devious little way, don't you know, I've obtained for myself and Churchill a key to your room. Not that a credit card wouldn't pop the flimsy lock in a second. But I'm high on appearances, you see. So how would it look for a retired copper to be sliding credit cards into doors?'

'Indeed.'

'Well, lad, damn me for a monkey if I didn't let out the key.'

'Let me guess. You gave Churchill the key so he wouldn't have to mess on that super linoleum.'

'If things could only not be so complicated, laddie. No, indeed. I gave the key to a lass I haven't seen in a year. My niece at that, and me her only uncle.'

'Your niece?'

'Ah, you are a forgetful sod. I suppose over there in the States, you have the girls just hanging around for a key to your pad. We here, we British, are so provincial, much as we try to deny it. My niece, Mary Buttons, you bloody Yank, who seems more taken with you than you with her.'

'Mary is here? In my room?' I believe I sounded like a fourteen-year-old boy after his first soul kiss.

'Indeed.'

'Mary's in my room. Right now?'

'Christmas in January, you might say.'

I stared into the amused eyes. 'Oh, wow,' I said.

'Your most intelligent observation, to date. So, lad, if your blood is pulsing, go to it. Or to her.'

'I don't believe this,' I said. 'I don't believe this at all. And where are you and Churchill going to be? On the floor?'

'Fact is, laddie, yes, we're going to be about. Not inside the Enchanted Cottage, of course, but about. I do think you might have needof us before sunrise wrinkles the black of night.'

He was right. What awaited me in number 11 was a Spielberg fantasy. Or maybe Disney. The drab room was lighted by candles. It was warm. Churchill slunk out as I came in. In the middle of the small room, stood a barefoot girl in a full skirt and a white blouse without shoulders, the blouse just covering her breasts. In her hand she had a wooden container enclosing a glass/flask, obviously filled with golden beer.

'I see you've dismounted your horse, sir. So you could come into the bar and look over the wenches. Decide which one you wish to mount. All of us wenches are at your beck and call sir, ready to raise our skirts. Just take your pick, sir.' Mary Buttons had the devil in her eye and in that candlelight, she was a challenge to Marilyn Monroe. I walked to the bed and sat down. Died and went to heaven.

'Jesus,' I said.

'He won't be here tonight, sir. Will Mary do?'

'I don't believe this, Mary Buttons.' She took the glass from the wooden holder and handed it to me. Then she raised her glass and clinked it against mine.

She swished her large skirt and sat down, very close, hip to hip. She grinned at me, leaned forward to put her glass on the floor and then made me take a sip before she did the same with mine. I sat staring down the front of the peasant blouse. Magnificent. Unreal.

'Uncle Ruff is a dear. He's also a pain. He's decided that you, American or not; are the laddie for me. So, he advised me to come up here and seduce you. He said you are the sort. Never leave a girl in the lurch. He likes you. Well, so do I, although you are older than the man of my dreams. But one can't have everything, can one?'

She put her arms around me and pulled me close and we kissed. Her tongue invited itself into my mouth. We fell backwards on the bed as you always see in the better movies. I could feel her warmth and I was out of my mind. This does not happen outside fairy-tales.

At this point in time, it does not. The door of number 11 burst open and I vividly recall a voice, almost a mimic of a cockney accent say: 'Another Yank taking one of our girls.' I remember seeing two bodies in black pea coats, and one of them swung what I thought was a baseball bat. It connected with my head.

I was still somehow conscious, but I knew I was on the linoleum floor and that nothing functioned. I couldn't move, but I could see. One of the pea jackets took a swing at Mary Buttons and she ducked the blow and, skirts flying, she said. 'I'll bust your bloody arse.'

And then suddenly, Ruff Lane was in the room, swinging a mighty club, and Churchill, that docile dog had a pea jacket on the linoleum next to me, sounding like a B-36 on take-off and apparently trying to chew the man a new windpipe.

And then it was all over. Mary Buttons was holding my head. I was propped up against the bed. At my feet a man in a pea jacket groaned and that lovely and peaceful dog still had him by the throat. I sipped some whiskey, Irish most likely. It burned. It also tasted good.

'Mary,' Ruff Lane said. He sounded now like a tough, a very tough cop.

'Mary, go up to the restaurant and call the airfield. Ask them for an ambulance for your lover, here. He's had a rather good blow to the head. I think they may also have smashed in his arm a bit. Ask the ambulance people to wait outside. I don't want them in here, you understand? And don't you come back here. You wait in the restaurant.'

There was no arguing with that command. One did what Anthony Lane ordered.

'Now, then,' he said, 'let this sod up, Churchill.' The dog backed away, obedient as Lassie. Anthony 'Ruff' Lane hauled the pea jacket onto the bed, pulled a knife from his own jacket and sliced the pea jacket, pants and all that went under, away. He then pushed the totally naked man on to the linoleum.

Naked, huddled on the cold linoleum, he did not look as big as he had appeared to me. The dog, Churchill, lay down facing him, inches from the man's bare hip.

The owner of Churchill showed no signs of worry, walking into my small bathroom to fix himself a stiff plastic cupful of Canadian. He came back and sat down next to me, stroking my back for a moment.

'Stand up,' he yelled suddenly and the dog rose, as did the hairs on his back. The nude man pushed himself up. He was not all that big.

'Now, there are only three things I wish you to tell me. The name of your accomplice is one. Who hired who and for how much is two. And if you know why.

'As you may have noticed, laddie, you are naked as a jaybird. You may also have noticed the dog standing before you. There'll be none of the so-called police brutality here, young sod. No policeman here, you see. However, my dog there, Churchill, is a bit weird. Loves chewing gonads. You know what they are? Balls, laddie. Balls. He mucks about with sheep all the time. No balls there and he loves balls.

'I give him the word you see, you naked jaybird, he'll have your balls for dinner. Loves them. Now then if you want to go to high mass and sing soprano the rest of your days, then go right ahead and insult my intelligence. Jaybird, are you reading me loud and very clear?' This was a different Ruff Lane that I knew. This was a very tough, very mean man. There were no laughter lines around the eyes. As I said before, I was some groggy during all this time, but I got a good look at Anthony Lane's eyes. There was murder there, as there was in the gentle Collie-like growls emanating from Churchill.

'If one word coming out of your mouth, my friend, is not true, you sing soprano.'

'Constable O'Brien hired us. Just five quid apiece. To bash this Yank's skull. My partner was Jeff Barnes. I don't know why. Constable O'Brien is a big man, hereabouts. He says, here's a fiver to bash a skull, we take the fiver.' He was now shivering. Heating unit or not, it was cold in that room.

'Take a message back, laddie. One, tell Jeff Barnes he's dead. Number two, tell Constable O'Brien it failed. Now, get dressed and get out of here. I'll keep your wallet for the time. Make sure you do what I say.'

I do remember being put on a cot and into an ambulance that screamed and had bells. I do remember a man in a white coat putting a huge needle into me, somewhere. Then, I floated.

18
Doctor and Nurse

There was no meeting the next morning in the temporary office of Major Henry DeWitt Mills. I awoke in the base hospital as it was getting dawn. The shades over the large window had not been closed. My head and my right wrist were in competition for which hurt most. I looked at the wrist, not moving my head from the pillow for fear something, certainly not brains, would spill out. I raised the arm gingerly. The wrist was wrapped and taped but not in a cast. Too swollen, probably. I lowered the right arm and put it next to me very slowly, then used my left to explore my skull. It felt padded and bandaged.

My mouth was so dry I could neither swallow nor move my tongue. I could see that there was a night light, that I was alone in a large room with two hospital beds. There were runners on the ceiling for curtains to separate the beds. I felt around with my good hand, gingerly, located a buzzer pinned to the bed sheets and pushed. I was also aware that the backless hospital gown which destroys the last vestige of dignity was up around my belly.

The door swished open. 'Well, Mr Helbig, up and at them, are you?'

A nurse, major's oak leaves on her collar, leaned over me, felt my forehead gently and then my pulse. 'Good thing the good Lord gave you a hard head, mister.'

I wanted to say something witty and dashing but nothing came out.

'Hold on there, buster.' She left the bedside and returned with a bottle with a straw in it and put the straw between dry lips. It was water which I sucked down as greedily as a hungry suckling. 'Swish it around in your mouth, love. And keep your head as still as you can. I'm going to dissolve some pain pills. Won't taste like Jamieson's best but it will help with what must be the most colossal hangover you've ever had.'

She disappeared from view for a few moments. The light from the window was now strong, or as strong as I'd seen it in sunny Britain. She returned with the bottle and I sipped from the straw again. She was right, it tasted something like milk gone sour. But I drank it like the little soldier I am.

'Will this make me dopey?' My tongue was still fuzzy, but I could taste saliva again.

She gave me a quick, impish grin, but didn't say what she was thinking. Then she pulled a stool up to the bed.

'I'm Major LaFarge, the day duty supervisor. Although my darling husband prefers to refer to me as Madame LaFarge. Which is because I'm older than he is and I outrank him. Your doctor is Jimmy Hung Low, the story of the ruptured Chinaman. The doctor has heard that one since he was a toddler, or so he says.

'You have a concussion, no fractures. Your wrist is bruised and sprained, not broken. I do not know very much about what happened to you, just what the evening nurses overheard and passed on to the night nurses who passed it along to the day shift. Hearsay, I suppose you would call it.'

'Hearsay on hearsay. Double hearsay,' I said. 'How long will I have to lie here like a mummy?'

'That, you can discuss with Dr Hung. I'm neither doctor nor radiologist. Just your typical step-and-fetch nurse.'

'Serving wench.'

'Well, I suppose you could put it that way. But I would not very much like it.'

'No disrespect intended, Major.'

'There is that. I outrank not just my husband but also Dr Hung.'
'About the medication, Major LaFarge?'
'Codeine and Tylenol. It may make you drowsy, but not impair your faculties.' The impish grin appeared again. She was a woman of about forty, with sparkling blue eyes, reddish hair and a pug nose. She filled out the starched white uniform just about right. I knew what she was thinking this time also. I knew she thought that I needed no drugs to make me either dopey or to impair my faculties. 'The concussion, however, may cause you some problems.'
'Like what?'
'Oh, it depends. May not happen at all. May slow down your thinking, make you forget for awhile.'
'Why do you think I'm an asshole, Major?'
She studied my face for a long moment and then shrugged her shoulders. 'The scuttlebutt is that you are a hot-shot New York lawyer here to defend a court martial. It further says that instead you were concentrating your efforts on the wife of one of the locals in your hotel room when the irate mate busted your skull. I don't know, you are a pretty quick read, particularly in your condition, to be dopey. I do not repeat the scuttlebutt because I do or do not believe it. Forwarned is forearmed, pal.'
'Thanks. But this time that is not the way it was.'
'This time?'
'This time. The last time, that was pretty much the scenario. The guy I'm here to defend. In his case it was the girl catching the twenty whacks. Because the law would take care of the Yank lover.'
She gave me a long, puzzled look. A very attractive woman. 'Are you saying, Counselor, a local done it?'
'The local done it, the local constable. Which is why the next twenty whacks were meant for me.'
'Wow,' she said, coloring slightly. 'You're saying Paul was framed for that Kellogg girl's murder and you found out and so he came after you? Wow. This sounds like a detective movie.'
'Except in the movies, the concussions aren't real. You know Paul?'

'Everybody knows Paul the clown. He comes here for his medication every month and always puts on a show.'

I had been dozing I suppose when Dr Hung breezed into the room, about 9.30. Doctor Hung did not look what I had pictured ... fresh-faced son of Charlie Chang. My first impression was that he had played Odd Job in one of the 007 movies, although the features were Chinese, not Korean. Also, he was dressed like one of my MASH doctors in days of old.

'Well, young buddy,' he said, breezing into the room. 'As the Chinese say, you one lucky fellow. Nothing broken, nothing that won't mend in a couple days. My boss here, Madame LaFarge says she took care of you. Does the catheter bother you?'

I didn't know about the catheter. 'No. Didn't know I had one.'

'Well, you do, for the night at least. I don't think, with a little pain killer, we'll have to keep you in the hotel long. I gave you something so you won't shit for awhile. I wanted your head dead center about twelve hours. We got more than that. Let me feel you up, kiddo.'

And he did. Gently, and I expect expertly. He then helped me to sit up, raising the electric bed and positioning my head against the pillows.

'Dizzy?'

'Little.'

'Good. I hate fucking heroes. Don't worry. We'll pull the catheter and let you have lunch. You are a thick-headed fucker, you know. Good thing. But ... big but ... no walking on your own. A concussion means that whatever brains you have got bounced against your skull. Now we know you got a skull. There's fluid of course, to cushion these things. God thought of everything. But you don't need a fall right about now. What I'm saying is, don't get out of bed without a nurse to help you. Sooner you are out of here, sooner I am out of here. Any questions?'

'When do I leave your hotel?'

'Tomorrow, we do another scan, X-rays, you know the works

that cost the taxpayers a fortune. Then, I'll tell you. There is a list of people want to yak with you. OK, after lunch. Just don't nod vigorously or shake your skull vehemently, OK? Your arm will be in a sling awhile when you're up. Thick skull, thick bones. Could have pulverized the wrist bone. You're lucky, Mr Lawyer, or thick, as the case may be.

'Next time you come to Merry England, get yourself a lady of the night, not a local farmer's wife. Safer. Much, much safer.' He grinned at me showing teeth that would do a horse justice.

'Fuck you, One Hung Low.'

The grin widened, almost ear to ear. 'That damn broad. She made it all up you know. Never heard it until she gave me all the crap. Good nurse but a wicked broad. Irish bitch, I think is the term.

'Need anything, she'll take care of it. As she says, she's still teaching me. And she is. Too bad she's married to King Kong. They can hardly fit him into a cockpit and he's the jealous type. Oh, well, I suppose I'll have to send to Hong Kong for a bride. Meantime, I got a golf date. Anything? What?'

'Doc, when you get out of this man's Air Force, let me know where you set up. I need a doctor.'

'San Francisco, Counselor, San Francisco. It's more than Tony Bennett ever imagined. I'll give you my card when I get one. Now, I still owe Uncle another two. But hell, I'll be the first Chink to win the Masters and the Open same year. If I can't come to par now, it's never. There's serious work to do when I get out of here. Shalom, old buddy.'

And the door swished and he was gone.

By lunchtime, I was hungry, my head was clear, probably clearer than anytime since I had boarded the British aircraft and met the lovely Mary Buttons. Which made me think of how nearly a fairytale had come true. Nurse LaFarge brought lunch, the usual tasteful, tepid hospital fare, and I vented my views.

'How right you are, Counselor. Any big city hospital emergency room, they'd have given you a couple of aspirin and sent you on your way. Here, too, in wartime. But Dr Hung is a cautious one and besides, he can't play golf all day, can he?' She grinned brightly.

'He really plays in this weather?'

'Winter, summer, rain, shine . . . it matters not. He wants to play scratch golf and he's sure once he gets out of the service and has to work for a living, there won't be time to perfect his game.'

'Makes sense.'

'I thought golf was a game. For fun. In sunshine.'

'Football's a game, too,' I said.

Major LaFarge had enough on that subject.

'Colonel Woolridge asked me to call him after you've finished your lunch. Wants to stop by.'

'Who's Colonel Woolridge?'

'The exec officer. Colonel Smith's step-and-fetch. And then Major Mills wants the same thing. I don't know who he is. Also Sergeant Conyers and a Mr Lane asked for you and about visiting hours.'

'But no word from the farmer's wife? The one who got me in here in the first place.'

Nurse Lafarge looked sharply at me and then grinned. '*Touché*, Counselor.'

19
Command Decision

Mills appeared within the hour with Major Sully and a stenographer in tow. Outside the window, tiny snowflakes were falling, or rather blowing about. I have been told that although you could freeze your butt off in London on the Fourth of July, it rarely snows in England. No sand trucks or snow shovels on the island. Not only snowing but snowing on Dr Hung's golf game. And God doesn't make little green apples.

The lawyers sat on the empty bed, the stenographer on the one chair or stool in the room.

'How are you feeling, Counselor?'

'OK, thanks. Should be out of here in the morning. Probably start in the p.m., Major.'

'You sure, old buddy?' Major Sully asked. 'I mean I gather, frankly, that you got one hell of a blow to the old noggin. And a broken arm.'

Major Sully seemed truly a nice man. 'Jack, I appreciate the concern. But they tell me here that my head is hard and my wrist's only sprained.'

'Fine, fine,' Major Mills said impatiently. He had passed up Spain, or Portugal, or wherever to hear an interesting murder case, not commiserate with some asshole who got his head stove in. 'Now look, Mr Helbig, there are some things I want on the record before this case proceeds. *If* it proceeds. I think rather that the shoe is on the other foot from our last conference.

'The fact is, officially all we know is that you were attacked in your motel room. You have made no police report, so far as I know. Air police have no jurisdiction off the base as you know. All they can report is that they accompanied an ambulance and transported you here. They reported seeing one man with half his clothes off leave your motel room when they carried you out. They reported the presence of another man, a dog, and what the Brits call a bird – a young lady.

'End of official report. There are two currently floating rumors, however. One is that you were dallying with the wife or daughter of a local, who came after you. The other is that an attempt was made to kill you. In connection with this trial. If the first is true, it is of no concern to me. Just my sympathy on your bad luck,' he said with a smile, a frosty smile. I took it to mean that Major Mills frowned upon dalliances with the wives or daughters of locals. I wondered if he would have approved dalliances with blueblooded London wives or daughters, but I kept my mouth shut. A considerable accomplishment for me.

'However,' he continued, and now he began to sound pedantic as hell, 'however, if there is any truth whatever to the latter, then I want to know it all now. And I want the record to reflect here and now what I will allow into the record of trial. What I am saying, Counselor, is that if this attack upon you was connected to this matter, in fact or in your opinion, I will not let it into the record. Is that clear?

'In our last pre-trial conference, as you may recall, you explicitly indicated your attempt to produce evidence sufficient for a British court of law to indict the investigating officer, Constable O'Brien, I think his name is. After that last conference, I could just see a media circus coming out of all this. *Perry Mason*, I think you called it.

'Not in my courtroom, mister.'

The heat of Major Mills's anger came at me as from a flame-thrower and I could have sworn my hair was beginning to singe. The only sound in the room was the tapping of the steno's ball point against her teeth, or, the teeth her dentist had provided. Universal medical and dental care in Great Britain. I'm not sure I knew what the major wanted. An abortion so he could go to Spain? A gag rule on the trial? A plea? A conviction? I couldn't fathom it. I'm not sure he knew what he wanted either. But the everything-by-the-book routine which makes the military so attractive was spinning off into the by-the-comic-book routine, and Major Mills didn't like it.

'Major, Hank, if I still may, I got off to a bad start with you at the last conference. I regret that. Maybe I have too big a mouth. Maybe my grasp of the language stinks. I did not mean it to come out as you understood it. I'm a lousy apologizer, if there is such a word.

'At any rate, my private investigator, his dog and his niece and I were at the motel. We had dinner. The investigator and his dog went for a walk. The niece, not a local incidentally, and I were having a glass of beer. Two men broke in and went after both of us. They hit her and busted me in the head. Before they could finish, a very angry, big dog and a very angry big man came on to the scene. That changed the odds considerably.

'One of the two men got away with no more than some meat bitten off his legs. The other was questioned by my investigator. I was pretty fogged about then. But to the best of my recollection, and my investigator can certainly illuminate all this, the man with the bat said the constable ... O'Brien ... hired them to bash in my skull. You can corroborate that with two witnesses. End of story, Major.'

Total silence again. The steno was now buffing her nails and that made no noise. The flame-thrower heat emanating from the major was shut down. Major Sully stared out the window at the swirling snowflakes.

'With proof that the constable sent two assassins after you ...' Major Mills said very softly, thinking hard.

'We have proof that the good constable doesn't like Yanks. Period?' I finished for the major.

'Maybe, just maybe,' Major Sully spoke into the silence, 'maybe your assassin lied. Hates the constable. Wants off the hook for trying to rob a rich American. Now what have you got?'

'Indeed,' I said. 'Not likely when a big, mean dog has you by the balls. But possible.'

'What are you saying, Major Sully?' Major Mills said.

'Well, frankly, my old buddy here comes into an 802 and tells us the butler did it,' he grinned, and pulled out a cigar. 'Next damn day, the butler, he says, sent two wolves after him. And he's got corroboration. Who? His investigator. Frankly, that's pretty thin. I'm not saying I doubt you, Counselor, but we are talking court of law here. You know the best evidence in every case is always ruled inadmissible for some damn technical reason or other.'

'You got that right, Jack.'

Major Henry DeWitt Mills motioned to the stenographer. 'On the record, gentlemen, meaning the presence of JAG, Major Sully for the United States and Mr Knute Helbig, private counselor retained by the accused in the case of the US versus Paul R. Kelly . . . fill in all the numbers and orders, please, Stenographer . . . it is agreed, stipulated and understood as follows:

'A. The trial Of the aforesaid shall proceed forthwith. In the event, no mention is to be made of any events or occurrences involving the said private counsel. None whatever. As if they never occurred. It is also agreed, stipulated and understood that the personality, or character, or either, or both shall not become an issue or be raised on this matter. If these stipulations are breached, I shall declare an immediate mistrial.

'B. If these terms and conditions are not acceptable to either counsel for the accused or JAG, I shall declare that no trial shall take place. The entire matter will be referred to the proper investigative agencies and this court martial board dissolved.

'You may have it either way, gentlemen. Major Sully?'

'I say let's try the damn thing, frankly.'

'Mr Helbig?'

'If I choose Plan B what happens to Paul?'

'While he is charged with murder, obviously, he remains incarcerated.'

'So a year from now, while he's going bonkers in the can, he still might be tried for murder?'

'Yes, Mr Helbig.'

'You still got your appeal route,' Major Sully said.

'That's another year in the can. And then, maybe a retrial. I don't much like my options.'

'Your decision, Counselor.'

'Yeah. It's easier when you're the prosecutor, you know?'

'If you asked to be relieved, you've got it. You aren't officially counsel of record yet.'

'How much time have I got to make this command decision, Major?'

'You are to be released in the morning. Let's make it 1400 hours tomorrow. Give you a chance to think this out, talk to your client. Oh, by the way, Colonel Woolridge sends his regrets. Hoped to stop by personally but had a staff conference at Southby. Said he wanted to invite you to move to the BOQ and enjoy the facilities of the O club. Said the commander was sorry he was gruff. Forgive him. Now, anything else?'

'Yeah, Major, there is one thing else.' I could feel heat rising to my face. It always happened when I was pissed off. 'There is one thing else. Yesterday, we had an in-camera pre-trial hearing. No steno. I laid my cards, all of them, on the table. Nobody but you, sir, and Major Sully here and CD and I, knew that I planned to go after O'Brien. No one. That night, two bully boys come around to bust my skull. One admits he was hired, or framed, or whatever, by the constable. Somebody in that off-the record, pre-trial conference talked. Not CD. Not me.'

Major Mills looked at a rapidly blushing Major Sully. 'Not I,' Major Mills said.

'Frankly, all we got to go on that this wasn't a run-of-the-mill robbery is some local ex-felon saying the constable did it. First it's the butler did it, now it's the constable did it. Who proves the connection? Who, in fact, knows you were in your room with your investigator's niece? Maybe, frankly, it was the farmer's niece? I don't mean any harm, but we don't exactly have hard evidence of any of this, do we?' Major Sully said angrily.

'No, we don't,' Major Mills said.

'OK, gentlemen. I got the picture. I'll be ready for trial at 1400 hours, tomorrow.'

'Command decision on the spur of the moment?' Major Mills asked.

'Set in stone, Major,' I said.

'The court martial will commence at 1400 hours tomorrow, gentlemen.'

20

Strategy Sessions

CD came in when the majors marched out. 'How're you feeling?' What a really nice man, I thought. The question was not perfunctory. 'My wife made some brownies for you,' he said extending a box. I opened it and ate a brownie.

'Tell your wife she's with the angels. All I've had since last night was the hospital lunch. These are very good. Best I ever had. And I'm feeling fine. Wrist throbs some and the lump on my noggin only hurts when I touch it.'

'Really?'

'Really, CD, really, I'll be OK. Couple of Bayer every four hours and nothing will hurt. Only, you'll have to do the writing. I don't think the wrist is operative at the moment.'

'That's no problem if you really feel OK.'

'I'm OK, OK? Let's go on to other things . . . our trial starts at two . . . 1400 hours to you . . . tomorrow.'

'How could they?' CD rose from the stool at my bedside, coloring a rosy pink. 'They just can't do that to you. There's more grounds for a mistrial. After a brutal beating, out of a hospital bed and into a courtroom. This is just too much.'

I had to grin. They just don't make lawyers like this where I come from. 'Relax, CD. I pushed them, they didn't push me.' I went very carefully through all of the events of the last twenty hours. CD, constantly shifting on the stool as though he were sitting on a hot stove, either scribbled rapidly in his notebook or sat staring at me, open mouthed.

While I was talking, Sergeant Chuck Conyers and Ruff Lane came into the room. 'Are we interrupting, old boy?' Lane asked.

'This is Lieutenant Clarence Darrow Day, my partner. Called CD. CD, this is Anthony Lane, known as Ruff, our investigator and a former constable himself. You know Chuck Conyers.'

CD rose to shake Ruff's hand.

'I really do hate to correct a famous barrister, particularly since he'll soon become family, but false pride which I know goeth before a fall forces me to correct His Eminence. It's former Inspector Lane, late of New Scotland Yard. Very pleased to make your acquaintance, Lieutenant.'

'I should have known. Sorry, Inspector. And when we're alone you'll explain our family relationship to be. I hope you mean I'll be your heir. In the meantime, after Dr One Hung Low has finished torturing me tomorrow morning, we go to work. Kick off is 1400 hours. I was just explaining to CD options A and B as explained to me. Let me run through it again.' And I did. And then former Inspector Lane outlined the attack on me and the subsequent confession.

And then we sat and all looked at each other. Chuck Conyers had not said a word, if you get my drift. After a few moments, he began rummaging in his fatigue jacket which had about six pockets. First he produced a pack of Marlboro and a throw-away lighter. Then six bottles of Canadian Mist, the kind of bottles airlines use. Then came a plastic ashtray and a sleeve of plastic low-ball glasses. He carefully poured the whiskey into four glasses and touched them all with water from the decanter at the bedside.

'Gentlemen,' he drawled, 'I'm just a hillbilly from West Virginia, but I do humbly believe that we need some spirits. And I do humbly believe we have us a slight problem, if you get my drift.'

I clawed open the pack of smokes and inhaled so deeply that for a few moments I was dizzy. Like when I first started inhaling coffin nails. Dizzy or not, I knew better than to ask where the goodies came from and why the authoritarian nurses had allowed three visitors to the room. The signs all said no more than two at a time.

'What problems, Chuck? I'm not sure I get your drift.'

'Well, Counselor, you laid all your cards on the table in your pre-trial conference, right? And that little shit, Sully, every man's friend, ran right back and puked it all out for the base commander, right? And our intrepid colonel got himself ahold of Constable O'Brien and told him 'Hey boy, our cover-up is falling apart because of that shit-head Yid from New York', right? So O'Brien, right, that mother-fucking murderer and a traitor to his race, he gets a couple of shit-heads to knock off our famous New York mouthpiece, right?

'So, they don't get to scatter your brains over the countryside, Counselor, right? Thanks to Ruff here. So what is our intrepid commander going to do? Lay it on the line to your so-called judge, Mills, and to the members of the court he himself appointed. If you get my drift here, gentlemen, Jesus H. Christ himself could come down off his cross to testify he saw who killed that little girl and this here court would not believe him. You may be mighty good, Counselor, but if the game is fixed, no way you can win, if you get my drift.'

'I'm open to hillbilly suggestions from West Virginia,' I said.

'Let Major Mills call off the dance, Noot.'

'OK, suppose I do. Maybe his investigation will take two months, maybe six. Paul stays in the can. Now we get a new trial. Another six months before we actually go to bat. That's a year out of a man's life, Chuck.'

'Beats facing a hanging jury, Counselor. Besides, maybe the Brits charge O'Brien. End of case. Paul's back.'

'He may be right,' CD said, thinking, frowning, moving about as though the stool under him was a hot seat. This was all pretty heavy shit for a clean-cut boy from Michigan.

There was another silence. It maybe made sense.

'Unfortunately,' Ruff Lane said, refilling all the plastic glasses, 'that will not fly. One of the really fine things about working for

New Scotland Yard is that we *never*, not hardly ever, but *never* make mistakes. This matter was looked at by our CID and Scotland Yard, no matter how quickly. They both decided your chap killed the lass. End of story.'

'You mean a cover-up?' CD asked, incredulity written all over that unlined face. What a lousy welcome to the real world.

Inspector Lane smiled his quizzically humorous smile at CD.

'Yes, lad . . . a cover-up. I agree with learned counsel. Let's get on with it.'

'We'll lose, damn it,' Chuck Conyers sighed wearily.

'Thanks for the vote of confidence,' I said.

'I don't mean it that way, Noot. Jesus H. Christ himself couldn't pull this one off.'

'You should hold Air Force officers in higher regard, Chuck. Some of them have integrity. Even Paul seems to think that. He waived having NCOs on the court,' I said.

'Sure, because he knows NCOs stick together, but they don't stick their necks on the line.'

'Well, at any rate, I'd like you and CD to get me all the files on the members of the court and Major Mills. Get them to me here soon as. CD, you'll handle all the rigamarole tomorrow, the mating dance. I looked at your manual. Reads like the script for a play. When I get out of here tomorrow, we'll go see Paul and prep him.'

'You going to put him on the stand?' CD asked.

'Yeah. We all know Paul is a con artist and one of the world's greatest bullshitters. We also know that he can charm the birds out of the trees and that butter doesn't melt in his mouth. I'd put him on the stand if he were guilty, he's that good. I think he'd beat a polygraph.'

'He's not very GI, you know. Or overly respectful,' CD said, still dubious.

'He will be, CD.'

'At any rate,' I said, 'Conyers, CD, get a move on.'

After they left, the sergeant kindly leaving behind the smokes and several little bottles, Ruff Lane moved from the bed to the stool. 'And now Counselor?'

'I think you know.'

'Perhaps. Stop me if I wander off the well-trodden path. Your whole case is O'Brien. You've got to shoot him out of the water. You'll now want me to risk my pension ferreting out all New Scotland Yard has on the sod. You want witnesses who saw O'Brien with the murder weapon at prior times. Am I getting warm, Counselor?'

'Except that I don't want your pension on the line, you are red hot, inspector. But that's not all I want. My defense, if I can swing it, will be two-pronged. The charge is murder, not manslaughter. That requires a motive. There was no motive. I need witnesses who knew them as love-birds. The Kellogg girl willing to do anything and everything for Paul. The jerk went AWOL to party with her. Why kill her? As Sergeant Conyers so well puts it, "you get my drift"?'

'Party with her? Is that what you chaps now call a night of coupling?' His eyes danced with amusement. 'Well, now, this is rather a tall order for a shepherd. How much time have I?'

'Not much. The prosecution case itself will probably take tomorrow afternoon and the next day, that's without cross. My cross will take a day. Then the defense kicks off. But if you need another day, I'll get a continuance if I have to.'

'How?'

'Lie,' I said. He sat and looked at me, wanting more of an answer. If I tell Dr Hung that I can't remember things, feel dizzy and have a continual blinding headache he'll order me back into the hospital.'

He nodded gravely. 'Very good. I see our trains run very much on the same track.'

'Speaking of that, Inspector, where is our favorite niece?'

'Regrettably, the only niece. My sis was not what you'd call a brood sow. Just four lads and one lass. Mary had to return to her position. No time to lollygag about while you're in the hospital.

She was terribly disappointed, I'll say that. Thought she had you seduced good and proper.'

'That young lady does not have to seduce me, Uncle.'

'All to the good. She's more than half on to being thirty. Up here in the country that's an old maid.'

'Meaning?'

'Fact is, I was never a Yank basher. But then, I also never thought I'd want a Yank for our little Mary.'

'Let's talk of cabbages and kings, Inspector.' I could feel myself blushing which is something I have fought since I was a kid. I was a terrible kid blusher. Over the years I had managed to pretty much psych myself out of it.

'Let's not talk at all. I've got work to do.' He got up, walked to the door, turned and smiled at me. 'Laddie, I've several shotguns.'

'Yeah?'

'Some beautiful and long-lasting weddings have taken place at the point of the barrel,' he said and walked out.

21
Members of the Court

I slept off the Canadian whiskey until early dinner arrived. It came not with Madame LaFarge but a black airman, Airman Second Class Justin Gallagher, his identification tag stated. I asked him to help me to the latrine – out of the service all these years and suddenly a john was a latrine again. Signs of premature senility.

The dinner was not as bad as the lunch and I was hungry. There was even apple pie à la mode. The pie was fresh. Airman Gallagher sat on the stool, pushed near the wall, while I ate. For a long time he just sat and stared out the window. It was only 5.30 in the evening but it was dark outside. I could not tell if the snow had stopped falling.

By the time I had finished the pot roast and spuds and vegetables and started on the pie, which was now swimming in melted ice cream, vanilla, Airman Gallagher cleared his throat. 'Tell me, sir, what's it like to be a big-shot lawyer in New York City?' He grinned, showing teeth a movie star would envy.

'Airman Gallagher, I am not from New York City, I'm from Suffolk County, which is fifty to one hundred and twenty miles from New York City, depending on where you live in the county. And I'm not a big-shot lawyer. I'm an assistant district attorney. Salaried, like you.'

The grin widened even further. 'No kidding. You mean you just a working stiff like me? How come you here?'

'Paul is or was my brother-in-law. I raised him.'
'No kidding?'
'No kidding.'
'So you ain't getting no cool half mill to come and defend his case?'
'I'm paying most of my expenses and it's not tax write off.'
'No kidding?'
'No kidding.' I would like it known that I was not bullshitting or wasting my time. I was beginning to rehearse for the jury, the court martial. If Airman Gallagher in food service had heard I was a hot-shot New York City defense attorney, then the whole base had that information, including the members of the court. The military does not like civilians. Never mind the only purpose of a military is to provide defense for the civilian population.

'You telling me Paul got a relative is the best he could do?'
'Yeah.'
'Oh, wow, that sure ain't the way I heard it. But, sir, there are hot-shot New York City lawyers making millions, right?'
'Yeah. Why?'
'Well, I got my GED equivalent degree and I'm taking correspondence courses from George Washington University and I thought it might be neat to be a big-shot lawyer.'
'It would probably be real neat. I don't know. But hot-shot black lawyers are scarce as hen's teeth. In big demand. So stick with it.'
'Sounds good, man.'

At this point Quirk McQuirk and Conyers came into the room. The airman gathered up the dishes and trays. 'Nice talking to you, sir,' he said.

'Conyers,' I said, 'I want you to locate my belongings. What I came in here with. I'm getting out of here, now.'

'Is that wise, Counselor? Without the doc discharging you?'

'There's a method to the madness, Chuck. Like if I need a continuance because of a relapse.'

He grinned at me and nodded. 'Using the old noddle. OK, take a little time to sneak you out. Quirk,' he said, turning, 'get wheels and tell our security detail.' He turned back to me. 'I understand you are now no longer barred from the BOQ or the O Club.'

'I want back to my room.'

'That gal ain't around no more, Counselor,' Conyers said.

'Sergeant Conyers, your mouth is just about as big as your nose. I've a mind to take a poke at both.' I did not say this kiddingly because I guess I was still pissed off about being called 'boy'. I don't know why that rankled me so much. But Conyers took no offense, giving me his goofy grin and shrugging in that relaxed way of his.

'Too bad you weren't so tough when those old boys paid a visit to your motel room. Drift I get, some old retired Brit and a little beagle had to pull your roasting chestnuts out of that there fire.'

'You are fucking lovable, Conyers.'

Goofy kept grinning. 'OK. Quirk, tell Ham. We'll set up security at the old live-in riding academy.'

'I don't need security. Just the files I asked you for ten years ago.'

Conyers tossed a fat red folder on to the foot of the bed. 'You are assuming you don't need security, Counselor. It's my understanding you don't much put a prize on assuming things. If you get my drift?'

I shrugged. Arguing or fighting with the sergeants was like shoveling sand at Jones Beach. Every time you dug a shovelful out of your hole, the waves would come in and refill it.

'All right, Conyers, you win. I got work to do tonight. I need some sleep. Tomorrow is a full day. OK?'

It went pretty smooth and quickly after that. Out of the hospital, back to room 11 with two air police sergeants in fatigues and boots, carrying M-16s as my guards. Weapons are not allowed off base, but Ham, the sergeant major, had allowed full loads. Live ammo. I invited them into the ice-box room but they stayed outside, front and rear. John Wayne types. The snow had ended, not more than an inch or so had fallen, but that was enough to leave cars and trucks stranded everywhere, the drivers drinking tea, or bitters, or whatever, waiting for spring. Socialism is debilitating, I thought. I had been brought from the hospital in a Jeep. Four-wheel drive and a driver who had seen snow before. No sweat, man, he had said.

No sweat in my room either. I punched the electric heater and filled the bath tub with scorching water, even turned on the towel warmer. My fingers stayed numb as I opened the big red file holder.

Major Mills: not much I didn't already know. Straight arrow, the NCOs thought. Family man, richer than God. Quick temper, very GI but also very fair. For an officer, the NCOs gave him good marks.

Lieutenant Colonel John Hawkins: age 47, born Lincoln, Nebraska. Married, four kids. President of the board. Command pilot, chestful of decorations. Academy graduate, top third. Engineering major, meticulous, mathematical mind, cool under pressure. Amateur tennis player. The NCOs said he would be fair. But no sense of humor.

Major Theodore (Ted.) Goodwin: 37, married, two kids, born Wichita, Kansas. Command pilot, commissioned as air cadet, earned a BS degree in engineering, Geo. Washington University, operation bootstrap. Two years a POW holding a Purple Heart, Silver Cross. Credited with three MiGs. The NCOs think he is not corruptible and also has no sense of humor. Another straight arrow.

Captain Igor Bazoudas: 38, married and divorced, two kids. Born, Assiti, Greece. Father was a communist resistance fighter during World War II. Became an American–Greek restaurater. Like me, pilot candidate school for wings and commission. Bombadier wings. No combat time. Now B-47 bombadier. One Pentagon tour, officer efficiency reports not above average. Reserve officer, turned down for regular. 'Will kiss ass,' the NCO report noted. Shit, I thought, already the weak link.

Major Hull N.M.I. Williams: 34, senior pilot, married, three kids, born Irvinq, Texas. Combat time, usual decorations, academy graduate, lowest third. Owned a World War I byplane and likes to fly it and jump parachutes. The NCOs noted that his crew, including enlisted, like him and trust him. Good old boy, loves bourbon, broads and tall tales. Played football three years at the academy, wide receiver. Very steady under pressure, flight commander. Known to have socialized with Paul Kelly. Two nice bullshit artists.

Captain Hugo Rudolph Schmidt: age 29, senior pilot, flight leader. Graduate Norwich University, ROTC, commissioned, called to active duty as an engineer. Went to flight school as an officer in time to get into combat. Married, three kids, divorced and remarried. Another straight arrow, very GI, very regimented. Good efficiency reports, given a regular commission. The NCOs rated him an 'asshole, by-the-book Nazi'. No imagination, no sense of humor. However, they conceded that Getty and Rockefeller combining their fortunes, couldn't buy him. However, NCOs noted, unless you were German and the Air Force charged you with a crime, you had to be guilty. Why else charge you?

22

Court Martial, Day One

For me to refer to the procedure to be followed in a so-called general court martial as a mating dance was undoubtedly gilding the lily, but all parties to the event have a written script that is to be followed word for word. Cross every t dot every i. There is also a diagram of where each party is to sit. This courtroom was the back of the legal office in the concrete block bunker which now served the forces of truth and justice for American airmen. I entered the bunker from the parking-lot behind the front of the building. The back door opened into a narrow hall which had waiting-rooms on either side as well as one his and one her latrine. A large paneled door opened into the square courtroom. That room was painted dark green and was brightly lit by fluorescent lights, there being no windows. Directly to the right of the door CD showed me the defense table, a sturdy wooden table with three hardwood captain's chairs arranged with military precision. A little forward and in the center of the room was the stenographer's small table and secretarial chair. To the far left, against the wall and elevated about a foot was the law officer's high desk and leather padded chair. In front of the defense table was the prosecutor's table, a slightly smaller table with two hardbacked captain's chairs. At the far end of the room was a long elevated conference table with five leather-padded swivel chairs. Behind the chairs was a door that I supposed led to the legal offices. There were glasses and a decanter on all the tables and the mandatory flags and presidential and commander's pictures were all neatly arranged. I did not recognize the Secretary of the Air Force nor the Air Force Chief of Staff. On active duty it's wise to know the Who's Who of military command, but it had been a while since my active duty days, even since my active reserve time.

The witness stand, also elevated, was next to the law officer's seat, between him and the end of the long table for the members of the board. A three-foot-high railing with its gate separated the actual operating area of the room from four rows of spectator seats.

'I see the judge and the court members will be comfortable while the rest of us squirm,' I said, dropping my files and papers on the defense table.

'Law officer,' CD mumbled. CD was skittish. He had obviously cut himself shaving and dabbed constantly at the white styptic-pencil mark on his chin. I didn't know anyone still shaved with razors that could cut you. CD probably used one handed down to him by his namesake, a straight edge.

'Whatever, you're going to do the rigmarole stuff.'

'I've only been assistant trial counsel in generals. Actually only tried specials, mostly all AWOLs,' he whispered.

I looked at this husky, good-looking hayseed from Michigan, barely out of law school, in his neatly pressed blue uniform without a single decoration, his shoes mirror-bright, the crease in his trousers sharp enough to slice bread. Scared to death though knowing all he had to do is read from the script and do some step and fetch if required. This is what Major Sully (call me Jack) had assigned to defend a capital case. This kid was who he had expected to take down – until it developed that there was a fly in his ointment. Paul Kelly once had a brother-in-law who maybe knew just a little more than the law-school graduate. And who didn't work for Colonel Smith.

I smiled at him as reassuringly as I knew how. What a good kid. I understand why he had made that phone call and then chewed me out. He knew how green he was and how unfair it would have been if he had to try this case. If I had been in his shoes, I might very well not have looked for help.

'You're a better man than I, Gunga Din,' I said softly.

'What?' Still a whisper.

'You don't have to whisper, CD. Nobody here but us mice. Besides, lawyers don't whisper, they boom. They shout, they scream, they pound tables, drop to one knee, recite *Hamlet*. Doctors whisper and murmur things behind their hands. Lawyers wave their hands and yell.'

He gave me a long look I did not understand. 'Why are we here an hour early, anyway?' He sounded like he had a lot of better things to do.

'Every actor likes to look over his stage. Every boxer looks over the ring before his bout. Golfers play practise rounds,' I said.

'Your sarcasm is showing, Mr Helbig.'

'You're right. Sorry. Just nerves.'

CD blew out a lungful of air. 'You? Nerves? Ha.'

'Before every trial, CD. Stomach clamps down, sarcasm and my acerbic sense of humor sets in. Even get that way with broads I like. Talk too much, say things supposed to be funny, come out stupid. Nerves, CD. Fortunately they don't attack my hands, or make jelly of my knees. But it's always there.'

He gave me another long look I did not understand. 'You're a hard one to figure out, Counselor,' he said.

'Well, let's save that for now, OK? I want to get comfortable in the room. More important, study the layout. Look, I like leaning close to a witness some of the time. Here,' I said, gesturing, 'it can't be done. If I stand right face to face with a witness, I got my back to the whole jury, the trial counsel and the stenographer. Unless I shout, the steno's going to ask me to repeat the question, the jury won't hear me and the trial counsel will jump up and down about not hearing what's going on. If I stand on one side of the jury box, the steno and judge won't hear me. The other side, I got my back to the jury and am blocking their view of the witness. Shit.'

CD grinned for the first time. 'Aren't state courts laid out like this?'

'State courts vary from courtroom to courtroom, even in the same building. They are laid out by architects wanting to leave something of themselves to posterity. And to administrative judges and clerks who've never tried a case seeking splendor for the majesty of the law. I've tried cases in village courts which were converted attics where the jurors had to sit hunched down under a sloping roof. And in grandeur of expensive wood paneling and massive jury boxes where nobody could see a witness unless he was Wilt Chamberlain.

'The military had someone lay out these courtrooms who hated defense lawyers. Except for this case, I don't really blame them. But shit, here I'm going to have to conduct this whole damn thing from right here, almost.'

CD grinned that good, honest grin I had come to like so much. 'I'm very, very glad that you have nerves, Knute. That you're nervous.'

'Everybody does, CD. A doctor, a surgeon, one of the few of their like I can tolerate, told me once he gets close to the shakes before a dicey one. He said that's why a lot of surgeons booze it up, even before surgery. No such thing as steel nerves. When I boxed, I used to piss ten times before every bout. About three drops each time. And there was usually a line for the urinal. When I wore a blue suit . . . not like yours . . . cop's blue suit, I knew I was a target. All the guys did. When we got out, alone at night in a hairy situation . . . any macho man tells you he's not about to shit his britches is either an idiot or a liar. Same in the military. Seen guys shit, literally, shit their britches. And then go out and do the job.

'Now look, I didn't come here early for Philosophy 103. I want you to stand there, behind our table, and in a normal speaking voice, read from the manual or whatever. I'm going to sit in every seat in this room. You just keep reading, OK?'

Which we did. And then we stepped back outside into the parking-lot and I had a smoke. CD came along. The sky looked as

123

sullen as ever. Long Island is pretty lousy in the winter, too. But once in a while the sun showed you it was still up there. Once in a while you got an ice day without a cloud in the sky. Cold as hell but invigorating. Here it seemed, there was no sun up there. But the sun must have been somewhere because the snow was mostly gone, even without snow shovels.

'I still haven't decided about Bazoudas,' I said. 'You read the files, what do you think?'

'This trial, Knute, capital case, all five got to vote a conviction. What difference does he make? You think he'll change the other's minds? All of them?'

'I know. I know. But he could hang the jury, maybe. And they passed him over for a regular commission. They think he's second string.'

'You put that much trust in the military mind then?'

Good point. Maybe.

23
Court Martial, Day One

Paul was first to arrive in the courtroom, in handcuffs which was depressing but to be expected, I guess. He was charged with murder. Two air policemen flanked him. Other than the cuffs, which were removed just inside the railing, he looked good. Class A uniform with several rows of ribbons, hair cut short, clean-shaven, shoes shined. CD and I had spent several hours with him in the morning. I pulled out a chair for him and he sat down and looked around.

'Jees, this is about the most fixed room on the whole damn base,' he said. 'How you like the arena, Knute?'

'Arena?'

'Yeah. That's what they call it in Rome. You know where the gladiators fought and they threw the Christians to the lions.'

'Novel, Paul,' I said. But the comparison was very good. We had our spectators, the ruler who made up the rules of the battle giving the spectators the final say, thumbs up or down. And, of course, the gladiators. Criminal trial lawyers go into a courtroom to do battle. As I'd said to CD what now seemed long ago, winning isn't everything, it's the only thing. There is no sportsmanship between opposing counsel, no Queensberry Rules. The judge is there to keep things within the rules, but there's an awful lot you can sneak past him. For instance, you ask a question you know is totally out of order. Even before opposing counsel can rant and rave and the judge has it stricken from the record, you withdraw the question.

It's stricken from the record, but you put an idea into one or two jurors' heads. Don't want to play dirty, don't try cases. I think Leo Durocher said it best, nice guys finish last.

There are a couple of lawyers in my county that I truly like and respect. But when we go up against each other in the courtroom, even if we were out boozing the night before, no quarter is given or taken. Within the confines of the arena we are adversaries, gladiators doing whatever we can to win, to stay alive. The more I thought about it, the more I liked Paul's name for the courtroom. Me, the mighty Viking gladiator slaying bad guys in the arena. Helbig, I thought to myself, sometimes you are an insufferable asshole.

Major Mills came into the room from behind the court members' long table, from the legal office, followed by the members of the court, first the light colonel, then the majors, then the captains. The colonel sat down in the center of the long table, a major and a captain on each side. Major Mills, 'Hank' in better times, strode forcefully to his little preserve climbed up on it and sat down. While this was happening, Lieutenant Day and Sergeant Kelly rose to a stiff attention.

Major Mills motioned with his hand at them. 'Not necessary for you to rise. Where is Major Sully and the stenographer?' The trace of West Texas was pronounced. Still pissed off.

OK, I thought, might as well get this war right off the ground. I was sitting down. 'I don't think, Major, with all due respect, it's our job to excuse Major Sully's lack of respect for this court.' I could feel Paul poke me like this was better than jelly beans. I could also see the major's color rising. Before anything else happened, Major Sully and his assistant and the old broad stenographer came in from the hallway behind me.

'Sorry,' he blurted out, smiling with difficulty 'had a little trouble sorting out which steno was going to handle this.' He arrived at his table and his assistant, a lieutenant, put down the files.

There was a nice, long silence, then Major Mills said, the drawl even more pronounced 'Major Sully, when I advise you that we shall proceed at 1400 hours, I do not mean 1402. I mean 1400. Your stenographic difficulties are of no concern to me or the members of this court. I hope that I have made myself abundantly clear.'

Major Sully had come into court in his Class As, no overcoat. It was a cold, damp, miserable English January day, and he was beet red or at least, pink to beet red and he had sweat in his forehead.

'I'm very sorry, sir, it won't happen again.' Majors do not usually call each other sir. He was rattled. Great start. He was also being mistreated. He had come into the courtroom a few seconds before 1401. I am certain of this because my only treasured possession is a watch given me by the PBA (Patrolmen's Benevolent Asssociation) when I switched from cop to district attorney investigator and prosecutor. The watch had the PBA shield on its face with my badge number. My watch keeps perfect time. Major Mills was doing in Major Sully for fifty seconds at the start of our mating dance, our clashing of gladiators. But then Major Mills knew as well as I that Major Sully (call me Jack) had taken our RCM 802 back to the base commander. I would guess he was pissed off at us, even Steven. Fair enough.

'See that it does not, Major.' Major Mills then nodded to the President of the Court, *el presidente*, cleared his throat. Nervous. OK, I'll take that. Thinks this job is on the level.

'The court will come to order,' he said. Hell, the court was in perfect order. No spectators, no visitors, just two APs, guarding the door.

Major Sully stood up, papers in hand. 'This court is convened by Special Order AB 93, Headquarters, 13th Air Division, as amended by Special Order AB 5, a copy of which has been furnished to the law officer/military judge, each member of the court, counsel and the accused and to the reporter for insertion at this point in the record.

'The following persons named in the appointing order are present.' He then named the members of the court. The script reading had begun and my mind began to wander. What to do about Bazoudas? I had the file for three officers waiting in the wings, the jury pool we called them.

Although unlike state and federal court trials, we had no real choice. The court, the jurors, were picked by the man who brought the charges, not from voter registration cards or drivers' licenses. Challenge one of Colonel Smith's choices, he's replaced by another.

'The prosecution is ready to proceed with the trial in the case of the United States against Paul R. Kelly, Technical Sergeant, 345th Light Bomb Wing, Headquarters Squadron, who is present in court.

'Mrs Willa Wadsworth has been appointed reporter for this court and will now be sworn,' Major Sully read from his script. He then swore the court reporter, the same one as had been in the hospital with Majors Mills and Sully. He continued on, setting up the legality of the court martial, the qualification or certification of the military lawyers, members of the court and our judge, Major Mills from JAG, Wiesbaden, Germany. He then gave CD a chance to get his one-liner read from the script.

CD stood up, red-faced, holding the *Manual for Court Martial* so tightly his knuckles were white. 'The legal qualifications of the appointed members of the defense are correctly stated in the appointing orders.' That was the end of the script. Now CD had to wing it. 'However,' he said, in a strained voice, reading from his own yellow legal pad, 'the defendant has requested Civilian Counsel as well as myself to represent him.' Colonel Hawkins looked over to Major Mills.

'Please give us the name of Civilian Individual Counsel,' Major Mills said.

'Knute Helbig.' CD spelled both my first and last name. 'Sir.'

Major Sully now turned his attention to me. 'Mr Helbig, are you certified as counsel by an appropriate judge advocate general, and if not, have you any of the legal qualifications enumerated in Article 27b (1)?'

I got up and looked around, feeling like I was in a high-school play, not a court martial that could vote a death sentence. 'No, no judge advocate general has certified me and I never read Article 27 or its sub-divisions. My legal qualifications are that I graduated from law school, was admitted to the practise of law in all of the courts of the State of New York, the Eastern and Southern Federal District Courts and the United States Supreme Court. My experience is that I've been a prosecutor for about eighteen years and I've tried quite a few homicides ... however I've never been a defense counsel. Never defended anybody before.' I sneaked that in to disabuse the jurors, members of the court, that I was the high-priced New York City mouthpiece as labelled.

Major Sully looked at Major Mills. Major Mills said, 'You have never defended anyone? In a civilian or a military court?'

'No, sir.'

'Do you feel, nevertheless, that you can defend this case? It's a capital case, Counselor.'

'I'm not sure I feel real cocky being here, Major. But Paul Kelly seems to think I can hack it. He asked for me; I didn't ask to come here.'

'Sergeant Kelly, you've heard this exchange. Are you certain you want to be represented in this capital case by an attorney who has never defended a criminal case?'

Paul rose smartly and came to attention. 'Yes, sir. My brother-in-law is about as good as lawyers get. I want him for my lawyer and Lieutenant Day here to help him.' Then his damn sense of humor had to let go. 'Old enough to work the other side of the street at least once.'

'Very well, let the record reflect that counsel for both sides have the requisite qualifications. Has the accused made a request in writing that the membership of this court include enlisted persons?' Major Mills said.

'The accused has not made such a request,' Major Sully read from his manual.

'Proceed to convene the court,' Major Mills said.

'The court will be sworn,' Major Sully said. The members of the court climbed to their feet so that everyone was now standing. As

Major Sully called out their names, starting with the colonel, they raised their right hands in turn and kept them up while Major Sully read off a long swearing in ceremony which finally ended with 'so help you God'. He then proceeded to swear in Major Mills and was in turn sworn in by Colonel Hawkins, then swore CD and me in. A lot of swearing going on. No place for agnostics. All of us now sat down except the prosecutor.

'The court is now convened,' Major Mills said gravely.

Major Sully went about more reading from his manual and various documents about charges and specifications and grounds for challenges but I tried to tune him out. I had seen enough of the script to know challenges to the court, our jury, was at hand and I was still debating about bouncing Captain Bazoudas. He advised the court that he had no challenges for cause nor any peremptory challenges. Then he turned slightly toward the defense table.

'Does the accused desire to challenge any member of the court or the law officer/military judge for cause?'

The mating game was now over. Time to copulate. Or to put it more nicely, the overture had finally ended and the curtain was going up. Or perhaps best put, the last strains of the National Anthem had faded and the cry was: 'Play Ball'. I sat for a long moment. Major Mills knew I wanted this trial now, he wasn't about to get bounced. But he watched me intently just the same.

'Can I have a *voir dire*, Judge?' If not Latin, use French. We could just say 'I want to ask the jurors some questions'.

'Obviously, you may, as you must be aware.' Not a nice sound at all.

'Thank you, Your Honor. I have no challenges peremptory or for cause against the judge. I would like to ask a few questions of the court, if I may.' Come around the table slowly, Mr Viking Gladiator, with papers in your hand. Your excuse for a broad sword. Stand and study your notes until you have everyone's attention.

'I'd like to ask this of all members of the court. It's my understanding that unlike a civilian trial, the prosecutor, Trial Counsel, makes an opening statement right about now, but the defense does not. I don't make an opening until the People... the United States, rests its case. That being so, it's my wish not to do very much cross-examining of the prosecution witnesses since without hearing how I want to try this case, my cross may not make much sense. If the judge allows it, I want the right to recall all the prosecution witnesses. Will you all accept that? Keep an open mind until the very end of the case, when I sum up?'

They all nodded vigorously. Major Mills did not nod. 'Mr Helbig, you know better than I do that you have that right. You also know that if you recall them, it's no longer cross-examination. They become your witnesses, you can't lead them, you can't badger them.'

'Not unless you declare them hostile witnesses, sir. And with my personality, that should take no time at all.'

Major Mills did not find that amusing, but several members of the court did. 'OK, let's move on. Captain Williams, I note from the files that you were at one time stationed at Westhampton Beach Air Force Base.'

'Yes sir.'

'That's in Suffolk County, New York. My home county. Where I prosecute the bad guys. You or any member of your family run afoul of the law in Suffolk County? We ever cross swords, sir?'

'Ah don't think so, Counselor.' The accent was pure Texas. 'Probably got a few tickets from your Smokies but never went to court. Just paid the fines, right or wrong. Actually, I liked it just fine out your way. First time I lived near an ocean. No, sir, Counselor, we never crossed swords.'

'Did you, or for that matter any member of the court run across me while I was on active duty? I was an RO. Any of you hear rumors I locked on to one of our own? Or called in air strikes from the ground, on friendlies?'

They all shook their heads. Some of the stiffness seemed to be leaving. I hadn't had to hit them over the head. They got the message. I'd been one of their own.

'OK, thank you. Captain Bazoudas ... I note from the file supplied to me' – and the file purloined for me – 'that you are not a pilot. Did you, like me, for some reason get bounced to the second team?'

'I don't think I understand your question, sir.'

'I mean, did you start out applying to be a bombadier or a pilot?'

'Pilot,' he mumbled.

'Care to tell me what happened?' I said, in as friendly a way as I could. Two kindred spirits screwed by the powers-that-be. It didn't work.

'I see no reason why I should.' Even better, I wasn't the one who got nasty first.

'Captain,' Major Mills said, 'a *voir dire* ... examining the members of the court to determine impartiality is Counsel's absolute right. The questions may be repetitive, insulting, even stupid and way off the mark. But the manual allows Counsel great latitude in this. Whether it bores us, insults us and stretches out the proceedings. If you don't feel that you wish to answer his questions, a challenge for cause will be granted, subject to approval of the rest of the court.' Nice going, Major Mills. This asshole civilian can outrage us or put us to sleep with his wasting of our time. He's got the right to put down one of the brethren.

'Major,' Captain Bazoudas said in a tight voice, 'I see no reason to submit myself to this man's interrogation. I'm not on trial here.' He sounded as though he was. Major Mills turned toward the members of the court. 'Gentlemen, I am required to excuse the captain, subject to the objection of any member of the court. Do you wish to withdraw to discuss this?'

We were not following the script now and there was some confusion up on the high bench.

'May we approach, Judge?' I asked. Major Mills nodded and CD, not knowing what was happening, and Major Sully, already appearing to smell a rat approached the bench with me on the side away from the court members, the side by the stenographer who would record this so called 'side bar'. Unless the judge specifically ordered the conference off the record, which is dangerous for a judge to do: reviewing authorities would have to wonder what the judge didn't want them to see in the record.

'Major, I don't want to embarrass the captain, nor do I want to put the court to sleep, or outrage them, or hold up this trial. I'll just challenge Captain Bazoudas peremptorily. Period. No muss, no fuss,' I said.

Major Mills's blue eyes tried boring holes in mine, like laser surgery. I didn't melt but bored back. Cops learn, not in the academy but on the street, very early in their careers about hard eyes. 'Very well, that will save time. Thank you. Is that all?' I nodded, which the stenographer duly noted as she watched us, hovering over her steno machine. We turned back to our respective tables. Behind me I heard Major Mills exhale softly, 'Cute, Helbig, real cute.' I am certain that did not make it on to the record. The steno undoubtedly had already recorded 'side bar ended'.

'Gentlemen, Civilian Counsel has indicated that he wishes to challenge the captain peremptorily, meaning he needs no cause. We therefore need not vote, or take testimony, or whatever,' Major Mills said. 'Therefore, Captain Bazoudas, you are excused with the thanks of the court.' The captain climbed off the high bench, marched in front of Colonel Hawkins, saluted and marched out of the courtroom. He didn't look over at me. Not much to see anyway. Major Sully now sent one of the APs out for a replacement. The replacement was Captain Donald John Leone. I flipped through my papers. He was 28, single, born Brooklyn, New York. Pilot, academy graduate, academy despite lousy high-school grades. His father had been killed in action, an automatic. Very young to command a B-47 carrying a nuke, I thought. Good ERs. The NCOs said he had a great sense of humor, sang opera, loved practical jokes, and big-breasted, *saftig* broads. They thought that if he didn't get jammed up kidding around or fooling around he could end up Air Force Chief of Staff. That is quite a recommendation. My kind of guy.

Major Sully and I now accepted the members of the court. Phase one was over. Major Mills, noting that we had spent more than two hours with these preliminaries suggested that the president of the court call a short recess. He did. Paul, CD and I went into one of the small, windowless witness waiting-rooms. The APs waited outside. They should have cuffed Paul but didn't. Probably because there was an AP Master Sergeant in the hallway.

Paul and I lighted up. 'How we doing, Counselor?' Paul asked.

'Haven't started yet, really.'

'Bullshit, big brother. You already got a feel for all this. You already made friends with the court there. I caught all that about first-team pilot regulars and second-string reserve bomb hurlers. And about you calling in air strikes from the ground. I got you, they got you. Why didn't you just come to court in your A1s, wearing your Purple Heart and CIB and the rest of the fruit salad?' He was grinning ear to ear and sucking on his, actually my, Marlboro like it was the last one before they put the blindfold on him in front of the firing squad. The tip was cherry red.

'How does he know about "feel"?' CD asked.

'Can't bullshit a bullshitter,' Paul said cheerfully, lighting another of my butts.

CD shook his head and swallowed several times. 'I don't know . . . you don't act like a man on trial for his life . . . or a lifetime in Leavenworth.'

'Oh, I did, when they first busted me. I pulled every string I had to get Knute over here. Called my sister I ain't spoken to in years, since she married that guinea mobster. Called my ma who always knew I was bad news. Got you all hyped up to get Knute here. Worked a lot on you to get you mad at him 'cause I knew he didn't want to come. Shit, man, I worked very hard to get the hell out of here. Did everything and anything I could. And when I did it all, that's all I could do. I pitched the first couple of innings. Hard as I could. Knute's on the mound now, I'm on the bench. His ballgame. I know my brother. He always played hard ball. Nothing more for me to do but say "yes, sir, no, sir, I don't know, sir".

'Worrying gets you ulcers. So does chewing your nails. I did what I could. Like the man said, if rape is inevitable, might as well lie back and enjoy.'

'CD, is this room wired?' I asked.

'What do you mean wired?'

'I mean is my pal, Major Sully, tape-recording every word we're saying in here?'

CD looked at me like I had just suggested he got it on with one of his cows. 'Of course not.' Indignant. 'I can't believe you'd even ask me that. He's an officer of the court.'

'So am I. Where I work, most places, we wire everything. No court orders. Can't use it in court. Can't even use what we get off the wire . . . it's called "fruit of the poisoned tree". Still, always nice knowing what's coming down. Sometimes you save a life that way. Sometimes opens up a whole new can of worms. In this business, ignorance is not bliss. Anyway, time's up.'

24

Court Martial, Day One

Major Sully was on his feet. 'By direction of the convening authority the prosecution wishes to Amend Article 120....' He continued on in rapid fire.

'What's he doing, CD?' I asked.

'Amending the rape to attempted rape,' he said, and then he suddenly got up and said, 'The accused consents.' He sat down.

'The reading of the charges may be omitted,' Major Mills said. CD leaned past Paul toward me. 'We got copies of the charges right here. As amended. Just waived the reading, they're in the record.'

I nodded as Major Sully went on with more of his script. Then he asked how the accused pleads. 'Before receiving your pleas, I advise you that any motions to dismiss any charge, or to grant other relief must be made at this time.'

CD looked past Paul's nose again, at me. I shook my head and CD rose to plead the defendant '... the accused ... not guilty to all charges and specifications.' We then went through some more mumbo jumbo about citing legal authority and such, which neither side wanted to present. We entered into no stipulations. Opposing counsel sometimes do stipulate, which means simply that they both agree, for example, that a handwriting expert from the FBI Lab is qualified as an expert in many prior trials. No sense spending an hour while the prosecutor elicits all of the expert's schooling, training and expertise, and where and how often other courts have qualified him an expert witness. They stipulate that he is an expert in his field. I wouldn't stipulate the time of day if I was staring at the Greenwich Mean Time Clock.

'We have only one expert witness, the psychiatrist who examined the accused right after the incident. I was hoping we could save the court a lot of time and stipulate to his expertise. After all, the Air Force hired him as a fully qualified psychiatrist,' Major Sully said, looking at the court with a sort of hurt expression on his face. Why can't this fucking civilian do one thing right, fellows?

'Nice try, Jack,' I said without getting up. 'No stipulations.'

'Major Sully,' Major Mills said coldly, 'You know as well as I do that becoming an Air Force physician or psychiatrist, or lawyer, for that matter, means nothing more than that the individual has graduated from his specialty and has been licensed. The Air Force, the entire military does not equate that with being an expert in his field or being qualified in a court of law as an expert witness. You know that and I know that, and Individual Counsel knows it better than either of us. If he didn't, if he were inexperienced in a court of law, I'd not allow such a stipulation.

'In this case, I see no need to protect the rights of the accused. He has excellent representation. I seriously doubt that Individual Counsel would stipulate that this is Tuesday, that this is a court martial, or that it is taking place at RAF Singlebury. Am I correct, Counsel?' He was having a good time now, taking over. I make the rules, sonny, don't play cute with me or I'll hand you your thick, Irish head. I nodded, appreciating that pissed off as the major was, he was going to be fair. Chew both of us a new asshole if we played games in his, courtroom. 'While I feel no need to assist Counsel in this matter, I do take very gravely the fact that our court is composed of non-lawyers, flyers all. I would hate to think that you would even consider misleading them in any way. Now, proceed with your opening statement if you have one.'

Major Sully stood like a statue, the red rising up from his blue collar and suit to his broad, open face. He hadn't been guilty of underestimating the enemy, but he sure as hell was guilty of underestimating the neutral observer. Cardinal rule of trial law: do not ever underestimate the enemy. If that's a cardinal rule, it's at least a pope's rule not to underestimate the judge. He stood there like a kid, caught with his finger in the proverbial cookie jar.

In the sudden quiet, suddenly another force was coming to the fore. 'I don't think so, Major,' Colonel Hawkins said very softly. 'I don't mean about stipulations, Major, I think we all understand what that's about. Flying B-47s doesn't mean we all took degrees in stupidity. What I mean is that it is now 1645 hours. I'm going to adjourn the court until 0900 tomorrow.'

Captain Leone was hardly able to contain himself. The other members of the court were also trying hard not to go into the team cheer. I could see it, sitting quiet without a word at my table. Know what they were thinking. A lieutenant colonel, unless he's on a ship, air or sea as passenger, outranks a major. Lawyers, even those with wings over their left uniform pockets, are not God's chosen. Major Mills was here to rule on things to do with lawyer stuff; Colonel Hawkins was the president of the court. He was also a light colonel. This was his courtroom and he had a wife and four kids on base. Things to do, places to go. Major Mills was TDY (temporary duty assignment) from Wiesbaden. He had a single-O dinner ahead of him and maybe a movie or TV in the BOQ. No things to do, no places to go. And he'd missed his trip to Spain and he wanted to get this over with and get home.

Colonel Hawkins was home and did not intend to spend the wee hours of the night in this bomb shelter, paneled or not. When you fly his kind of missions, seventy-two-hour TDYs anywhere in the world are routine, rubbing your eyes to stay awake and feeling like you have a beachful of sand under the eyelids, you take the slack where you find it. Colonel Hawkins and the rest of the board were standing down a few days from their grueling hours. They wouldn't fly again until the case was over. God knows they deserved it.

25
On the Economy

Totally against his better judgement, CD let me put my suit jacket on him instead of his uniform blouse and join me in the NCO club. He had never set foot inside it. Few officers ever did. If an officer is invited there, it beats winning the Air Medal. Invitations like that are about as common as hen's teeth. And never in uniform. I know he felt like he was breaking every rule in the *Officer's Guide*, a booklet which was the only training doctors and lawyers received before entry on to active duty. But he was mellowing and I think he was beginning to think that he'd take his chances with Iceland or Greenland or whatever.

Also, like a good lawyer, he wanted to know what was happening. I do believe the NCOs were beginning to rub off on him and he liked being around them. We sat at the same table where I had lunched, although more crowded now. Sitting in my seat was Sergeant Major Hamilton. McQuirk was there and Conyers, of course, and Sergeants Phillippi, Russo and Jansen and about six others, including the master sergeant AP I had seen in court.

Sounds from the bar reminded me of a muted Coney Island with the pinballs and their bells and the shouting and laughter. The dining-room was nearly empty, however, and most of the sound came from a speaker hooked up to the juke box. As the sergeant major waved us into seats, I could hear rock music booming out.

'Gents, please,' Ham boomed in his deep drawl, 'we have the

honor of esteemed learned counsel with us. Welcome. How did it go today?' The table was suddenly quiet.

Our little waitress appeared. I heard CD order a Coke, saw Ham grin and wave and place his own order. The plump waitress removed as many empty steins as her tray would hold.

'I think everybody succeeded in getting everybody pissed off royally,' I said. The drinks arrived, heavy, good-sized shot-glasses with tankards of beer. Ham picked up his shot glass and motioned it toward CD. He looked around the table. We had all raised our shots. CD blew out a deep breath and picked up his tumbler.

'Lieutenant, welcome to our club. You'll be getting a card, free. You and yours are welcome, anytime. Here's to you, sir, down the hatch.'

The waitress now appeared with two bottles of Canadian Windsor and Ham and Jansen immediately refilled all the shot glasses. 'It's a shame, Lieutenant, that the military now brings all lawyers in as commissioned. Used to be otherwise. I, for instance was a so-called Flying Sergeant. Time was, they didn't let the commissioned ranks do any of the real things war's all about. Just had them around to sign the paperwork. Hell's bells, Patton didn't know how to drive a tank. Old Ike couldn't drive a car.' We tossed down our second shots.

The sergeant major whispered behind his hand to one of his sergeants who left the table immediately and then turned toward me. 'Well, sounds like you had a hard day, Counselor.'

'He didn't have a bad day today, Sergeant, he had a brilliant day.' All talk stopped and all eyes turned to CD. Three quick shots of whiskey and part of a beer, after an early and nervous light lunch. We hadn't been here half an hour. CD was shit-faced. His ears were cherry-colored but his face was now white. Almost chuck-up time.

'Lieutenant, that's why you have the run of this club. You did the right thing for an NCO. Won't win you Brownie points, but I guarantee you, it won't hurt your ERs,' Ham said.

'The only Brownie points you'll ever get, Sergeant Major, is for fixing the last Bingo for me.' We all turned to look at Anthony Ruff

Lane. He was in work clothes and his heavy jacket, except for a bowler hat.

'Ruff, you son-of-a-bitch,' Ham said, grinning. 'Who in hell let you in?'

'Your card, you sodding hillbilly. I've come to collect our barrister.'

'He nowhere near ready to leave.'

'He has, unlike you, work to do.'

'Aw. You've got a point, you bloody Limey. Take him then, he's yours. But our security detail goes along.'

'Not bloody likely. He's coming to the estate for a bite and then I'll deliver him back to the motel. About ten. That's where you pick up your so-called security. To be brutal, Sergeant Major, he'd be safer with Churchill sleeping by his bed than your sodding APs with their Israeli Uzis they never fire.'

I realized during this exchange that I could feel my drinks. Also, that in normal times – home – I never drank during a trial. 'I'm ready, Inspector, and thank you,' I said, standing up.

'I might just have one more,' CD said, grinning stupidly.

'Don't let him drive home, Sergeant Major. And not too late. He also has to work tomorrow,' the inspector said tartly. Ham nodded benignly.

We drove along through the dark, overcast night without speaking, in an English version of a pick-up truck, a lorry. The open back was just about big enough for two Churchills, the front, the cab, was cramped and unheated. At first we were on the highway on which my motel was, then we cut off this two-lane super highway on to rutted dirt tracks. It felt like the truck had no springs and it looked like the headlights were kerosene lamps, but Ruff drove purposefully, knowing each really bad hole or bump and slowing for them, shifting.

'Some of your Yank military, they live off-station. Places like this. Only way they can get their families over here. Our RAF bases weren't built for families and your people don't want to spend their quid on a lease air station. They call it living off the economy. Our ladies are used to shopping for the night's repast every day, and cooking on a coal-fired range. Your lasses don't much take to it.

'My sis and me, we grew up like this. Maybe got a bit spoiled in London, in service, but easy enough to revert back. For your lasses, it is no tea and scones. I don't blame them, understand, it's how they grew up. No, I don't blame them at all.'

'Enough of that . . . come in and meet another Mary, Mary Beth, my kept woman. I told her you're partial to steak and kidney pie and she bakes a fair one.'

'Inspector,' I said, seeing my breath in the small cab despite the near total darkness, 'I don't think I can get out of this car. I think my feet are frozen to the deck.'

'Ah, laddie, I like your sense of humor.' He clapped me on the shoulder, chuckling. I did manage to leave the cab on my icicle feet and follow him to the cottage, Churchill jumping around us. The cottage doorway opened into what the Brits call a sitting room. No hallway. Ruff hung his big jacket on a hook by the door. I kept my overcoat on. There was a coal stove across the room and I stood by it, finally taking my hands out of my pockets to hold them over the heat. I stood as close as I could to try to bring circulation back into the ice my feet now were.

The inspector went off into what I assumed was the kitchen. I stood with my hands over the cast-iron monstrosity that was pouring out heat, my shoes on a slab under it, shivering in my lined topcoat. The room was perfectly square. In its center, two easy chairs were shoved back to back under a lightbulb, bare, hanging down, giving off about forty watts. One wall was covered with pictures and other knick-knacks. The other three walls were bare, save windows with drawn curtains. There was also a couch and a rocker. The floor was wide-plank wood, oak maybe, also bare.

In one corner was a heavy ladder going up to a half loft. The loft covered half the room, the other half allowed a view of a vaulted ceiling, huge beams, no apparent insulation.

Anthony Ruff Lane came through the swinging door of what I now knew had to be the kitchen, carrying a tray. He set the tray on a small table, hidden in a dark corner, pulled the two chairs under the lamp bulb next to each other and then pulled the small table in front of the chairs. 'Right,' he said, 'come rest the weary bones.' I reluctantly left the thawing out and sat next to him.

'Now, we've got good whiskey, Canadian, we have a bit of beer my woman fetched for us, we have some cheese and bit of sausage. To hold us 'til din din.' The blue eyes sparkled with devilment. 'Chairs are here so we can both read under the bulb, you see. Poor old generator does not charge up the poor old batteries very much. Costs an arm and a leg for petrol. There is a bit of light in the loo, also, if you have the need.'

I drank a whiskey and some beer chaser. Then, beginning to thaw out, went to the one decorated wall. The light wasn't much. I could see photographs of my host, in military uniform, in front of the tourist spots in Egypt, in what I had to presume was Northern Ireland, in front of the Chrysler building in New York, the Leaning Tower of Pisa, the Singapore Men's Club. Also pictures with men and women in formal dress, the inspector as a bobby, the inspector in civvies, plaques, decorations, and above them all, a ceremonial sword.

I came back to my chair and a full shot glass. 'Thank you, but that is it. I have, as you told Ham, work to do. Places to go and things to do. I would very much like to have dinner and then go back before washing dishes.'

'Soon, laddie, soon. Mary Beth had no way of knowing when I'd drag you away from your compatriots. By the by, we'll dine in the kitchen. You won't need your topcoat in there. It's jolly warm.'

I stood up, dropped the coat and walked around the room. 'You do love to play the country bumpkin, don't you?'

He glanced at me with his laughing eyes but did not answer because the door to the kitchen swung open and Mary Beth came into the sitting-room. I had anticipated a middle-aged, plump missus. She came to move the tray from the small table between us.

'Thank you for coming all this way for my humble meal,' she said, giving me what I'd swear was a sort of curtsy.

In true Helbig fashion, I said nothing, just sat and stared. I believe to this day that Mary Beth was the most beautiful young girl I had ever seen. Not sexy, earthy and appealing in the Mary Buttons serving-wench way, but tall, lithe and graceful, like a swan, I thought. I sat and gaped, I suppose, as she took our beer tankards into the kitchen.

'You're in shock, laddie,' Ruff Lane grinned at me mischievously. 'Didn't expect to see a beauty out here in the wilds with an old bugger like me, now did you?' He pulled me to my feet and directed me into a large, cheery kitchen, well lit by a fluorescent ceiling fixture. I sat where he indicated, watching the girl at the stove and the small counter. 'Pulled her out of the Thames near ten years ago. Where her dear old dad pitched her. Mother had actually run off with a circus years before. Old Dad substituted her for the wife, she was all of ten years of age. She was twelve when I pulled her out of the bloody river. Decided, finally to hop it, which got old Dad downright mean.

'We've been together since. No other kin. She was a daughter to me until a few years ago. Then Mary Beth decided we should be lovers. Not so hard for an old sod to take. However, she's not that much about these days. Second year medical school now. I think she should be in the films, but she wants to bandage up bloody knees.'

While the inspector was talking she had piled the table with steaming dishes and sat down across from me. She wiped a stray lock of her blonde hair from her face with a forearm several times. There were a few pale freckles across the bridge of her nose and on her bare arms. She watched him as he spoke and the look of pure adoration was overwhelming.

'Let's eat,' she said, and began to load the plates. 'Pediatrician, that's what I intend. To do for the little ones all that I missed out on. I'm surprised Old Bumptious told you my sad tale. Mostly he just says I'm his daughter.'

'He's to become family, you see,' he said.

'Ah, of course, Mary Buttons. But he's an American and you know how Mary feels about them.'

'Not about this one. Of course, there will be some logistical problems.'

'Of course, always.' She smiled. Absolutely gorgeous. She should be in the movies. 'Have you proposed and she accepted?'

'I've known Mary about five, six hours. No, I haven't even thought about proposing.'

'Old Bumptious decided?'

'Both Sis and I together. He's the first one she ever cast an eye to. My God, girl, she's halfway to thirty and she's still a bloody virgin.

'What a horrid disgrace,' she said, touching his arm lightly. 'Let's eat before things get cold and the American will think me a worse cook than I am.'

Which we did. Splendidly. Whether it was all the drinks or the intoxication of Mary Beth I do not know, but suddenly we were back in the little truck and then at my motel. The inspector passed me along to my two guardians. On the bed I found a regulation Air Force parka, fur-lined hood. The note attached to it said: 'Stay warm, Counsellor, and stay off-base with it on. Ham.'

26

Court Martial, Day Two

'The United States versus Technical Sergeant Paul R. Kelly, when all little legal details are gotten out of the way, is a rather simple case.' Major Sully's opening statement. 'All of you have the charges and specifications in front of you so I will not read them again. They are entered into the record. The only change made was that the rape charge was changed to attempted rape. You have that before you also.

'We also changed the desertion ... a technicality since the accused was not off-base long enough to be charged with desertion, just a simple old absence without official leave ... AWOL.' Major Sully stopped to smile at an impassive group of court martial members. 'We must and we will prove these underlying charges however, because they form the background for the major charge and specification. Murder, gentlemen. Violation of Article 118 subsections 1 and 4 of the *Manual for Court Martial*, United States. A violation of law in every land on this earth. A violation of the Ten Commandments. . . .' He was warming up pretty good now.

'Sorry to interrupt your opening,' I said, jumping up with a loud scratch of chair, 'but I have to object. It has always been my understanding that an opening outlines the evidence to be presented under the charges before the court. This man is not accused or charged with violating any law in all the countries on earth, nor of violating one of the Ten Commandments. Whichever one. Which commandment are you referring to, anyway?'

'That will be quite enough, Individual Counsel,' Major Mills interjected. 'This is a court martial, not a Bible study class. However, I do instruct Trial Counsel to outline his case, his evidence, and to stay away, far away, from histrionics. The accused is charged under Article 118. All members of the court have the charges before them. They also have copies of the manual. They all know he is charged with murder. Let's get on with how you are going to prove it.'

'Thank you very much, Judge. That is just what I intend to do. Gentlemen,' he said, turning back toward the long bench, 'as I said, the basic case is not complicated. We are going to prove that the accused left this base without authority . . . AWOL. We are going to prove he took a room in the Huntington Arms. We are going to prove that he met that unfortunate girl there, Margot Kellogg, that he somehow got her to his room. And that when she resisted his advances, he bashed in her skull. Killed her. Murder.

'We therefore have a rather uncomplicated case. But, for the record, we must take you step by step through that dreadful day. Thank you, gentlemen. The United States is ready to proceed.'

'Individual Counsel,' Major Mills intoned, 'I know that in the federal and state courts, the defense at this point also makes an opening statement. Those, as you know are not the rules here. However, if you wish to make a small statement at this time, you may do so.'

'I don't think so, Major.' Colonel Hawkins was back in the ball game. 'If Mr Helbig would be more comfortable making his opening now, I think we'd oblige him. He's never defended a case, never been in a court martial. This is a pretty heavy case. The accused could be executed. I don't think a little leeway would hurt all that much. We can vote on it if you want.'

'Colonel,' Major Mills said, the color rising in his face and his voice tight with anger, 'my job here is to see that this court martial is carried out as prescribed in the manual. That manual states that the counsel for the accused makes his opening statement, *if any*, after trial Counsel rests for the United States. I hope that's clear, sir.'

Aw, Jesus. You don't really want the judge and jury playing cat and dog.

'Colonel. Sir, if I may be heard. I greatly appreciate your consideration. But I knew the rules coming in here. I've prepared my defense accordingly. I'll live by the rules. And the only thing I want to say at this point . . . back home I have five suits as well as some sports jackets and trousers. All Brooks Brothers, very conservative. Here I just brought two. I just hope you understand. I can't shower where I'm staying, but there is a bath. And no matter how they look, I don't sleep in my only two suits.'

That lightened things up considerably. 'Very well, Trial Counsel, proceed with your witnesses,' Colonel Hawkins said.

'Yes, sir. Thank you, sir.' He then began his case. First the clerk that does the morning report, attendance. Then a young AP who saw Paul drive off the base at about lunchtime. He had not returned by the time this AP was relieved at 1600 hours, four p.m. The next young AP had the gate until midnight. Paul had not returned.

'Airman,' I said, 'for the record, what you are saying is that between 1600 hours and 2400 hours, you did not see Sergeant Kelly drive himself back on to the base. Or anyone else drive him back on to base. Correct?'

'Yes, sir.'

'The official reports indicate he was brought back in an ambulance about 2200 hours. Did you see an ambulance about that time?'

'Yes, sir.'

'Look inside, search it?'

'No, sir.'

We next had three airmen testify that, although they worked for Paul, they did not see him after lunch. No cross indicated. Then Innkeeper Rudman took the stand. Dressed in a tan, nubby wool suit, shirt and tie, a cherub face, reddish and happy with some broken blood vessels. Every man's dream of the perfect innkeeper.

Major Sully swore him in. 'Do you swear or affirm that the evidence you shall give in this case now in hearing will be the truth, the whole truth and nothing but the truth? So help you God?'

'Well, now. I'm a Unitarian don't you see. I'll affirm to tell the truth and nothing but. Without God, however.' His first name was Irving. And Irving was enjoying himself.

'Please take your seat. Now, let us go back to December twelfth of last year. Sometime after noon. Were you then working at the Huntington Arms, here in Maspeth, England?'

'Of course, lad. As you Americans say, "I own the joint".' He giggled and the court members tried to hide grins behind papers or hands.

'At that time and place, did you see the accused, Paul Kelly?'

'Oh, yes indeed.'

'If he's in this court, would you point him out, please?'

'Oh, certainly. Sitting between the young lieutenant and the man in civvies. Hello Paul,' he said, giving a little wave.

'Let the record show that the witness has identified the accused. Now, sir, tell us step by step.'

'Very well, sir. Paul came in about half past twelve. Took his usual room, thirteen, top of the stairs. Paid cash. Had a couple of drinks in the bar. Didn't eat. About two, when I close the bar he went upstairs. Guests can stay on you know, but he left with the rest.

'Next time I saw Paul was about five, five-thirty that night.'

'All right. Now from between two in the afternoon, 1400 hours about, and nine, nine-thirty, what happened in your hotel?'

'Objection as to form. What if *anything* happened.'

'Sustained,' Major Mills said.

'What's that supposed to mean?' asked Major Sully.

'Don't ask leading questions, Trial Counsel,' said Major Mills.

'I just asked what happened during that time.'

'Form, Major,' Major Mills said disgustedly. 'Individual Counsel, spell out your objection.'

'With all due respect, Judge, I'm not required to do that. You said this is a court martial not a Bible study class. It's also not a course on evidence.'

Major Mills gave me his first sincere grin since we had become antogonists. 'Rephrase the question, Major Sully.'

'All right, but I don't know why. This case's going to go on all year, way we're going.'

'Major Sully, if you have any criticisms of the way I run this trial, put them on paper and send them up the line,' Major Mills snapped.

'Let me get this straight,' said Colonel Hawkins.' It was my understanding that I run, this court, as President of the Court. I was given to understand that you, like Counsel here for each side, are to keep things within the rules. *In my court*. If that is not correct . . . if that's not the way it is, we better talk to Colonel Smith and your superiors.'

'I'm sorry, sir. It's your court. I was upset and used the wrong terminology.'

'Major, you do your job, we'll try to do ours. You rule on the legal fine points. In *my court*.'

'Yes, sir.'

'Major, some of us, not as pure as you and the driven snow, like a smoke. Since it is pushing 1200 hours, I am going to adjourn until 1400 hours. Is there a problem with that?'

No one had a problem with that. It was now obvious that Colonel Hawkins did not like Major Mills. Also, obviously, vice versa. If the colonel didn't like Major Mills, then the entire court martial board would feel that way. They all flew together. Where I practiced law, it was a little easier. My jurors did not outrank the judge. And back there, the judge did own the courtroom. I was not at all sure that I liked this turf war.

27

Court Martial, Day Two

It was 1403 hours and Irving Rudman was back on the stand. He looked even rosier than he had in the morning. 'So, as I was saying, sir, Paul came on down to the bar about five, five-thirty not much after I reopened. Place gets right busy then most evenings. Then, not much later, my missus comes along to help getting out the dinners and such. About six, six-thirty, the lass comes in.'

'Meaning Margot Kellogg?'

'That's the lass, yes, sir.'

'What, if anything, happened then?'

'Well, she knew a few of the gents. Had a drink with a group of them. Gin, if I recollect.'

'Was the accused with the group she had a drink with?'

'Who? You mean Paul? Yes, he was in the group.'

'Go on.'

'Well, most of the lads from the air station here, they stop in for just a touch or two, on their way home you see. Don't stay the evening. Last I noticed, the lass and Paul had taken a seat near the fire, you see. Having a bite. I think it was a rare roast, but I can't be sure. My missus, though, she'd remember, if you want to ask her.'

'What they ate is not important, Mr Rudman. Just please go on.'

'Well, sir, the bar being quiet now, I went round to the front desk, in the lobby. Doing my bills and accounts and like that. The missus and I dine late, after the dinner hour, you see.'

Mr Rudman's rambling explanations and asides were clearly annoying Trial Counsel. 'Please go on, Mr Rudman,' he said.

'Well, sir, what do you want me to say?'

'I want you to tell the court what, if anything, happened next?'

'You mean about my bills and such as that?'

'Major Sully, without leading the witness in any way, I would like precise questions. Not "go on" or "what, if anything happened then". Ask direct questions,' Major Mills said.

'Very well. Mr Rudman did there come a time when Paul, I mean the accused here, came out of the bar?'

'Oh, yes. Yes, sir.'

'When? What time?'

'Well, sir. The clock, the old grandfather my dear old dad left me, it's in the bar you see. Keeps perfect time, the old darling. So, not carrying a timepiece on my person, you see, it's hard to be sure.'

'Approximately what time?' Major Sully's impatience was clear in his voice. I realized suddenly that he had not interviewed this witness personally. That is not only lazy, in my book that's criminal. You can't rely on reports, statements taken by others. You are the guy who puts the witness on the stand. Cops, investigators, mostly don't think like court-room lawyers. My cops, when they interviewed, I sat in, took notes. They knew how to interview. But there were always things I wanted to know that they hadn't gotten into. I wondered if he'd interviewed the shrink. Probably not. Just read his evaluation. Probably didn't know I had talked to the old doc. Dangerous shit.

'Well, sir. I heard the old grandfather chime eight. Accurate to the minute, he is. Somewhere after that.'

'How much after eight, 2000 hours, would you say. Half an hour, an hour?'

'Oh, no, no, no. Shortly after my Big Ben, I like to call grandfather that, shortly after he chimed eight.'

'Did the accused come into the lobby where you were?'

'Nooo . . . no, you see the desk, my desk where I do my papers and such, that's near the front door. Just inside the front door.

When you come in the front, the Great Door I like to call it – very fine, old wood, all hand carved, you see – well, when you come in, there's a place for brollies and a coat-rack and walking sticks, you see. Then my desk. Then the bar is off to the left, same side my desk is on. The going up is beyond the bar. If you come in the Great Door and march straight ahead, there's the stairs.'

'But you did see the accused come out of the bar?'

'Objection as to form.' My hardwood chair on the hardwood floor scratched with a rasp almost as bad as a fingernail on a blackboard.

'Sustained. Reword the question.'

'Judge, I just asked a question,' Major Sully said.

'No, you did not. You just made an exclamatory statement. That's called leading the witness, Major. This is direct, not cross-examination. Reword the question.'

'May I have the stenographer read back my question?'

The stenographer pulled up the tape full of dots and dashes that emanated from her machine. 'Question: But you did see the accused come out of the bar.' She did the read back in an almost cockney accent, or what *My Fair Lady* led me to believe cockney sounded like.

'Oh, very well. Mr Rudman, did you see the accused come out of the bar shortly after eight?'

'Yes, indeed. He and the lass.'

'The lass?'

'Maggie, of course. Maggie Kellogg.'

'Together?'

'Indeed, sir.'

'And what did they do when they came out of the bar together?'

'Went up the stairs . . . to his room, thirteen, head of the stairs.'

'And then what happened, if anything?'

'I'm sorry, Mr Barrister . . . what do you want me to say?'

I thought about making a speech about now. This was the second time old Irv had asked what he was supposed to say. But I didn't. Old Irv was testifying like molasses running uphill in

January. Sounded like he was programmed to say what the prosecution wanted. But I knew that was not so and I thought the members of the court could read that as well. Even Major Mills let it pass.

'Did there come a time when a constable, Constable O'Brien came into your hotel?'

'Oh, lordy, I don't keep a hotel. Just a country inn, sir. Small, just the bar and thirteen rooms. Small kitchen. Just a wee country inn, but a fine one, sir. Yes indeed. Clean rooms, lots of hot water for the bath. And my cook, although he is me brother-in-law, is as good as you'll find hereabouts. Good fare, and plentiful. Don't penny-pinch when it comes to me fare.'

'Mr Rudman,' Major Sully said. He was sounding tired and surly. 'Did there come a time when the constable came into your inn?'

'He did that, indeed he did. Just a minute or so after Paul and the lass took the stairs.'

'And then, what, if anything, happened?'

'Well, sir, leaned on the desk for a bit. Turned round the register to look over the guest list. Then, oh yes, I remember this real clear. He says to me, "What's the rumpus up there? What's all the rumpus?" he asks me. Well, sir, I didn't hear a rumpus, but my old ears aren't what they were. Up he goes, upstairs. Little later he calls down for an ambulance. Telephone is on my desk, you see. None in the rooms.

'Well, sir, pretty soon, my establishment is full of lads from the station here, pounding up and down the stairs, using me telephone. All kinds coming and going, you see.'

'I have no further questions.'

'Cross, Counsel?'

I got up. God, they were hard chairs. 'Mr Rudman, would you mind very much coming back another day.'

'Oh, no, sir. Not at all. Just glad I can be of help. Anytime, sir. No bother at all.'

'Sure would love to own a Big Ben like yours, sir. Can you hear him chime all over the inn?'

'Not so sure about all the rooms upstairs. But he sounds off downstairs. The missus and I stay downstairs, behind the kitchen, you see. Might be able to assist you to find one. But my Big Ben, I could not sell.'

'And you can hear Big Ben in your bedroom, from the bar past the kitchen? Great.'

'Oh, yes. Clear's a bell. Fine clear tone he has. Beautiful to hear. Come to the inn, Mr Barrister, hear him yourself.'

'That I will. I have no further questions at this time. Thank you, sir.'

Major Mills now asked if the court had questions. I'm sure they did. They conferred for a few moments, and thanks be to God, decided to wait. He was to be recalled. They did not jump into the middle of my case. Chalk one up for the colonel, I thought.

'It now being after 1600 hours, Trial Counsel, who is your next witness?' asked Colonel Hawkins.

'I intend to call the air police at the scene, the CID personnel. Get that out of the way today.'

'I think we'll get to that tomorrow. 0900 hours. Court's adjourned.'

28

Court Martial, Day Three

Another grey, sullen day, this time the air base shrouded in a wispy fog with no sun to burn it off. Major Sully spent most of the morning with his air policemen and criminal investigations people. He introduced a pile of photographs, room measurements and much, much trivia. I had no cause to cross-examine or object to the exhibits. What did concern me was why Trial Counsel was not staying in sequence. Logically, Constable O'Brien would have followed the innkeeper to the stand, then the cops.

All of the testimony thus far was follow-up. His photographs clearly established that a girl, ten times now identified as Margot Kellogg, had suffered a bloody and violent death. But without the constable, there was not a single link to Paul. All they could say was that Paul was partially in the bed when they arrived, appeared or acted dopey, drugged perhaps. They put some pants on him and hauled his ass out of there in an ambulance. There had been no confession. None of the witnesses were smug or gave a word more than they were asked. No innuendo. The enlisted and noncom fraternity versus the officer corps.

Except the last witness, Captain Burns, OIC of the Criminal Investigators (Officer in Charge). 'In my opinion, the accused was faking his state of mind.'

'Meaning?'

'Meaning, sir, that he was in fact not as spaced out as he acted.'

'Objection.' Scraping the hardwood chair.

'Counselor, I'm well aware of your aversion to educating us on the rules of evidence, but I'd like to know why you are objecting. I really don't know. And if I don't know, how can I rule on your objection?'

'Very well, Judge, let me spell it out. The witness is here as the boss of the investigators. We have his schooling and military experience in the record. Nowhere in that record has he been qualified to make a medical evaluation, nor a psychiatric one, nor schooling in the behavior of pathological liars or sociopaths.

'Give me about five questions of cross, and then decide if he is capable of making the statement he just made.'

'It's my understanding that police officers routinely make such evaluations ... drunk driving cases, for instance, or public intoxication.'

'You're right. The cops run the defendant through a series of tests. Walk a straight line, pick up coins, put your hands out and then touch the nose. They also observe the defendant, how he walks, slurred speech, glassy eyes, smelled of booze. Sometimes there is a film shown the court so it can observe the behavior, make up its own mind. There could have been a film here. God knows they took enough pictures of the deceased.'

'Well, I'll just say this is a laymen's opinion, a trained layman however, giving his opinion. What do you say to that?'

Before I could tell Major Mills that he was setting the groundwork for reversible error, Colonel Hawkins came on to the scene. 'Major, all your rulings must be agreed to by this court. In order to save some time, let's give Counsel his five Questions.'

'Yes, sir.'

'Captain Burns,' I said, coming around the front of the defense table. 'You ever hear of a pain killer which consists of codeine and Tylenol?'

'I believe I have, yes.'

'Know what happens when you mix that pain killer with alcohol?'

'No, not exactly.'

'You know what a synergistic reaction is?'

Captain Burns was thinking hard. He didn't want to say no, but he also didn't want me to ask him to explain it to the court.

'No.'

'If it please the court,' – Major Sully was on his feet – 'I will just withdraw my last question and ask the answer be stricken.'

'Is that satisfactory, Mr Helbig?'

'Yes, sir, if I can have my last two questions.' Major Mills nodded and looked to Colonel Hawkins, who also nodded.

'Captain, are you in charge of this investigation? Is it your case?'

'Yes, sir.'

'So if you locked up the wrong man for this murder, is it your ass in the sling?'

'Objection.'

'Withdraw the last question.' I sat down. CD slid a sheet of yellow paper past Paul to me. It said in block letters: You are a real SOB. You just destroyed a man. I had to grin. CD will never be a criminal lawyer. I wrote back: Right, a man who wants to send an innocent man to the gallows.'

'I have no more questions of the witness. Do you wish to cross-examine?'

What a temptation. If CD thought I had destroyed this guy, he should wait for my cross. But the red light went on immediately. If CD thought I'd already done the job, so would the court. I'd now start kicking a guy after he's down. Whipping a dead horse. Defense counsel always seems to do that.

'No questions,' I said. The court adjourned for lunch. I asked CD to get our NCOs to get us Cokes and sandwiches at the stockade. I wanted to talk to Paul. We ate in the interview-room.

'Paul, can't you remember one thing?'

'I told you, Knute. You know I know what the pills do for me. I just drink beer. That day, I was so pissed off I drank whiskey. Irv Rudman said I had a roast beef dinner with Maggie. News to me. I was zonked. Don't know how I got to the room. Next thing I remember clearly is old Doc back at the base, telling me I got a nasty gash here.' He pointed to the rear base of his skull, within the hairline. 'I remember he said he wouldn't stitch it because it wouldn't show anyway. Sorry, that's it.'

'How'd you get that?' CD asked, getting mustard on his chin from the cheese and ham sandwich.

'I wish I knew, Counselor. I wish to God Almighty I had stuck to beer. I can handle that, even with the pain pills. I was just so pissed off, getting turned down for housing again.'

'It's OK, Paul. Not that big a deal. What I can't figure, why did Sully put up all the cop witnesses and not put up the next logical witness, the constable? It's out of sequence. He can't be saving him for the finale, can he? Makes no sense. He must have something up his sleeve. I can't figure it.'

'He's dumb as shit,' Paul said. The trial, I noted, had not interfered with his appetite. Paul always ate like a starving horse and he always stayed like a rail. Very tall, but not an ounce of fat. He ate so much when he was a kid I was convinced he had a tape worm. Took him to a doctor. No tape worm. And guzzled beer by the bucket.

'Never underestimate the opposition, Pauli.'

'He's a numb nuts, Knute. Guys tell me. Why else he's in this godforsaken hole making twenty G a year?'

'I've seen him try cases,' CD said, his mouth still full. 'Does like to save the best for the last.'

'A numb nuts.'

'But he hasn't connected his evidence. You weren't mentioned all morning. And that gave me an idea that might just fly. Just bullshit, of course, because no matter what you have stricken from the record, the jury heard it. You can wipe the record. You don't wipe a juror's mind like he had a blackboard up there.'

After the lunch break, Major Sully called the autopsy doctor to the stand, a local doctor. English jurisdiction, I suppose. He looked about seventy and wore one of those suits the Brits seemed to love, all nubby wool, three piece. The old doc even had a big pocket watch in his vest, gold chain. He was dry, accurate, good. Head wounds bleed a lot, but in itself that doesn't mean much. He said the victim suffered two massive blows to the skull, one left, one right. Thirty-eight fractures of the skull. Death almost instantaneous. He identified the victim from the photographs in evidence. Time for cross.

'Doctor, do you know what a synergistic reaction is?'

'Well, I had damn well better.'

'Would you then kindly explain to us, who do not know?'

'Not an easy one. It's like, if you take different compounds, say like blue mixed with yellow, you get green. That's how it's supposed to be. But if you mix some compounds together and expect that two and two equal four, they don't. You get five, say, or six or seven. Let's just say it's not a natural mix and you don't know what you'll come up with. If that makes any sense.'

'Makes a lot of sense, Doctor. I'd love to have you as a regular witness in my trials. Now. . . .'

'Objection. What Individual Counsel would like in his trials is irrevelant and immaterial.'

'For heaven's sake, Counsel is just trying to make the doctor comfortable. We up here can see he's a bit nervous,' Colonel Hawkins said.

'Quite right, Your Honor,' the little doctor said. 'Plenty of coroners' inquests under the belt, you see, but never a Yank ... American trial.'

'Objection is overruled. Proceed Mr Helbig.' Major Mills was wanting in.

'Doc, in your professional opinion, having as Trial has shown, practiced forty some years, tell me what happens when you mix together codeine, Tylenol and lots of booze, alcohol?'

'Aha, aha.' He grinned at me through not very good false teeth. 'You get a synergistic reaction. No telling what will come out. Not like say whiskey and marijuana, where you get a sort of high and then a low. Not like say, whiskey and aspirin, where you get sleepy and the pain goes. Don't know what you'd get. My best guess, you get a Zombie.'

I let that sink in, happy I had not taken Captain Burns any further.

'Thank you, Doctor. Now, you said there were two massive blows to the victim's head, one left, one right you said. How powerful?'

'Oh, do the damage they did? Very powerful, indeed. Just two blows, like swinging once from each side.'

'In your professional opinion, what kind of instrument? Fist?'

'Fist, Barrister? Impossible. Break a fist before you fracture a skull. Blunt instrument, not a cutting one.'

'Like?'

'Club of some sort, possibly lead weighted. But not lead or steel. That would have cut, different lacerations. A cricket bat, perhaps. But they have sharp edges. No, blunt and round, and, I suspect, wood. Maybe weighted, but I'd think wood.'

'In your professional opinion, Doctor, could a person, theoretically, in the synergistic condition we have talked about and using this blunt instrument, have inflicted the blows you described?'

'Oh, no. These two blows were struck by a very strong, very angry person. The synergistic chap, if he could function at all, would have needed a great number of whacks.' There was that great word again.

'Objection. There has been no showing of this reaction to the accused. Pure speculation.'

'That's true, Judge, but this is cross. I have the right to ask you to take this subject to connection. However, all of this morning's testimony was on direct and did not ever connect to the defendant, the accused. I therefore ask you to strike it all.'

'Counsel,' Colonel Hawkins said tiredly, close to exasperation. 'We hear and see, and whatever you do or do not strike from the record we know what we see and hear. When you cross-examine, we listen carefully. But the technical objections. . . .'

'He does have the right to make his record, sir,' Major Mills said.

'And it is my function to rule on objections. Now, I will allow the doctor's testimony, subject to connection. I will also allow this morning's testimony although I agree the order of witnesses might have been better. With the permission of the members of the court, of course.'

'Let's get on with it, Trial Counsel,' Colonel Hawkins said.

'Yes, sir. If Counsel for the accused, the judge and members of the court have no questions, the witness is excused, subject to recall. Gentlemen of the court, Military Judge, I have taken the witnesses out of order out of respect for the wishes of the government. Constable O'Brien works for the British. He has long duty days over a great deal of territory, I would want, in consideration of our sometimes delicate relations with our host country, to be obliging in every way. Our hosts would like the constable to be in and out as it were. Not back and forth like a ping-pong ball. I have only two witnesses left to complete this case, the psychiatrist who examined the accused and found him totally in command of his faculties, and Constable O'Brien.

'I would beg the court's indulgence that I call the doctor to sort of wrap up this day, and then have the constable here tomorrow, for both direct and cross.'

'Individual Counsel?'

I climbed out of the chair giving me a backache. 'I have no objection to Counsel's weird order of trial. Happy to have the doctor on next. I don't really mind all this prior testimony taken subject to connection because I know this court can sort all that out.

'I do sort of take exception to this little closing argument by Trial Counsel. And I object most strenuously to the notion that when Trial Counsel finishes with the constable tomorrow, that then I'm forced to follow with my cross. I made it plain at the outset, I want to try my case my way. That was agreed.

'I do not plan to call the constable tomorrow, no matter when direct is done. When I'm ready. And I do not give a particular damn about delicate relations with the host country. This is a capital case. Trial Counsel can run his case, he sure as hell can't run mine.'

'Major Sully, there being no objection to your calling your witness as you wish, you may proceed. When you have rested your case, Individual Counsel will run his case in any order he wishes. And I do share his view regarding delicate relations and all that. If the court agrees?'

'The court agrees. Call your next witness, Trial Counsel.'

29

Court Martial, Day Three

'I call Captain I.A. Shaw,' Major Sully said.

The little Indian doctor came into the room slowly, filled with trepidation, it seemed to me. He was sworn and seated in the witness stand. In his office, he had looked bigger and darker.

'Captain, would you tell the court where you are stationed and what your duty assignment is?'

'Yes, sir, I'm on staff at the 3334th Base Medical Hospital at Alconbury. My duty assignment is Wing Psychiatrist.'

'Now, sir, would you give us your educational background? Schooling, work experience, and when and where you have testified before?'

'Objection. *If* he's testified before.' That, of course, that kind of objection is pure bullshit. The kind of bullshit that just antagonizes a jury. Makes you a smart alec. A Kunstler technique. But I chanced it with this court because I wanted right off the bat that the little shit on the stand knew I was here, waiting for him. It worked better than I expected.

'The objection is sustained. Rephrase the question, Trial Counsel.'

'May I say something, sir?' the witness said, addressing Major Mills.

'You don't want to answer the question, Captain?'

'It's not that, sir. It's just that . . . well, I'd like to say something now.'

Major Sully said, 'This is most unusual, most unusual.'

'You object, Trial Counsel?'

'No sir. But this is highly unusual.'

'Individual Counsel?' I shook my head, doing my best to hide the good things I felt perking inside. 'Individual Counsel shakes his head, indicating he has no objections . . . for the record. Members of the court?'

They all shook their heads. 'The members of the court indicate, for the record, by shaking their heads that they have no objection. Proceed, Doctor.'

The little doctor shifted uneasily in his chair, the liquid brown eyes darting around the courtroom. He fingered the slim folder in his lap. 'What I want to say is that on the day Paul R. Kelly, Sergeant, was brought to my office . . . well, it was late in the day. I had seven crew-member interviews that day. Flying personnel with extreme, even traumatic problems. I was given to understand that my assignment was to do everything in my power to keep the air crews flying.

'Seven air crew members, none from the same aircraft. That meant seven aircraft that couldn't fly the next mission. Please understand, gentlemen, flight crews can have tremendous psychological problems. They are sent to me by the flight surgeon for evaluation and counseling. I know the mission of the Air Wing. I spent the day with these airmen. I knew I would spend the night on their various psychiatric disorders.

'They brought in this sergeant. I was tired. I had much to do to try to get some of these men back on course so they could fly. I had a whole night ahead of me. My records show I spent all of thirty minutes with the sergeant, about another ten to write a report and get these people out of my office so I could get back to my main task, assignment.

'I must now,' he said, looking around and almost crouching in the witness stand, 'retract what is in my hastily written report.

Under normal circumstances I would have to spend ten, fifteen hours to come to the conclusions in this evaluation. Therefore... much as I regret it, I must ask you to disregard the evaluation. I just wrote what those people wanted to get rid of them. It's something I should not have done and would not have done if the importance of the mission had not been foremost in my mind.' Beads of perspiration covered his brow, the hands moved and twitched on the slim folder he held.

'Move the witness be excused,' I said, glancing down at a yellow sheet CD had slid across the table. It said: Nice going, you bastard.

'As Trial Counsel has said, this is most unusual. Does Ttrial Counsel wish to continue with this witness? And subject him to cross?' Major Mills added with a wolfish grin.

'A moment, if you please,' Major Sully said. He sat down at his table and conferred with his young assistant behind hands.

'We'll take a ten-minute smoke break here, while you decide, Trial Counsel,' Colonel Hawkins said. Major Sully rose to give the usual instructions which by now were beginning to sound to me like church liturgy. We adjourned. Paul was jubilant, CD kept grinning and shaking his head. 'Golly,' he said, 'we spent so much time prepping to take him down.'

'Yeah. And he knew it.' In a way, I resented the smart, early capitulation. I was loaded for bear for this shit bird and it looked like I wouldn't get a shot. Like setting out on an expensive safari and finding the lion committed suicide. I also knew that very few of us hot-dog prosecutors or defense did not often lose sight of what we were here to do. We are never there to look good. We go into the arena to win, not to grandstand. Jesus, I thought, what a total asshole you are, Helbig.

'The Government will accept the motion made by Individual Counsel. The witness may be excused,' Major Sully said.

'Very well. Captain you are excused with the thanks of the court for your forthrightness.' Captain I.A. Shaw crawled off the stand, and like all the professionals hired into the military, had not read his manual of how to become an overnight officer and gentleman by an act of Congress. He did not march to the front of the long bench and salute the president of the court. He slunk out. Colonel Hawkins smiled and let it ride. He was a pilot, and the Air Force was never that stuck on ceremony. It had been part of the army until 1948 and the traditions were not yet, are not yet, set in marble.

'Are you ready to proceed, Trial Counsel?'

'Well, no, sir. I've scheduled Constable O'Brien for the morning. Thought this witness would fill up the afternoon.'

'Understood. Very well, it's now 1533 hours.. We'll adjourn until 0900 tomorrow.' With the exception of Major Mills, I believe we were all very content with that ruling. Major Mills voiced no exception.

30
Court Martial, Day Four

Constable John J. O'Brien's blue-uniformed bulk filled the witness chair. He looked around casually, the light-blue eyes moving from face to face with studied professionalism, arms resting on the sides of the witness chair. Occasionally he smoothed the walrus mustache with thumb and forefinger. He looked comfortable, at home in a courtroom. After solemnly swearing before God to tell the truth, I thought, more lies come from all the witness stands around the world than they do from husbands to wives or wives to husbands.

CD and I had spent a good part of the evening going over the interview we had had with the constable. I asked CD to take copious notes of his direct testimony so we could compare it with the tale he had spun for us in his office. The steno was giving us daily transcripts, but she was hopelessly behind. Hard work to strain to hear every word said in a courtroom all day, and then spend the night typing it up. Back home, our stenos divide up the work since they all used identical machines. The one in court turned over her squibbles and scratches to one who had not worked that day to do the transcribing.

Essentially, the constable told the tale he had told CD and me in his office. Essentially, it matched the written statement he had made at the time. Major Sully offered the statement into evidence. I had a copy.

'Individual Counsel?' said Major Mills.

I rose. 'Judge, normally I'd have to object. Best evidence rule. But, I'd like the court to have his statement so they can compare it to my cross. No objection.'

'Very well, sir. If you had objected, you would have been sustained, but I certainly don't want to try your case.'

'I'm pleased to hear that, Major,' said Colonel Hawkins.

We were now at the point in the trial where Colonel Hawkins and his court were showing open dislike for Major Mills. Major Mills returned the feeling in addition to having no use for either counsel. Major Sully was mad at me and terrified of both Major Mills and Colonel Hawkins. And behind all this conviviality lurked the presence of the wing commander, Colonel Smith. He had picked the investigating officer, he had picked the members of the court, he had given the dubious honor to Major Sully to prosecute. He had not picked Major Mills. Nor me. The flies in the ointment.

'I am aware, as are my fellow court members, Mr Military Judge or Law Officer, whichever the manual now calls you, that Mr Helbig has never defended a case nor been involved in a court martial. However, we all believe that this counsel knows what he is about. We'll give him a wide range on the technical stuff, Major. But we are all convinced that the accused has himself a top-notch attorney. So, please do not attempt to help him try his case.'

Major Mills colored visibly, biting his lower lip. I didn't have a mirror, but I'm sure I went the other way, turning white. Colonel Hawkins, I thought, was Colonel Smith's man. He had just put into the record how much help the court was giving me. On review, that would read beautifully. I hadn't even sniffed around the cheese and he had managed to spring the trap on me. He motioned to Major Sully, who was standing before his table like a statue, to proceed.

Major Sully marked the next exhibit for identification, had a tag put on it by the stenographer and walked it toward the witness stand. He handed it to the constable.

'I show you Government Exhibit 15, and ask you if you know what this is?'

The constable, knowing exactly what he was handed, like the professional witness that he was, took his time. He turned it over in his hands, felt it, seemed to weigh it lovingly in his hands. 'Yes, sir, it's what you'd call a billy club. I found it between the lass and the bed, where the accused was. Covered with blood, it was. The dark brown here, it don't look like blood, you might say, but that's the color it dries. The poor lass's blood.'

'Objection.' I was on my feet, scraping the chair loudly as I could. 'He doesn't know what the brown is. Or if he does, he hasn't been qualified at all as an expert in the field. Well, on the other hand, perhaps I should withdraw the objection. From what I've seen of the constable's record, he probably is an expert on dried blood on a billy club.'

Captain Leone hid a grin. He already knew where I was planning, or hoping, to go.

'I offer it into evidence as Government Exhibit 15.'

'Counsel?'

'Judge, I have stipulated as to the constable's knowledge of what blood looks like, fresh flown or dried. I will not stipulate that he knows whose blood has dried there. That would require a DNA Specialist. In addition Judge, it's customary where I come from that I am given the exhibit marked 15 for identification only, before it's offered into evidence. Even the opportunity of *voir dire*.'

'You want a *voir dire*?'

'In due time. Right now I just would like it be admitted into evidence without reference from what head the brown came from. That blood could have come from fifty different bashed skulls. All a blood test can do is identify type. You need DNA to make a positive, and we have none.'

'Trial Counsel, show the exhibit to Individual Counsel before offering it into evidence. Those are the rules, and you must know that.' Major Mills was well pissed off again. Major Sully dropped the club on my desk. It looked like a piece of hardwood two by four had been used to make the club. It was no more than a foot long, with a ridged handle and a weighted, round end. I could see a line, a thin line, at the end of the club. The thin end piece had been sawn off and indicated a hole had been drilled up the wood in the middle, and filled with something heavy, steel, concrete, lead.

'*Voir dire?*'

'Just one question, O'Brien.' I scraped my chair and stood up. 'Ever see one of these before?'

'Maybe ... possibly. Can't be sure.'

'That's all for now. Subject to recall.'

The constable lumbered off the stand, threw a hand forward salute and left the courtroom. There was no one in the spectator seats, just the two air police.

'The Government rests.'

'Is Individual Counsel ready to proceed?'

'No. The withdrawal of the psychiatrist has thrown off my timing as it did that of Trial Counsel. I had expected to start in the p.m. today.'

'It's just past 1100. Surely your opening is prepared? If your witnesses aren't?' Major Mills, thinking about Spain.

'For the record, objection. But yes, I can proceed.'

'Then do,' said Colonel Hawkins. I scraped back my chair and came around the defense table. Unlike the courts I was used to, there was no lectern to lean on, place notes, hide behind. 'Very well. I would like the record to note that my last objection was not ruled on.'

'It is now. Overruled.' Major Mills was testy again.

'Gentlemen of the court. The defendant is accused of attempting to rape and then kill this girl, Maggie. What I will attempt to show you, through witnesses, is that Maggie and Paul were lovers. I will attempt to show you that Paul and Maggie spent many happy days and nights at the Huntington Arms. Although admittedly, Paul left base five hours early the day, December 12, his interest and intent was to be with his girlfriend.

'It is *my* intent to show you that Paul, a victim of an injury he sustained during his military duty, required him to take pain medication. When he mixed that with booze he would become a

Zombie. And he did. Wrecked him. On that night, December 12, Paul did intentionally wreck himself. Denied again, after a year, of having his wife and kids join him. Disgusted, he took off at lunch, called his girlfriend and registered at the Huntington Arms. As they had done many times. We'll prove that.

'Exhibit 15 is very important. The murder weapon. Did Paul bring that to his assignation? Did he build himself a weighted billy? He went to the Huntington Arms for tea and sympathy. And he got it from a young local girl who worked at the NCO club. Liked Paul. No motive. Why would Paul kill his best friend here? She gave him succor. She dined with him. She had sex with him. He never told her he was single. They were having an affair and they both knew he was a married man and likely to remain so.

'I think we can prove to you that Paul had drinks, combined with his painkillers, and passed out. I think we can also prove to you that a very frustrated constable, filled with rage and jealousy, burst into that room. Laid out Paul with one blow. Killed the girl with two. Using the billy club he had never seen before. If the court gives me the leeway, I will prove that Paul didn't kill anybody.'

'Are you saying the constable killed the girl?'

'That's not my job, sir. My job is only to prove that Paul didn't kill her. Ever occur to you, Colonel, why a murder on English soil is here in this court martial? Technically, no jurisdiction. It's been done before, but why now? It's not my intent to prove the constable guilty. Not my job. My job is to raise a reasonable doubt that Paul killed the girl. If I can do that, I've done my job. We here have no jurisdiction over the constable. The locals will have to sort that out.'

'But that's what you're saying. You are, are you not, saying that Constable O'Brien killed the girl?'

'Yes, colonel, that's what I'm saying. But I don't intend to prove that. That's not my job. My job is merely to raise a reasonable doubt that Paul did the whacking with Government Exhibit 15.'

'I see,' the colonel said, thoughtfully. 'Major Mills?' he asked.

Major Mills was not up to par. He sat back in his chair. 'I think, sir, that we should adjourn for the day to sort things out and let Individual Counsel proceed as he planned, tomorrow.'

'So ordered.'

So ended the court day.

31

Court Martial, Day Five

'Are you ready to proceed, Counselor?' It was exactly one minute after 0900 hours and Major Sully had already run through the usual liturgy about all who were in court are now again in court and so forth. For Colonel Hawkins and the other members of the board, flyers all, starting the work day at 0900 hours, probably seemed almost indecent, like starting after lunch rather than breakfast.

CD rose somewhat unsteadily to his feet, his face red and his hands a trifle unsteady. 'The defense is ready to proceed, sir. The defense calls Cindy Ashwood.'

We, CD and Ruff Lane and I had had dinner together at the table where the wind blew least through the Sunbury dining-room. I had kept my newly acquired parka on during dinner. And today, for almost a full minute I glimpsed the sun. It had suddenly brightened and I could just see the outlines of a bright whitish ball through the perpetually sullen grey of the sky. I believe that I will forever think of grey overcast as English weather. I learned that the colonists came to the States seeking religious freedom. I doubt it now: they came to see what the sun looked like.

Major Sully swore Cynthia Ashwood. I had last seen her at the NCO club, a short, plump girl with a pretty smile and a nondescript uniform. She was now rather garishly dressed in a sort of purple suit, her hair swept up and held with a large comb beaded with rhinestones, and deep red lipstick, nylons and high heels. She clutched a rosary in both hands. Scared shitless. Totally unlike the carefree girl with the pretty smile I had met briefly at the NCO club.

CD sat down and I stood up. Behind the defense table. I missed the lectern. 'Cindy, you look very pretty today, but I do think you are scared out of your wits. Are you?'

'God, yes,' she managed.

'Never been in a courtroom before, Cindy?'

'Oh, no, sir.'

'Would you like a glass of water? To wet your whistle? Can't offer you anything stronger.'

Behind me, I could hear the door separating the courtroom from the hallway, opening and closing. I could also hear people taking seats on the benches. After four days of operating in an almost vacuum, our trial seemed to be drawing spectators.

'I could use a stiff gin, sir, but I'll settle for the water.' Members of the court grinned or chuckled. I filled a glass from the tray on my table and brought it to her. She took a couple of big mouthfuls and, very unlady-like, wiped her right hand across her mouth. She gave me her nice smile. 'Thanks, governor.' Even Major Mills smiled tightly.

'Now, Cindy. Sit back. Relax. This is not like taking a test, or applying for a job. Just a few things we all want to know. For instance, did you know Maggie Kellogg?'

'Oh, yes, sir,' she said, finding her voice. 'We was roommates. Her and me and Iona and Shelby. Flat in Huntington, Oxfordshire. Gossamer Lane. 31B.

'Where, if anywhere, do you work?'

'You know, sir, at the NCO. I served you drinks there.'

'Cindy, you know that, and I know that, but members of the court do not know that. I'm asking you questions I know the answers to. But all these gentlemen don't. Got it?'

The quick, pretty smile. 'Got it. I work there, Maggie worked there. We was not just roommates, you know, also best friends. We was going to buy a car together. Used of course.'

'As roommates and best friends, did there come a time when you met Paul Kelly?'

'You mean Pauli there?' she said, pointing. 'Of course, he was around all the time. They liked each other, see?' She grinned conspiratorialy. 'We was four girls in the flat, you see. No hanky panky there. Pauli was always a real gent. They'd go to the Huntington Arms, you see. For what they had in mind.'

'Objection, pure speculation,' said Major Sully.

'It ain't speculation, sir. I often had a bite with them there. Saw them off upstairs and all. Ask Mr Rudman, he's the one who knows, if you don't believe me?'

'The objection is overruled. The line of questions, I have to speculate, are offered subject to connection.'

I ignored Major Mills and walked to the Trial Counsel table to pick up Government Exhibit 15.

'Cindy,' I said, walking over to her, 'ever see this, Exhibit 15, or anything like it before?'

She took the billy club in her hand, then put it down on the armrest of her chair. 'You mean the Constable's whacker? Surely; he always carried it. Showed it off. He was in the flat a lot, coming on to Maggie. She'd have none of it, of course, him being not our sort. I think he's the one who done her in. He's a brute.'

'Objection.' Major Sully was now red-faced.

'Strike that sentence from the record. Miss, we don't want to know what you think; we want to know what you know.'

'What I know, you say? Well, I know he's a brute. I know his wife left him. I know he was always after Maggie. That's what I know.' Cindy was no longer frightened.

'Objection, I want it all struck as immaterial. Constable O'Brien is not on trial here.'

'It will be struck from the record. Proceed, Counsel.'

'Judge, I have no more questions. But I take exception to your sustaining the objection. She said it was what she knew. A witness is permitted to testify to what they know. That's what trials are all about, Major. Telling what you know. She said she *knew*.'

I had the impression that Major Mills, pilot-lawyer, inheritor of a huge Texas oil and cattle ranch, was about to come over the top of his magnificent desk.

'I had the same impression,' remarked Colonel Hawkins. 'Young lady, what is it you know, for a fact, about the constable?'

'Well, sir, I seen him time and again, coming round, asking Maggie out. Always saying she shouldn't work for the ruddy Yanks. Always sitting with that club in his hands, saying if people don't do like he says, they'll have blood on them. I also saw his wife, Sarah, when she finally left him, all black and blue with shiners for eyes. That's what I *know*, sir. He's a bloody brute, sir, if you ask me.'

'I am again going to rule the last sentence struck. Individual Counsel, I have the feeling that we are turning this court martial into a circus. Yesterday afternoon, you indicated that you would prove the accused innocent, and the constable guilty. Today, we have a full courtroom, including, I suspect, the Press. Now, I can't bar the public from this trial, nor the Press, but, subject to the objection of any member of the court, I'm going rule all of this young lady's testimony struck. I will note your objection to my ruling. Proceed.'

'Judge, you know I don't do much stipulating. So when you note my objection before I say it, that's a stipulation. I want my objection on the record, Major.'

'Overruled. Proceed.'

'Just a doggone minute, Major,' said Colonel Hawkins. 'We find the young lady's testimony very interesting. Particularly about the constable and your Exhibit 15. The court, therefore, does not want her testimony struck. Not at all. This young lady testified that the weapon, your Exhibit 15, had been seen often before all this happened, in the constable's hands. The court will take her testimony, Major.'

There was absolute silence in the courtroom. Behind me, I could hear people, unseen by me, moving about.

'Colonel, Mr President of the Court, I believe you will find rules and regulations for deciding to call off this trial . . . mistrial, and of relieving me as Military Judge. . . .'

'No way, Major. I do not believe in wasting the government's time, or money. All of us have already stood down for a week. We'll proceed.'

My next two witnesses were Conyers and McQuirk, and I wanted CD to do the asking. Major Sully had stayed away from Cindy Ashwood like she was on fire. No questions. He did the same with the NCOs. They testified that Paul and Maggie were a pair. Common knowledge. Major Sully objected to their testimony, which I argued should be taken subject to connection since they went to the question of motive.

'The charge here is not manslaughter or negligent homicide; it's murder, and to establish murder you must prove a motive. That's why we have the underlying felony of attempted rape. To establish motive. The last three witnesses, we contend, show that the defendant . . . accused . . . had been having an affair with the victim. He didn't go to the Huntington Arms with murder on his mind. Who goes to an assignation with a billy club? Why attempted rape with a willing paramour?'

'Individual Counsel is summing up,' Major Sully said harshly. 'Objection.'

Major Mills smiled at me like the wolf in Little Red Riding Hood. 'It does seem, Counselor, for someone who doesn't want to give a class in evidence that you have proceeded to do just that. However, this is a capital case and as the president of the court has pointed out, you will be allowed considerable room to roam. If the court agrees, I will overrule the objections and let stand defense witnesses' testimony.' The court agreed. Major Sully sat down. Behind me, there were coughs, sneezes and the shuffling of feet as Dr One Hung Low ambled up to the bench, threw a sloppy salute and took the oath from Major Sully.

'Will the court take judicial notice of the fact that Dr Hung is the wing flight surgeon? Save a lot of time.'

'Trial Counsel?'

'No objection.'

'Members of the court? The members of the court, for the record, nod, indicating that such notice is taken.' Major Mills appeared somewhat mollified.

'Doc, were you on duty the evening of December 12 last?'

'Regrettably, yes.'

'And at somewhere between 2130 hours and 2200 hours, did you come to see the accused, Paul Kelly?'

He opened a file folder. A professional witness, like the constable, would have asked if he could use his notes to 'refresh my memory'. The huge Chinaman was not an expert witness. He obviously also had not very seriously read his Air Force manual on how to become an officer and a gentleman in ten easy steps. Witnesses salute the president of the court after testifying, not before. But then Dr Hung apparently was very casual about everything, except his medicine. 'Paul, there,' he nodded in our direction – 'was brought in by two APs at 2145 hours.'

'You know Paul Kelly?'

'Everyone knows Paul. Not only hung around bringing donuts and kidding with the nurses, also came regularly for condoms. I always wondered if he actually used them all or sold them to the locals.' For the first time, there was laughter from behind us, and grins on the faces of the court members. All of them knew the doctor, of course. He was their flight surgeon and none of them appeared to look down on this 'short termer' just passing through to repay the government for its largese in his education. 'If he used all that rubber personally, with his back, I'd put him up there with Errol Flynn and all the great swordsmen of history.' More laughter, and for the first time Colonel Hawkins used his gavel.

'As the judge has stated earlier, court martials are open to the public. But, I warn you, not if the public interferes with the serious business at hand. This is not the *Rowan and Martin Laugh-In* and if you cannot contain your merriment, out you go. I hope that's clear.' The room became tomb quiet. 'Proceed, Counsel.'

'Let's talk about that back, Doc.'

'Medically or plain?' Doctor One Hung Low was enjoying himself. A whole new branch of medicine. Forensic.

'Plain.'

'OK, Counselor. Paul's medical charts show that he was swept off the wing of an aircraft he was servicing. Bad wind. Hit the concrete on his spine. Crushed a disk. Operation too risky. Could paralyze him. Without wanting to disparage his surgeons of that time, I'd say he should have gotten a medical discharge. That was about six years ago. Instead, he was given pain killers. He comes round to the hospital for them 'bout once a month.'

'Bad pain?'

'Bad pain,' he agreed.

'Did you test him for drugs when he was brought in on that night?'

'No, no need. He'd come around about noon that day for a fresh supply. So I knew when he was brought in that he'd been taking his medication. The nurses dispense the drugs, but I was there when he came in. One look at his ugly mug, I knew he was in pain. But when I saw him that night, I knew what he'd done.'

'Go on.'

'I told Paul, more than damn well once, a few beers he could handle, but no hard booze. One look at him, I knew he'd been into the booze. Took a blood test for booze just to be sure.'

'And?'

'He blew a .18. That's .08 over the medical and legal definition of intoxication. Soused, man. Stinko.'

'Plus his medication. What is his medication?'

He looked briefly at his notes. 'He gets 50 miligrams. That's heavy duty stuff for heavy duty pain. It's codeine and Tylenol.'

'And the result of that combination of drugs, Doctor?'

'You got a space cadet on your hands. Like totally out of it. I sure didn't need medication for him that night. Just gave him an IV to keep his fluids up and wash him out. And a catheter. In the state he was in, you don't hear nature's call and we didn't want a messy bed.' There were a few snickers, quickly suppressed. 'Next morning, he had a head like a balloon, but he was OK. Thirsty mostly. APs took him on out. Last time I saw Paul 'til today.'

'Your witness, Counsel.'

Major Sully stood up with a sheaf of papers. Probably blank. The investigating officer had not interviewed the doctor. Most likely, Trial Counsel hadn't either.

'Gentlemen,' he began, 'I realize the court took judicial notice of Dr Hung's being the base flight surgeon, but since he has testified extensively on the condition of the accused and the results of mixing drugs and alcohol, I should like to examine his familiarity with such things, his study of them.'

'Examine away, buddy. I spent a fair amount of my residency working the drunk tank and the detox center.'

'Excuse me, Doctor,' Major Mills said mildly. 'But the court has to rule on this. I'll let you enquire, with the consent of the court.'

'Trial Counsel, you are not a flying officer. This witness, Dr Hung, is our doctor. All of us, the lives of our flight crew depend on his judgement. Are you now serious about questioning his judgement?'

'Sir, these are special circumstances . . . drugs.'

'And you don't think drugs and liquor are a problem for flight crews? Move on, you are wasting time.'

'Yes, sir. Doctor, you have testified to the accused's condition when you saw him.'

'Obviously, Counselor.'

'But you don't know what his condition was like earlier, before you saw him, do you?'

'No. Not say at five in the afternoon. But I can give you a fair idea of about two-three hours before I saw him.'

'Please just answer the question, Doctor.'

'He'd have been zonked for hours.'

Major Sully stood and glared at the huge doctor. Should have interviewed him, you careless bastard. If you had, you'd know the court would have to decide between the testimony of Captain Hung and Constable O'Brien. Dr Hung was the court's physician.

You silly, careless bastard. It explained why Major Sully was a career air force lawyer. In the city criminal courts, he'd have to chase traffic cases. 'I have no further questions.'

'Redirect?'

'Yes, sir, please. Doc, within say two hours before you saw Paul, in your opinion as a doctor, could he have committed rape?'

Dr Hung grinned and blew out a lungful of air. 'In my opinion, after the first or second shot of booze, he couldn't have got it up for Marilyn Monroe.' More suppressed merriment behind us. Captain Leone was hidden behind papers, but I could see his broad shoulders shaking. Even hatchet-face Colonel Hawkins was fighting for control.

'Could Paul, in two whacks, causing thirty-eight fractures of the skull, have done this?' I walked over to pick up Exhibit 15 and handed it to the doctor.

'In my opinion, he couldn't even have picked this thing up.' Murmurs behind us, subsiding quickly. 'Frankly, if he had drinks downstairs, I don't know how he made it up the stairs to his bed before he passed out.'

'By the way, Doctor, did you Mirandarize Paul?'

'Don't even know what that means, bucko.'

'Read him his rights against self-incrimination? There's a California case, went to the Supreme Court. Says that you can take blood from an unconscious man for evidence of driving while intoxicated. But the court was very specific. Said having a license, driving a car – that's a privilege, not a right, but in a criminal case, a clear violation of the Fourth Amendment.'

'Well, now, Counselor, being from California and all, maybe I should have known all this. Fact is, I studied medicine, not law. Don't know the Fourth Amendment from a hole in the wall. And, no, I read him no rights.'

'Thanks be to God,' I said softly. That blood test, which the investigating officer omitted from his report, was a Godsend. We had to thank Captain I.A. Shaw for inadvertently showing it to us. Sloppy. 'No further redirect.'

'Do you want to rest now, Captain Helbig?' Wow, Captain Helbig! Major Mills, obviously, had found reasonable doubt. But Major Mills was from Wiesbaden. He had not been appointed to the court by Colonel J.J. Smith.

'For lunch, sir.'

'For lunch. Very well, if the court is agreeable to an early break?'

'Yes, until 1400 hours. Adjourned.'

32

Court Martial, Day Five

Major Sully swore in Anthony Lane. 'Your witness.'
'Mr Lane, would you tell the court about yourself? Your background?'

'I'm English, grew up in north London. Spent eight years in the military. Did a number of overseas tours. Joined the Constabulary. Retired about one and half years ago. Raise some sheep now, hereabouts.'

'Retired as what?'

'Plain inspector, New Scotland Yard.'

'Inspector, how many years of police work?'

'Twenty-one, give or take a month or so.' Inspector Anthony 'Ruff' Lane was a personage to be reckoned with. On the stand, no muddy boots, no Churchill, no heavy mackinaw. Instead, a Savile Row sort of suit, vest, subdued regimental tie. Black shoes shined. Another very professional witness.

'Inspector, is it a fact that I engaged you to do some work for the defense in this case?'

The deep-blue eyes sparkled across the room. 'Well, not "engaged" actually. Except for two working dinners in a draughty second-rate eatery, I haven't heard a word about being "engaged". Took on the job, you might say, partly boredom, partly because of a friend of yours, relative of mine. Been to the States you know. Let's just call it reverse Lend Lease.'

Oh, Lord, I thought, how many times have you been on the stand, charming the birds out of the trees?

I turned toward the court. 'If Trial Counsel would like a *voir dire*?'

'No.' Truculent.

'Very well, Inspector. What had I asked you to do?'

'Oh, muck about a bit. Get some background on Constable O'Brien, get some witnesses.'

'Which you did?'

'Of course.'

'Specifically, I asked you to check into the Government Exhibit 15, did I not?'

'Most specifically, Barrister.'

'I now show you Government Exhibit 15,' I said taking it once more from Major Sully's desk to the witness stand. 'What, in your opinion as a police officer, can you tell me about it?'

Inspector Lane was seeing the exhibit for, the first time. He took his time inspecting it. 'Right. Fairly common, but well done. Handle made to fit the hand. Bottom drilled, filled with lead or cement. Reglued. Well made. Very well made.'

'Ever see this particular club before?'

'No. Not for certain. But I found three lads for you. All saw a weapon like this. None can swear it's the same. Looks the same.'

'Objection. Hearsay.'

'Sustained, subject to the court.'

'Your witness, Trial Counsel.'

'Any person in the whole wide world could have made this weapon, correct?'

'Not so. Example: no young children, no persons without arms and so on and so forth.' The inspector's eyes were twinkling.

'Very well, Inspector. Millions of able-bodied adults could have made this weapon, billy club, Exhibit 15.'

'Yes, if they're a mite handy and have access to a lathe.'

'There's a woodworking shop on this base. It has a lathe.'

'That so, Major?'

'Yes, that's so. And it is also so that you have never seen this particular Exhibit before, isn't it?'

'And it's entirely possible that the accused made this weapon right here at the base woodworking shop, isn't it?'

'Possible. Not probable.'

'Oh, and why is that?'

'A bit bulky, as you can see. Your chaps carry a club that's easy to hide in a back pocket, and it's even more lethal than this. A woman could be deadly with it. Whereas this monstrosity needs a bit of wielding, a bit of beef behind it.'

Major Sully glared at the witness who looked back at him benignly, now crossing one knife-edged pant leg over the other. All the books, law books and fiction say one should never ask a question to which one doesn't already know the answer. You can do that with your own witnesses on direct examination, but never on cross. You don't normally interview witnesses for the other side. Cross-examination can destroy a witness. It can also destroy you and your case. The maxim is 'fools rush in where angels fear to tread'. Major Sully was astute enough to realize where he was treading.

'No further questions.' And no redirect. The witness was excused, marching smartly before the bench and delivering a palm-out salute.

We next called Willie Randall, local milkman, duly sworn. He wore a well-used garberdine suit and held a cap tightly in his hand.

'Mr Randall, I show you what we call Government Exhibit 15,' I said, handing it to him. 'Ever see it before?' He took it up gingerly and turned it round and round in his hands.

'Not going to get whacked with it again if I say yes, will I?' There were giggles behind me and grins on the bench.

'Objection.'

'Are you objecting to the question or the answer, Trial Counsel?'

'The answer.'

'But the answer was a question. With the concurrence of the court, I am going to overrule the objection. Proceed, then. It was the first genuine smile I had seen on Major Mills's handsome face since the trial began.

'I do not believe you'll get whacked with it again. It's now the property of the United States. Have you seen it before?'

'Can't be certain, sir. It, or one just like it.'

'When and where was that, Mr Randall?'

'Say a year past. This cold, bloody time of the year. Me and some lads had quaffed a few at O'Malley's over in Huntington. Singing a bit, having fun. Before you could say Jack Robinson, whack, whack, whack with that thing. Laid me up three days, it did. Passed blood in me urine for days. Never knew having a quiet little bit of fun, even singing off-key, was a crime.'

The British surely did like that word. More popular than sod, bugger, or bloody at least ten to one. 'Who delivered the whacks, Mr Randall?'

'The Constable, of course. Who else'd carry such a ruddy bruiser? O'Brien, he's the only one we got up there.'

'Objection. Objection. Judge, this is a collateral attack on a government witness. May we approach the bench?' We did. Major Sully was red-faced, breathing hard and very excited. 'Judge, he can't impeach my witness.'

'I'm not impeaching his witness. I'm trying to show where this club came from. The murder weapon.'

'Judge, the witness couldn't identify it. He said he saw "it or one like it". There may be millions of clubs like this around.'

'He said "it or one *just* like it".'

'Interesting legal point, gentlemen. In a sense, you are impeaching the constable. He testified he found the weapon at the crime scene.'

'And this witness puts it or one *just* like it in the hands of the main accuser. He didn't call O'Brien a liar, or refute his testimony.'

Major Mills looked at me steadily for several long moments, his face expressionless. 'Counsel, I presume the other witnesses the inspector rounded up for you will also testify that constable belted them with this billy, Exhibit 15, or one just like it.'

'Perhaps one of them can make a definite i.d.'

'Not likely, and you know it. I presume they were also struck with it. Not bidders examining it at a weapons auction. Counsel, and I know this is on the record, you are one cute piece of work. You already know that your witness, Lane, slid in that the three men he found to identify this weapon were on call to testify. You also know that if I strike this testimony from the record, it won't strike it from the minds of the court. And the court also knows, whether I let your other victims of O'Brien's propensities testify or not, that they were there, in the wings to say O'Brien beat them with this or a similar weapon.

'What I am going to do, gentlemen, I am going to allow this testimony with a caution to the court. But I will not allow any further testimony of this sort. Please return to your seats.' We did. Major Mills addressed the members of the court. 'Gentlemen, we have just had some legal argument about the admissibility of this last witness's testimony, and that of following witnesses as to essentially the same thing.

'With the consent of the court, I am going to allow this testimony to stand. However, again with your consent, I am not going to permit further testimony to buttress this witness. I must further caution you that the rules of evidence do not allow an attack on the credibility of any witness, except, of course, the accused, if he chooses to testify. In this particular situation, we have a fuzzy, at least to me, area of the law. Trial Counsel contends this is impeachment. Individual Counsel argues that he is trying to establish ownership of the murder weapon. This witness, and the ones to follow which I wish to bar, can only testify that this "looks just like" the weapon with which they were struck.

'One cannot allow testimony that say, a gun or knife *looks* like the murder weapon. It is or is not. Individual Counsel cannot, through this or his other witnesses, establish that Constable O'Brien was in possession of the murder weapon prior to the murder. The constable may very well have dozens of similar weapons. That does not prove he had ever before seen this particular one. Nor does it disprove that the accused also had such a weapon, or weapons. On that basis, I will allow the testimony if the court concurs. This is a capital case, and I agree with the president of the court that we should allow Defense Counsel as much room as the rules of evidence allow. And since I am not certain about this, I believe we should allow the defense the benefit of the doubt.'

The members of the court conferred in whispers. 'Proceed with cross-examination,' Colonel Hawkins said.

'Mr Randall, if you had been 'quaffing a few' as you put it, how can you remember by whom, or with what, you were struck?'

'Well, I'll answer that, sir. I quaff a few tans every night of me life. Might make me merry; don't make me drunk. And if you're lying on your bloody arse or your poor side, you get a pretty good idea of who and what is whacking hell out of you. Try it sometime, sir, you'll get my meaning in a flash.' Major Sully had no further cross.

'Gentlemen, I realize we are a good hour away from quitting time. However, I had planned on two more witnesses this afternoon. They are here. I scheduled Mr Rudman, the innkeeper, for the morning. If I roust him out from behind his bar, he'd be an hour getting here.'

'Understood. 0900 hours tomorrow then.'

'Sir, tomorrow is Saturday.' Major Sully looked panic-stricken.

Colonel Hawkins smiled. 'So it is. And the day after, Sunday. And so on. And so what?'

'Well, sir, the legal office is normally closed Saturday and Sunday. Chance to gear up, sir.'

Colonel Hawkins continued to smile. 'Major, the killing we are trying here took place December 12, I believe. If you aren't "geared up" by now, you might have a problem. This court, the members of this court martial, even our judge and our defense counsel are all, or were, flying officers. We are not used to standing down because it's a weekend. Normally, we stand down when we've completed our mission. Well, sir, we haven't completed this mission. And we'll stand down when we do. 0900 hours sharp ... tomorrow. Court adjourned.'

33

Court Martial, Day Six

The heavy ground fog was clearing rapidly by the time we arrived at the court, revealing another sullen, grey sky. Warmer today, but there was a penetrating dampness. We went through the usual liturgy about everyone who was present when court adjourned is again here and so forth, and my witness was advised that he was still under oath. Innkeeper Rudman had this day picked a checkered suit with brown vest, making him look even shorter and wider. However, he was as pink-cheeked, well barbered and bright-eyed as his last time on the stand.

'Mr Rudman,' I began, 'between your last time here and this morning, have you discussed your testimony with anyone?'

'Well, sir, I was told not to.' Slightly indignant.

'That does not answer my question, sir. But I'm not referring to the patrons; I mean anybody connected with this case?'

'Ah, so you know, eh? But I swear to you, I told the constable I was forbidden to talk to him. You won't find me putting my license on the line.'

'Objection, hearsay.'

'What hearsay?'

'Well. . . .'

'The witness is telling us what he said. That's not hearsay. Overruled, with the permission of the court.'

'Very good, Mr Rudman. Now—'

'Why not call me Irv? I've been Irv to everybody since my dear old Mum rocked me in the cradle. Mr Rudman was me father.' He fairly beamed at this witticism.

'OK, Irv it is. Irv, can you hear me all right?'

'Right enough, I'd say. Like a bell.'

'Irv, your Big Ben, the grandfather clock, is in your bar, correct?'

'As you say.'

'And your bedroom is past the kitchen, or behind the kitchen, correct?'

'As you say, sir.'

'And can you hear Big Ben when you're in your bedroom?'

'Like a bell, I dare say. I can hear him with one ear on me pillow. I mean he's so clear. Not another grandfather like him anywheres, I dare say.'

'I don't doubt that one bit, Irv. Tell us, when you are in bed listening to those beautiful chimes, is the bedroom door open or closed to the kitchen? Is the door between the bar and kitchen open or closed?'

Slight offense now in the look he gave me. But still cheerful. 'Well, sir, no bartender worth his onions would ever leave doors such as that open. Bars have their smell, you know, beer, spirits, smoke. Who'd allow that into his kitchen, I ask you? And,' he said, eyes twinkling gaily, 'who of my girth and appetite would want to go beddy-byes smelling the delights from my kitchen? I serve fine fare, fit for a king, or a prince at the very least.' Irv was having a ball and doing a bit of advertising on the side.

'Irv, I guarantee I'll sample your fare when this trial is over. Now—'

'Objection. I don't care where Counsel plans to dine, and all of this testimony is immaterial and irrelevant. This is cross-examination: it's limited to cross of my direct.' Major Sully was impatient and agitated.

'It's ranging far afield, agreed. Individual Counsel, would you like to reply before the court rules?'

'Yes, sir. Specifically, the witness testified that he and Constable

O'Brien were together at his guest register in the foyer of the inn. The constable was examining the register. From the desk where they were, it is a short distance to the stairs leading to the second floor. And Room 13 is just at the head of the stairs. No closed doorways or around corners.'

'Proving what, Counselor? Where are we going?'

Major Mills smiled his best wolf grin. 'I believe I now know exactly where Individual Counsel is going. Correct me if I'm wrong, but it's my recollection that the constable, to quote Mr Rudman, "heard a rumpus upstairs. Me hearing ain't all that good." Counsel, I suspect, wishes to challenge the faultiness of the witness's hearing. Witness heard no rumpus. Am I correct, Counselor? Very well, with the permission of the court, I'll allow all of the testimony. It does closely relate to his direct. Objection overruled. Proceed, Mr Helbig.'

'Ah, that's where we're headed is it? That's why I've been asked back,' the innkeeper said, twiddling thumbs in the hands resting in his lap. 'Well, I confess. Me hearing ain't all that bad. Except, of course, when the missus starts on me. I suppose at times such as that, no man in this room has twenty-twenty hearing, I dare say.' There were fewer spectators this day than on a normal working day, but there were giggles behind me and grins in front. I had to like some of the English. Irv Rudman was a regular father of Eliza Doolittle.

'Trial Counsel, we could ask Individual Counsel to elicit what has just been testified to. That would be redundant and a waste of time. If the court concurs, we'll let the testimony stand.'

'Irv, it appears your hearing is better than twenty-twenty. I ask you now, as an innkeeper who never wants to put his license on the line, aren't you always listening for any sort of trouble in your inn?'

'As you say, sir.'

'*Any* sort of trouble? *Any* sort of rumpus?'

'I dare say there's not another establishment in the district with fewer calls to the Bobbies. I like things genteel, you see. No rowdies on my premises. Don't need their sort. Respectable, that's what my place be. A point of pride with me, bring your old maiden aunt.'

'And your premises are as genteel and respectable because you always have an ear out for *any* trouble, *any* rumpus?'

'You can safely bet your bottom dollar on it, sir.' My witness was now expansive and content. Madison Avenue could have used his low-pressure approach.

'Irv, we have no doubt, not a one. Let's look now at when you and Constable O'Brien were at your guest register. Shortly after Paul left the bar with Maggie and went upstairs, did you hear a rumpus?'

'No, sir. But I'm not one to argue with the constable. He can cause you a barrel-load of trouble even if you're pure as the driven snow. He's the law hereabouts, you see. Want to keep your license? You say to yourself, and I hope there'll be no 'percussions for what I say, Constable O'Brien hears a rumpus, there's a rumpus. That's how it is; there's a rumpus. Not what made the Empire great, I dare say. But I'm just an innkeeper.'

'Was there a rumpus coming from the top of the stairs?'

'If there was, I didn't hear it. But if the constable said there was a rumpus. . . .' He shrugged.

'Thank you, Irv. Now, on to something else. In your direct testimony, you said that Paul, as always, paid cash. Is that correct?'

'As you say. Never on tick. Cash on the barrel.'

'How many times did he put cash on the barrel when he registered?'

'Lordy, now that's a tough one. How many times? Three, four, maybe five times a month, I dare say. He and the bird . . . I mean Maggie, they were my best regulars.'

'For how many months, approximately?'

He thought about that for a time. 'Close to a year, I'd say. Haven't me register with me which would tell exactly. Would you be wanting it? The register, I mean?'

'No, that's not necessary. Now, on all those occasions, what if anything did they do?'

'Always started in the bar, just like the last time. Had a few before the fire. I don't always have a fire, as you can gather. When it gets as hot as Hell, you want the cool the thick walls offer up. Escape the heat in the bar. Had the windows double-glazed so we'd be cool in summer. But, soon as a bit of damp is in the air, even a rainy summer day, on go the logs. Never spare the expense. Not penny wise and pound foolish: they all like a fire crackling.

'To get back to it, then. Paul and the girl always had a few in the bar, sometimes just themselves, sometimes with other Americans from the base. Then, they'd have a bite of me brother-in-law's fine vittles. Good cook, he is, not a chef I'd say, but a good cook. Then, maybe a snort after supper and up they'd go. Usually had breakfast sent up. Mostly I'd take it up because the missus cooks the breakfast and I do the carting. Can't afford the girls to do the waiting round-the-clock, you see.'

'How many times, roughly, very roughly, did you take up breakfast?'

'Lordy now. Twenty, thirty times, maybe more.'

'On any of those occasions, Irv, did you ever see this anywhere in the room?' I asked, handing Government Exhibit 15.

'Of course not, sir. That ain't Paul's; that belongs to the constable.'

'Objection.' Sully fairly screamed it.

'With the concurrence of the court, I will strike the latter part of the answer, leaving only "of course not, sir". Unless, of course, Counsel can lay a foundation.' The court concurred.

'Irv, can you positively identify Government Exhibit 15?'

He looked at me quizzically.

'The thing you're holding in your hand is known as Government Exhibit 15, Irv.'

'Can I identify it, do you ask? Is my name Irv,? Do you know how many times the constable laid it on me table and told me its history? I know this thing here like the back of my hand. See here, on the top of the grip? It says J.J. That don't stand for jelly.'

There was noise in the room and for the second time, Colonel

Hawkins, who had been unobtrusive all morning, banged his gavel.

'Showed me the blood, the brown crust here. Scared hell out of me, I can tell you. Don't want to come up against a head basher, not me.'

'Objection.'

'Operation of witness's mind. Subject to the members of the court, I'll let it stand.'

'Let's move on to one other thing, Irv, and then I'll let you off to go back to making your living. You told us about those windows you've had double-glazed so the summer couldn't get in, and the warm couldn't get out. Is that right?'

'As you say, sir.'

'If you're on the outside of the windows looking in, can you see the whole bar?'

'That's why I have them. Put the menu there daily. Me missus does it by hand, and she's got a fair hand. Let the public read the menu, look in, see my guests enjoying the wonderful food me brother-in-law dishes up. See the girls serving like the queen was at the table. You can jolly well see all of the bar. See the crackling fire, see me three taps of beer and the ales. If you ain't blind, sir, you can sure see the lot and want to come in. And lovely taps they are. Finest draught, always fresh, never a flat glass or tankard. We do it all proper, sir.'

'I'm sure you do, Irv. Thank you very much. Your witness.'

'Mr Rudman, the fact that you didn't *hear* a ruckus doesn't mean there was no ruckus, does it?'

'As you say, sir.'

'You don't know if the constable has better hearing than you do?'

'I don't, no, sir.'

'So he could very well have heard the ruckus?'

'He said he did.'

'Right. And so just because you didn't hear a ruckus proves nothing, isn't that so?'

'Well, sir. . . .'

Major Sully raised a menacing hand. 'I'm not interested in a speech, sir. Answer the question yes or no, that's all.'

'Could I hear your question again, sir?' The court stenographer read back the question.

'I'm going to have to object, Judge. He's asking the witness to testify to a conclusion. That's for the court to decide. He can only ask if, in the witness's opinion, it proves nothing.'

'Subject to the court, I'll sustain the objection. Trial Counsel, are you asking his opinion?'

Major Sully glared at Major Mills. He damn well did not want the innkeeper's opinion. If he asked the question he would undoubtedly not like what he heard. If he didn't rephrase the question, the record would be clean but the members of the court were not ciphers. They were not supposed to infer what the innkeeper would say, but they surely would. He walked to his table, picked up Exhibit 15 and approached the witness stand.

'I hand you Exhibit 15, which you have testified to before. Now, sir, how is it you recognize it?'

'Like I told the nice gent in mufti I seen it often before.'

'Aren't they fairly common, more or less the same?'

'As you say, sir, except for the initials.'

'Ah, yes, the initials. Could they stand for John Jones or Jack Jackson?'

'I suppose. But why would Constable O'Brien have another bugger's billy?'

'Every time you saw this club, or one like it, you didn't look to see if those initials were there, did you?

'So one time or another you saw a club with the initials, J.J., and at other times you saw a club but couldn't know if that club had those initials, or other initials, or no initials, could you?'

'As you say, sir.'

'Anybody could have made this club, Exhibit 15, isn't that right?'

'I suppose.'

'Anybody could put those same initials on fifty different clubs, right?'

'I suppose.'

'The accused could have put these initials there, right?'

'Objection. Speculation. No offer of proof, no foundation.'

'Sustained. Although Trial Counsel can go into hypotheticals.'

'He's an innkeeper not a billy-club expert, Judge.'

'Quite so. Trial Counsel do you wish to try to qualify the witness to answer hypothetical questions?'

Major Sully glared some more and then slowly shook his head. He sat down at his table and conferred with his young aide. After a few moments he said he had no further questions of the witness.

'The People call Paul Kelly,' I said.

Major Sully was on his feet. 'I presume that you mean the *defense* calls the accused, Paul R. Kelly?'

'Slip of the tongue, Major.' Like hell it was. Let's remind the court that a prosecutor is defending his one-time brother-in-law. Paul was duly sworn, advised of his rights against self-incrimination. He took the stand and looked around from this new perspective, arms resting on the sides of the witness chair, feet together, back as straight as his pinched vertebrae allowed.

'Paul, starting with the morning of December 12 last, tell us step by step what you did.'

'Objection. To the informality with the accused here. He's a noncom in the United States Air Force, not Individual Counsel's fraternity brother. Also, I believe rules call for questions and answers, not Hamlet-like soliloquies.'

'Counsel?'

'He is decidedly not my fraternity brother. I brought him up in my home from the age of thirteen until he joined the United States Air Force. If the court sees fit to order me to call him Sergeant Kelly, I will do so, my objection in the record. As for the Hamlet crack, I was not seeking philosophical meanderings but a straight account without wasting more time. I have here a copy of *Prince on Evidence*. I'll think that you will agree, Judge, that all trials are run according to Dean Prince. I'd like Opposing Counsel to show me where my question was improper.'

'Counselor, please approach the bench.'

'Wait, please, Major. Since any legal ruling you make has to have the approval of the members of the court, let me tell you the feelings of the court now, rather than going through rule books and closed-door legal arguments,' said Colonel Hawkins.

'How can you tell me how the court will rule on my decision when you haven't had a conference, Colonel?' Major Mills was not upset but honestly perplexed.

Colonel Hawkins studied Major Mills with calm, expressionless eyes. After a long silence when even the foot shuffling and sneezing and coughing behind me had ceased, a flicker of a smile crossed his face.

'Trust me, Major, this is, as has been much noted, a capital case. If Counsel for the Accused is more comfortable calling his relative by his given name, he can use his given name, or for that matter any name he chooses. He can call him Irv, for all the court cares.'

Sharp character, this colonel. Nobody had objected to Irv.

'As for the Hamlet stuff, we will allow the accused and his counsel to tell their account any way they wish. And if Paul wants to agonize about "to be or not to be" we will even hear that within reason. Now, you lawyers have your conference while we take a smoke break. Ten minutes.' He banged the gavel, something he had not done before except to quiet spectators.

The court filed out and Major Mills waved us to the bench.

'I have, as you know, the power to declare a mistrial. After six days I'm not so inclined. In addition, while I would rule that the accused be addressed by his military title, I agree that *Prince* does not bar a straight recital. Have you authority to the contrary, Major?'

'Not without research. If you'd give us the weekend, Major....'

Major Mills fairly beamed at Major Sully. 'How would you like to make that request to Colonel Hawkins, Major?' Major Sully looked away and said nothing. 'Very well then. There is nothing in the manual as to how Individual Counsel is to address an accused and we'll let Colonel Hawkins win the field on that. If you wish to grab a smoke now, be back before the court is. That's all.'

I wanted a smoke all right and the AP at the door said he'd call me. CD rushed out with me. Paul came down from the stand but couldn't go for a smoke. He probably needed one more than I did, but you can push just so far before the rubber band snaps back in your face.

34
Court Martial, Day Six

'Paul, I'm sorry you couldn't get a smoke break. You probably needed one more than I. But, let's get back to my last question if you recall it.'

'Yes, sir. I got to my office at 0730 hours. We had two crews to run through that day. I set out the films from the safe, in proper order. We had one morning run and one in the p.m. The first crew came in around 0800. we had coffee up by then—'

'Excuse me, Sergeant,' Colonel Hawkins interjected, 'all of us up here have been through your shop. And the coffee that melts spoons. So save us some time here, let's start when you left your shop.'

'Yes, sir, Colonel. I waited for the first crew to do their run, set up the p.m. run and went to the base housing office. I've been here fourteen months. Every month I go to base housing. Every month there ain't no base housing. I haven't seen my wife or kids for fourteen months. They've been in a basement apartment near my last base, Kelly, in Texas.

'I been in the service seventeen years. I never felt so fucked-over before. Jees, Colonel, when the docs said a broken back ain't a reason to get discharged, I was happy as hell about it. I love this man's air force. I've flown airborne radar, been in a war, did all kinds of ground maintenance. Locked up once for a barroom brawl but cleared. Been froze and steam-cleaned. Been around the world with some of the best buddies a guy can have. Been unfaithful to my wife in some pretty great places.

'Knute there made me join up. I hated him in basic and thanked him ever since. This rank and this job I got now, greatest. I never finished high school, but the air force got me a Ph.D. I got a great job, maybe the most responsible on a base.'

'Objection, this is not testimony.'

'Sorry, Major. You're right. I'm rambling along here like some Texan playing his guitar. Guess it's just I feel like among friends. All those officers up there been through my shop and choked on my coffee.

'Fact is, I come out of that housing office feeling lower than a garden snake. Fuck it, I said to myself. My back was giving me a lot of grief, even with the pills. So, I called Guernsey, my buck sergeant. Told him to run the afternoon crew through and secure the film. Then I called Maggie and asked her to meet me. She can always get off when she wants.

'Went to the Arms, checked us in, waited for Mag in the bar. She came, we had drinks at the table by the fire, our favorite. Ate, had a brandy, I think. I'm not supposed to drink hard booze with the pills. I just didn't give a shit. When I got up from the table, it was Disneyworld. I could hardly stand. Mag helped me walk, held me up really. Not proud of myself, I was in uniform. I don't much like a disgrace to the uniform, but I was bombed and I knew it.

'Mag helped me upstairs. I told her I wasn't about to take her on a trip around the world. That's what we called it when we got it on. I remember she helped me to the bed and took off my shoes. And that's about it until the door bust open and the constable came in. I'm vague here, but I remember him swinging his club and belting Mag, who was just sitting next to me on the bed. I couldn't move. That's it, Knute. Like I told you in the stockade, that's all I can remember. If I walked out of the Arms, like they say, it was a Zombie walk.'

'Thank you, Paul. Your witness, Major.'

Major Sully was on his feet instantly. An angry pit bull. 'Sergeant

Kelly, let's take it from the top. There is no doubt, is there, that you left your duty station at lunchtime with no intent to return to duty?'

'Not that day, no, sir. When my back starts making me see stars and I pop my prescription, I'm not fit to run the simulator. Dr Hung told me that.'

'I'm not interested in opinion or hearsay, Sergeant yes or no will do very nicely. Now, you left the base with no intent to finish your shift? Yes or no.'

'No, sir.'

'No what, Sergeant?'

'Objection. He instructs the witness to answer "yes" or "no" and when he does, then Counsel wants an explanation. Counsel should make up his mind.'

'Judge, I'm being badgered here by this eminent counsel, Individual Counsel from New York.' Major Sully was red of face and obviously angry. What I wanted. I was badgering him and I had no thought of stopping. An angry lawyer is a lousy lawyer.

'Trial Counsel, I think you are absolutely right. But trials, court martials, are adversarial proceedings. Individual Counsel is your adversary, as he should be. It's not his job to make yours any easier. And you did demand a yes or no answer. And you did then demand further explanation. With the concurrence of the court, I'm going to ask you to rephrase your question so that when we hear yes, or no, we'll all know and understand the answer.'

'Sergeant, when you left the housing office, did you intend to return to duty that day, December 12?'

'No, sir, I intended to go out and drown my sorrows that day.'

'Exactly. So that shortly after noon of that day, you were AWOL. Absent Without Official Leave.'

'Is that a question, Major Sully?' Paul said it like butter wouldn't melt in his mouth.

'Yes,' through gritted teeth, 'that's a question, Sergeant.'

'I don't figure I can answer that just "yes" or "no", Major.'

'Just answer it then.'

COMMAND INFLUENCE

'Well, sir, I don't think there's an NCO, or an officer on this or any other base who hasn't taken an afternoon off now and then. We are supposed to take one afternoon a week for PT ... physical training. I can't take PT, sir. I take a prescription drug and lie down. So, no, sir, I would not say I was AWOL on December 12.'

'Very well, you left the base before the end of your tour with no intent to return to duty. Is that correct?'

'Yes, sir.'

'And you did that because of your pining for your wife and children. Is that correct?'

'Partly correct, sir. I was also feeling sorry for myself because I hurt awful bad.'

'So, feeling sorrow for yourself and pining for your wife, you called your paramour to arrange another of your frequent assignations. Is that correct?'

Paul lost for the first time his perfect military bearing. He grinned his disarming grin. 'Could be, sir. I plain don't know them thirty-dollar words.' The court grinned with him, briefly and fairly well hidden. It was now becoming a battle of wits between an attorney-at-law, four years of college, three years of law school, and a high-school drop-out. A well-prepped, high-school drop-out.

'Very well, Sergeant. If you lack a basic comprehension of the English language, 'let's try it this way. Pining away for your beloved wife, you called your local whore to come and have sex. Is that about it?'

'Oh, no, sir. When I'm on those drugs, when I'm in pain, I ain't man enough to have sex. I was just looking for some T and S.'

'Have you no friends, Sergeant, who could have given you tea and sympathy instead of booze and sex?'

'No, sir, no way. NCOs I know don't drink tea and they are not full of sympathy. They'd say "shit happens, kid". Maggie was my friend, NCOs are buddies. There's a difference, sir, in the enlisted ranks.'

'Well, you had no tea, did you?'

'I had grog. Lots of it, I suppose. Maggie had to help me stand even though I ate pretty good.'

'And then you conveniently passed out and remember only that the constable broke into your room and hit the victim. Is that your testimony?'

'Major, why in God's name would I ever hurt a girl who was my friend and my girl. She'd do anything I wanted of her. Why would I bash in her skull? For being good to me? For sleeping with me? She was my best friend, Major.'

'And if your wife were to come over, what then?'

'I'd probably see her a bit less, maybe.'

'You mean to tell this court that you have been unfaithful to your wife almost since you landed here, and that you'd continue that sort of adulterous conduct?'

'Oh, yes, sir. I'm an NCO. We don't have the education or the high morals of officers. And I wouldn't be upset, Major, if my wife out there at Kelly decided to spend Christmas or New Year's or whatever with some NCO who could keep her from the Foggy, Foggy Dew. That's an Earl Ives song, Major. Makes sense.'

'You are the most immoral person I have ever had the misfortune of meeting. There is no dastardly deed, including murder, that I would put past you.'

I could sure as hell object to that. Paul did it for me. 'Is that a question, sir?'

Major Sully, red-faced, frustrated and angry. 'No, I have no further questions.' He sat down.

'Mr Helbig, would you wish me to declare a mistrial, based on Trial Counsel's words? Or have him removed as counsel?'

I stood up slowly. 'No Major Mills, neither. We don't have a jury of Sarah Lawrence freshmen. We have all flying officers here. I think they can sort things out all right. Major Sully is just upset. It happens. He's a very competent trial attorney.'

35

Court Martial, Day Six

'Very well, Individual Counsel, I agree. Please call your next witness,' said Colonel Hawkins.

'People... the accused recall Constable John J. O'Brien.' One of the APs went out to the witness waiting-room. Coming back into the courtroom he said, 'Not here, sir.'

'Did you subpoena him, Mr Helbig?'

'Yes, sir. Personally served. I have the affidavit of service here.'

'For today, this morning?' Major Mills asked. I took the subpoena from my file and walked over to hand it up to Major Mills. He read it slowly. 'It's perfectly proper. But it's our subpoena. I don't know if it applies to a British subject. Have you ever had this problem before, Trial Counsel?'

'No, sir.'

'Never ran into it in Germany, either.

'Very well, it's a bit early, but we'll break for lunch now and give Trial Counsel time to round him up. He answered this subpoena when you called him as *your* witness and he damn well better answer this one. We'll adjourn until 1330 hours. I want that witness here then, you understand me, Major Sully?'

Major Sully understood and we broke for lunch. CD, Paul and I went into the witness-room. Paul and I lighted up. We all sat around a small conference table.

'How'd you know O'Brien tried to get to old Irv?' Paul asked.

'I had Inspector Lane watching him. We anticipated.'

'I told you, CD, didn't I tell you?' Paul asked, grinning. 'Guy gets up mighty early in the morning. Hey, Knute, how did I do?'

'A touch of the wise-guy, as always, but you did manage to come off very military. You threw a real snappy salute at Colonel Hawkins, I'll give you that, Pauli.'

'I didn't like that crack about officers. You offended them, I think,' CD offered. Paul looked at the well scrubbed, unlined, boyish face and grinned.

'Naw, no way. They're flying officers. I've kidded around with all of them in my shop, heard them talking. Right, Knute?'

'I wouldn't know, Paul. Long time since I was a flying officer and I was single most of that time.'

'Shee-it,' he said grinning and lighting another cigarette, 'way I heard it you were bedding down a farmer's wife when you got your noggin split.'

'Don't believe everything you hear, kid, it'll only get you into trouble.'

'Me? I'm never in trouble.' We all chuckled. Paul had that way about him.

'Your trouble is why we're here. And we're sitting here like we're just killing time 'til the second-half kickoff.'

'What happens if they can't locate the constable?' CD asked.

'I most fervently hope he's gone underground back to Northern Ireland.'

'Why, Knute?' asked CD.

'Because he's a professional witness and a congenital liar. They believe their own lies and this one can do it professionally. I won't be able to take him apart. Maybe dent him a little, that's all. But if he disappears, that's as good as an admission of guilt.'

'He knows that too,' Paul said somberly.

'I think he's pretty stupid, myself,' CD said, obviously trying to cheer Paul up.

'Yeah, dumb as a fox, CD. He's no fast thinker but he's wily and he's been around, seen it all. I'd be happy if he's disappeared.'

'He won't,' Paul said, 'he's just trying to shake you up, get you off stride. He'll be here after lunch, eating humble pie with some excuse or other. I'll lay odds on it.'

'Speaking of lunch, let's get at it. We'll see you later, Pauli. Keep your apples up.'

'Don't worry, they're up and you'll make mincemeat of the fat fuck.'

'Keep your apples up?' CD asked.

'From when he was a kid. When you smile, your cheeks go way up.' I watched CD trying this out as he drove us to his kitchen for sandwiches.

Paul was right. At 1330 hours Constable John J. O'Brien was sworn in by Trial Counsel.

Major Mills said, 'I have a duly executed service of subpoena here. Will you explain to the court why you were not in attendance at 0900 hours? Why Trial Counsel had to send out the air police to round you up?'

'Forgive me, Major, gentlemen of the court. Just plain slipped me mind, sir. It being Saturday, you see, sir and knowing you Yanks knock off for the weekend. I wasn't hard to find, mind you. Right at me post filling out reports.' His 'sir'-studded excuse sounded as humble pie as Paul had predicted, but the body language told me a different story. The constable sat back in the witness chair, ankles crossed, arms and hands resting relaxed on the polished wooden arms of the chairs, a bulging blue mass composed and totally at ease. In the British court system, witnesses stand in the jury box. For the constable, this was like his home away from home. I hoped I could make him a little less comfortable.

It occurred to me that as a British subject, I couldn't even threaten him with a charge of perjury delivered overt or covert. Judges frown on such scare tactics, but you could always sneak them in and get the point across. This congenital liar had nothing to fear.

'Let's proceed. Your witness, Mr Helbig.'

'Thank you, sir.' I stood up went to the trial counsel table and picked up Exhibit 15. I walked across the room and handed the billy to the bully.

'I show you Exhibit 15 in evidence. Your last time on the witness stand, you said you had seen hundreds of similar billy clubs, as you called them. My information is that you would have first seen them in Northern Ireland.'

'I'd say you're right, Barrister.'

'Did you fashion yourself one while on duty there?'

'I suppose I did. Lots of lads carried them, still do. But anyone can make one of these. They ain't illegal, you know. Probably every farmer hereabouts has one, I'm betting.'

'My information, constable, is the same as yours. The billy club migrated back to dear old England and found its way into the police. The Constabulary. Is that correct?'

'Found its way into the home of every bloke hereabouts.'

'Including your home, Constable?'

He hesitated for a moment, the hands on the arms of the chair tightening momentarily. 'I deal all alone with some pretty tough buggers 'round here. All by meself. I carry it sometimes when I suspect trouble and the truncheon isn't enough.'

'So you don't have it with you now. You don't suspect trouble here, or do you?'

He smirked instead of smiling and relaxed again. 'No, Barrister, I don't expect no trouble here.'

'Not the kind you could settle with a billy, right?'

'I'm not sure I get your meaning?'

'I mean you and I both know that I mean to give you a downright bad time up here. You wouldn't want to come out of that chair with a billy in your hand, would you?'

'Objection. He's badgering the witness.'

'Subject to the concurrence of the court, the objection is sustained. Counsel, so far, this is your witness and it's direct, no cross.'

'But when there are no witnesses, isn't that what you do when you're angry, Constable, use the club to bash heads?'

'Objection.'

'I'll withdraw the question.'

'That's all very well, Individual Counsel but you know better. I just admonished you. I don't want to find you in contempt of court.'

'Maybe I *should* have brought my old pal,' the witness muttered, having reddened considerably. The close-set pig eyes stared balefully at me.

'I would like witness's last answer to my withdrawn question read back.'

'Why, Counsel?'

'Because if a witness tells his examiner that he wished he had brought his billy club to court to use on him, I think we have grounds to declare the witness hostile.'

'Objection. He never said that.'

'Very well, Reporter, please read it back.'

' "Maybe I should have brought my old pal",' the stenographer read back.

'You see, there is no reference to any club. All he said he should have brought a pal.'

'Major Sully,' Colonel Hawkins said quietly, 'we all heard what the witness said and the context in which he said it. We are not, as you seem to think, all of us deaf, dumb and blind. Without wanting to overstep into Major Mills's area of expertise, we know that sooner or later Captain Helbig will make the witness hostile. Instead of wasting a lot of time let's put into the record that we all heard the witness say in so many words that he would indeed like to use his billy club on the defense counsel. I therefore take it upon myself to declare the witness hostile. Can I do that, Major Mills?'

'Yes, sir, if the other members of the court concur.' He had done it again, and again got the bland stare from Colonel Hawkins. 'Believe me, Major, they do. Let's get on with it, Counselor.'

The first feeling is one of victory. It looked like I had the court solidly on my side. Most every ruling had been in the defense's favor. Great, except that is exactly how it would look to the reviewing authorities on appeal. They all leaned over for the defense and still found the accused guilty as charged. The record shows that Counsel was more than competent. The verdict must stand. The record, the *holy* record makes no mention of 'command influence.' So that little problem doesn't exist. Bullshit. I had the feeling along about then that I had been set up.

'Back to the fray, Constable. Please look at the exhibit in your hands. On it you see a brown substance which you testified was dried blood.

'You've been qualified as an expert on blood and dried blood. Now look at the top of the handle. Do you see the initials J.J. on the top?'

'Yes.'

'Do you know the full name of the accused?'

'Paul R. Kelly.'

'And your full name, Constable?'

'John O'Brien.' Surly answer now, anger barely concealed.

'Excuse me, Constable, is it not John J. O'Brien? John Joseph O'Brien, as it says on your commission here?'

He glared at me and hesitated.

'You don't have to answer. I'm putting your birth certificate into evidence.'

'Objection, I want a show of evidence, of proof.'

I walked over to Trial Counsel and handed him the birth certificate.

'This is a duly authenticated copy of a birth certificate. I offer it as Defense Exhibit 1.' Major Sully studied it for several minutes.

'Perhaps, Trial Counsel, you will let me see the offered exhibit?' Major Mills sounded annoyed again at what he probably thought was stalling. Major Sully handed it up. 'Do you object to the offer?'

'No, sir.'

'With the concurrence of the court, Exhibit 1 for the defense is now in evidence. Proceed, Counsel.'

'Constable, your initials are J.J., yes or no?'

'I'm known as John O'Brien. Constable John O'Brien.'

'Constable, your initials are J.J., yes or no?'
'Yes.'
'Very well. Judge, I'd like the exhibit returned to Trial Counsel.' An AP took the exhibit and returned it to Major Sully. 'Constable, Cindy Ashwood testified here, under oath, that you came around to see the deceased, Maggie Kellogg. That you wanted to date her, go out with her. Is that your recollection?'

'She was a fine-looking lass.' The hands had returned from Exhibit 15 to the arms of the chair. They no longer looked relaxed and resting. They were now gripping. I thought that a good sign. No sweat yet on the brow, but the casually resting crossed ankles had come undone.

'Cindy said Maggie refused your advances. She never went with you. True or false?'

'We playing telly games now?'

Major Mills said, 'The witness is instructed to answer questions, not ask them. You are not in your police station interrogating a suspect now. Answer the questions.'

'What was the question, sir?' Cute, stalling for time. He couldn't know what Cindy Ashwood had testified. The question was read back.

'The Ashwood girl exaggerates. I took a shine to the lass after me wife run off with some Yank, that's true. I come 'round once, maybe twice. She weren't interested, seeing as I'm old enough to be her old dad. That's all there was to it.'

'You're under oath Constable.'

'Maybe a few times more 'til I got the message. Nothing to it.'

'Well now, Constable, here's what we have so far. We have a billy club left at the scene of a murder, forensically identified as the murder weapon. A type of weapon you carry when you expect trouble. This particular weapon has the initials J.J. carved on it and your initials are J.J. And the victim is a girl you were after. Would you agree to that statement of facts?'

'Objection.'

'Why?'

'Who . . . who could answer such a long drawn-out, convoluted question?'

'With the concurrence of the court, I'll sustain the objection. Rephrase the question, Counsel.'

'Just a minute, Major. It so happens the court doesn't concur. We think the question was understandable and proper.'

Major Mills was right, of course. He and Major Sully both knew I was making a small summation where it did not belong. Colonel Hawkins, the pilot was not a lawyer. Maybe he wanted to let the question and answer stand. Maybe he wanted it to look to the reviewing authorities like the court was leaning over backwards for the defense. I decided I had to get the colonel pissed off at me so he would not be so damn kind.

'Proceed, Counsel.'

'Sir, with all due respect, I withdraw the question. If you have the question read back, you'll find it more summation then question. That's improper.'

The colonel's color rose to his face. He gave me a long, hard look. One does not tell a colonel, even a light colonel that he is wrong and a major is right. 'Read the question back,' he growled. The question was read back. 'There is nothing wrong with that question, sir. It will be answered.'

'With all due respect, the President of the Court is overriding the conclusion of all the lawyers. The record will reflect that, sir.'

'Major,' – the tone now was coated in three inches of ice – 'this court doesn't give a particular damn about the opinion of lawyers. Our function here, as I understand it, is to get at the truth; yours is to advise us. You have advised. Thank you. I now want the witness to answer the damn question.'

All eyes turned toward the witness box. 'She was just one of many lasses I fancied after me wife ran off.'

'Let's go now to the evening of December 12, Constable. The flight surgeon has testified that a combination of drugs and alcohol that afternoon and evening made the defendant, the accused rather, a hardly walking Zombie. Would you agree with that?'

212

'Walking Zombie you say? I came in that room, like I told you. Bashing her skull in, he was. Whacking the bloody brains out of the poor lass.'

'Then is it your testimony that the flight surgeon, who is a licensed and qualified physician, is wrong?'

'I know what me eyes saw. That's a fact.'

'Did you use your billy to stop him?'

'Didn't have me old pal. Just hit him a slap and he fell over. But 'twas too late.'

'The flight surgeon examined Paul. Found evidence of a blow. You say there was no blow?'

'I just told you that, laddie.'

'The flight surgeon must be wrong again?'

'Maybe he wasn't all that sharp that night.'

'It's your testimony, correct me if I'm wrong, it's your testimony that you burst in, saw Paul attempting to kill the girl, Maggie, and that he succeeded before you punched him out. Yes or no?'

'You got it right for once.'

'I'm glad to hear that. Let's now get to how you knew there was trouble in that room. What made you run up those stairs, burst into a private hotel-room without a warrant? With no authority to invade a private hotel-room?'

'I heard a rumpus. I told you before.'

'Mr Rudman and you were at his desk when you heard this "rumpus"?'

'Looking at the register. Often do that.'

'Why?'

'Make sure nothing funny's going on. That's all.'

'What does that mean?'

'Damn, don't you know? Making sure it's all respectable, like that.'

'It's in your rules and regulations that only married people can rent a hotel-room?'

'I'm the constable hereabouts. I do what I think to keep law and order, that's my job.'

'Do your rules and regulations allow you to carry your billy club?'

A long pause, looking for a trap, knowing I probably had a copy of them. 'Nothing in them forbids it, mate.' Good answer and quite right.

'Constable, you had a good view of the bar at the Huntington Arms from the front window. Where the menu is put. You looked in there that evening. Didn't you?'

'I don't recollect that.'

'You don't routinely look in to quote your words, "make sure nothing funny's going on?"'

'Not every night.'

'We are talking here about the evening of December 12, Constable.' He hesitated again, looking around the room. He could have been seen. People coming and going. Hard not to see that big, blue bulk looking in the window. He knew I could have elicited such testimony. Not a smart man, slow thinking, but wily.

'Could be, could be not. I don't recall.'

'And there by the fire, real chummy, was the girl you wanted to go with, who had rejected you, and a damn Yank. Right?'

'I told you, sonny, I don't remember looking in. Probably saw nothing, or didn't look in. I checked the register. I don't do that every night.'

'Did you know that Maggie and Paul were lovers?'

'No bloody way. Respectable girl, she was.'

'Lots of testimony in this record, Constable. All wrong?'

'I'd not believe it, mate.'

'She was in a hotel-room with Paul maybe forty, fifty times over the last year, Constable. And you didn't know. Always checking to make sure nothing funny's going on?'

'Don't believe a bit of it.'

'Why was she in his hotel-room?'

'Probably drugged her. Or got her drunk.' Constable O'Brien was beginning to fidget.

'Why was she at the Huntington Arms having drinks and dinner?'

'We all know the young lasses. Out for an innocent lark is all. We all know you Yanks have the money for it.'

'The testimony we heard is that she helped him up to the room. He was the one drugged and drunk.'

'Probably a ploy he used to get the lass up to his room. I know his kind.'

'The flight surgeon testified that by the time she helped him up to bed, he was a Zombie. Was he wrong?'

'Inexperienced in such matters.'

'The innkeeper testified to the same thing. Was he wrong?'

'Irv's a doddering old fool.'

'And hard of hearing, is that right?'

'Good God, I ain't his bloody doctor.'

'So you don't know if his hearing is impaired?'

'What do you take me for? I don't test the hearing of old fools, or young ones for that matter. I'm a policeman.'

'Mr Rudman testified that while you and he were at the front desk he didn't hear a rumpus upstairs. He also testified that his hearing is clear as a bell. Can you tell this court why you heard a rumpus and he didn't?'

'Mister,' he said, leaning forward menacingly, 'I don't have the foggiest idea about Rudman's hearing. I am telling you now that I heard a rumpus. I rushed up the stairs burst into the room to see a murder in progress.'

'Excuse me, Captain Helbig.'

'Colonel Hawkins?' I said.

'The witness has been on the stand since 1300 hours, and the court has been on the bench for the same time. I think we could all use a ten-minute break. Court adjourned for exactly ten minutes.'

This time, the APs let Paul join us in the witness-room for a smoke. No handcuffs. They had been in court throughout the trial and had made up their minds. Unfortunately they were not members of the court. And they had not been briefed by their supreme commander.

36

Court Martial, Day Six

'What, exactly, is a "rumpus" Constable?'
'Eh? I don't get your meaning.'
'Very well. Constable, based on your years of experience in police work and your intimate knowledge of the Huntington Arms, would you say that a loud scream would be heard all over the inn?'
'I suppose it would.'
'Even in the bar?'
'If the door to the hall was open.'
'You didn't hear a scream, did you, Constable?'
'Tricky question, right snide.' He glared at me.
'Please answer it.' The constable continued to glare at me. He knew where we were going and the blood rose again to his face. He had returned to the stand with his professional calm which now evaporated.
'No scream.'
'Then let's go back to my first question. What's a rumpus?'
'Noise.'
'Any kind of noise? A train going by, a jet screaming overhead?'
He stared at me without blinking, slowly raising his hand to stroke the mustache. 'Everybody knows what a rumpus is. You're playing games with me, sonny.'
'Maybe everybody else in the world, Constable, but I don't know and I'm asking the questions.'

'I told you, noise, sounds coming from a room that shouldn't be coming from a hotel-room. Based on my experience in police matters, it sounded like trouble at hand.'

'The dictionary defines a rumpus-room as a place for people to play, have parties. Sometimes people yell, laugh and knock over the chairs? That kind of rumpus, Constable?'

'No, you damn bugger, not that kind of rumpus.'

'Constable O'Brien, you are in a court of law.' Major Mills was almost menacing.

'Sorry, Your Honor. The man gets under me skin with all the stupid questions, same over and over again. Bugging me, Your Honor.'

'Constable. you are an experienced witness. You know that's his job. You also know Trial Counsel will object if the questions are improper. You're a bit old to have to be reminded of your manners.' The constable shifted in his chair and glared at an imperturbable Major Mills, who stared back, the handsome face set like a scene from *Thirty Seconds Over Tokyo*. The constable shifted his bulk so he again glared at me.

'No, Mr Barrister, not a fun-and-games sort of noise; a trouble-at-hand sort of noise.' He was still under control, teeth gritted, face flushed.

'You knew exactly which room?'

'Exactly.'

'You didn't knock to enquire?'

'No time for such nonsense.'

'Could the occupants of that room not have been playing blind man's bluff, or pin the tail on the donkey?'

'No.'

'Or a fun wrestling match?'

'No.'

'Or wild and passionate love?'

'No.' The voice was now rising.

'No knock to enquire?'

'No. I told you.'

'No search warrant?'
'I've told you.'
'Love to have that billy in your hands now, wouldn't you?'
'Objection.'
'I withdraw the question,' I said turning my back and going around the defense table. 'I have no further questions.' There were, of course a lot more questions. But I knew I wouldn't get answers, only denials. Questions like that are useless, defeating.

Major Sully conferred briefly with his co-counsel and advised the court he had no questions.

'Defense rests.'

Major Sully, read from his script: 'The prosecution has nothing further to offer. Does the defense have any further evidence to offer?'

'Defense rests,' I said, probably too sharply.

'Does the court wish to have witnesses called or recalled?'

'No.'

'Is the defense going to offer closing argument?'

'Yes.'

'Then the prosecution reserves its right to make closing argument.'

'Oh, very well, Trial Counsel. It's Saturday afternoon. I'll give you both time to prepare. We'll adjourn until 0900 hours tomorrow.' Colonel Hawkins banged his gavel. He got up wearily.

'I'd like to see Counsel in chambers,' Major Mills said, gathering his papers and following the court members out.

We all sat around Major Mills's desk, waiting while he carefully cut and lighted a long, black cigar. When it was billowing smoke and glowing red he smiled at us all.

'A difficult trial, gentlemen, quite taxing. I'm sure there will be hell to pay here in the good old UK. Trying to sweep their garbage under our rug. Typically British.'

'What do you mean, Major?' Major Sully asked.

'Well, naturally, I'm going to order that a transcript of this case be sent to their Home Office and New Scotland Yard. Give them back their garbage.'

'I still don't think I understand, Major.'

Major Mills puffed his cigar and stared at Major Sully uncomprehendingly. 'And I don't think I understand you, Major. One of their own has murdered a young girl. They've got to bring him to trial. Nice try giving us jurisdiction of what should have been their trial. Now the garbage is back in their backyard and they'll have to live with it. I should imagine the tabloids here will have a field day. Don't understand why the base commander went along.'

'But Paul Kelly?'

'Good God, man. The only thing they can find Paul guilty of is being AWOL a couple of hours.'

Major Sully stared at Major Mills. I do not think that it had occurred to him that Paul had not killed the girl. He did not gape, open-mouthed as people do in all the better novels; he just sat and stared, digesting what the law officer had said so offhandedly.

'You forgot one thing, Major,' I said. The cigar swung in my direction. 'Command influence.' The words hung there like dirty linen.

After a long, uncomfortable silence, Major Mills removed the cigar from his mouth. 'I'll not listen to anything of that sort. Frankly, I think that's beneath you, Captain. Well, how long will you be in summation?'

'It's not beneath Colonel J.J. Smith, Major. I'll be an hour or less.'

'Major Sully?'

'Half-hour or less.'

'Fine. So by the latest, the court will be closed by 1100 hours. If I know the colonel, they'll go right through lunch if necessary. Have a decision by 1300 hours, 1400 if they break for lunch.' He was talking to himself, not us. By 1500 hours, we'll be on our way. Pack tonight, be home tomorrow.'

37

Court Martial, Day Seven

'Members of the court,' I began, nervous as always, 'I hope, most fervently, that you will listen to the instructions from the judge at the close of the case. I know how boring it can get up there where you sit. The law is a ponderous, slow and tedious machine, but ultimately, it grinds very fine. Imperfect as it all is, it remains the best system of justice so far that mankind has been able to devise.

'In his instructions, Major Mills will make four points. Those are not his views or opinions. That's the law. He will say the accused stands before you innocent and so presumed until proven otherwise. Point one. He will say the law is that if you have a reasonable doubt as to guilt, it must ... *must* be resolved in favor of the accused. Point two.

'He will say you must find a lower degree of crime if the higher one is not satisfactory to you beyond a reasonable doubt. Point three. And lastly and most important to any defendant, the burden of proof is upon the government. We don't have to prove Paul innocent. We have to prove nothing. Paul, by law, is cloaked in the presumption of innocence unless and until he is found on the legal evidence to be guilty of the crimes charged ... beyond a reasonable doubt.

'Major Mills is not required to charge you, as is customary in the state and federal courts, as to what constitutes a reasonable doubt. I hereby request he do so before you begin your deliberations. I request it because the burden on the prosecution is awesome. But then, the way a case is set up against a defendant, an accused faces an awesome opponent. In New York, the case would be listed as "The People of the State of New York versus Paul R. Kelly". That's pretty heavy. But no way near as heavy as "The United States versus Paul R. Kelly".

'Heavy? No, actually overwhelming. The United States against one airman. All of the might and majesty of the greatest nation on earth pitted against one lone airman. An airman who had to get himself one freebie lawyer, a relative. Appointed Counsel, Military Counsel, has freely admitted that he is a novice who has never tried a major case.

'And so the Government of the United States of America has aligned itself against one airman, a sergeant, and his brother-in-law. The resources of the United States are unlimited; the resources of Paul Kelly are non-existent. In fairness, therefore, the government, by law, lays the heaviest of burdens on its prosecutors. It says, in effect, you got all the juice, so you must bear the burden of proof beyond any reasonable doubt.

'In the case of the United States versus Paul R. Kelly, has the government met that burden of proof? You have been a most attentive jury. I will not insult your collective intelligence by reviewing the case, witness for witness. I think every person in this room knows that Paul Kelly didn't kill. He didn't intend to rape. And the so-called AWOL was no more or less than any man in this room has done. Take off from work a couple of hours early.

'Paul has a wife and kids back in the States. Separated for fourteen months. He wasn't away from his family two months when he started an illicit, extra-marital affair. If he was charged with that, I wouldn't be here. I suspect that Paul would have carried on that affair if his wife and kids had been able to join him. I've known Paul a long time. He's no saint; he's probably not even a very moral person, and I know he's no church-goer. If he were charged with any of those things, he'd be on his own as far as I'm concerned.

'But that is not what he is charged with. He is charged with attempting to rape and then murdering his paramour.

'The scenario here is pretty clear, I think. Constable J.J. O'Brien's wife ran off with an American. Constable J.J. O'Brien spent many years in the R.U.C. in Northern Ireland. We know from both testimony and our observations that he is a violent man whom you do not dare cross. A man who whacks people.

'On the night of December 12, Constable J.J. O'Brien peered in the window of the bar of the Huntington Arms. And there, lovey-dovey with an American was a young lady who had spurned his advances.

'I seriously doubt that Constable J.J. O'Brien has ever considered that if it had not been for us, he'd be writing his parking tickets in German. What he does know is that his wife ran off with an American and that the object of his affection was holding hands with one – having told him to buzz off.

'He saw them leave the bar, ran into the inn and grabbed the register to see which room the lovers had gone to. Then he pounded up the stairs, burst into the room, and in a rage, beat Maggie Kellogg to death.

'This is all so obvious, I will not the labor the point, I'm not here to prove it, although I think it's proved itself. My burden is not to prove Paul innocent. My burden is merely to establish a reasonable doubt as to his guilt.

'I think we've succeeded in that. I remind you only of the testimony of Dr Hung, our flight surgeon.

'What I think that I have to overcome in this courtroom is not showing that the Govenment of the United States has failed to meet its burden of proof; what I believe we have to overcome is something more ominous than the non-existent case assembled against Paul.'

'Mr President, may I have one moment?'

Colonel Hawkins nodded. I left the side of the table, sat down next to Paul and leaned across to CD. 'You still think I'm wrong?' I asked CD.

'You'll insult the court, the entire military,' CD whispered.

'If it's not in the record, it will never be part of the review.'

CD stared straight ahead and shrugged, his face flushed.

'Do it, Knute. God damn, my money's riding on you. Do it. I'd as soon be hung for a cattle-thief as a horse-thief. Do it,' Paul whispered. I got up, took a gulp of water and took my place next to the table. This courtroom had no lectern.

'Thank you, Mr President. Gentlemen of the court. The fact is, in this case, it is not really the entire Government of the United States that wants Paul hung out to dry. The charges were brought, the court martial convened by a very local convening authority. Paul is charged not by the United States but by the Wing Commander of RAF Singlebury, on behalf of our government.

'If you want to know, as I want to know, why a killing on British soil of a British subject is being tried in an American court, don't expect an answer. Not a real answer. I asked the question. The answer was that it was by agreement between Her Majesty's Government and the Government of the United States. There is, I was told, precedent. Although that precedent was in Germany, an occupied country at the time.

'The true answer is that the convening authority has no authority in a British court. But he does have authority over a court martial he convenes on his base. He appoints the investigating officer; he appoints the trial counsel and defense.

'And . . . he appoints the members of the court.

'Colonel Smith gave me a very few minutes of his valuable time. He advised me that "no Jew-boy New York City shyster" was going to come between him and a conviction. I was very flattered he thought I was a Jewish lawyer from New York City. They are among the very best trial lawyers in the country. But I was very disturbed by the implications.

'The implications are the dirtiest word in the military: "command influence".

'I pray that it has nothing to do with this trial. Thank you.'

The courtroom was utterly still. No leather soles scraping on the concrete floor, no rustling of papers, no coughs. The unpardonable had been uttered and entered forever into the transcript of trial.

Telling a roomful of cardinals that the pope had syphilis would not be as shocking. Major Mills looked at me quizzically. Colonel Hawkins stared at me with open hostility. Except for Captain Leone, the other members of the court stared straight ahead. Captain Leone looked at me with interest. He had not been on the original team. He was a sub. He had not attended the wing commander's briefing of the other members of the court.

I drank some water and waited. Paul slouched in his chair for the first time. CD, his face flushed, stared at a far wall, his fingers turning a pencil over between thumb and forefinger, over and over.

'Major Sully,' Major Mills said at last. Major Sully's back had been turned while I spoke. He had not turned to look at me. Now he rose and looked at me steadily before turning back to address the court. The normally cherubic face was drained of all blood, like a skull left to bleach in a desert sun. His hands shook with his anger.

'In all my years in the military,' he began in a raspy voice, 'in all my years as a trial counsel, I have never for myself, my base commander, and for the court, felt so abused. Never has an opposing counsel stooped so low. I gave Counsel every courtesy, even when he took it upon himself to charge the jury, the job for our judge.

'But,' he now fairly shouted as the blood raced back into his face, 'but what has happened here is quite unforgivable. Counsel's job in summation is to comment on the evidence. To stress what is helpful to his side and gloss over damaging evidence. Here, there is no way he can gloss over the evidence, no way to stress anything helpful. Instead he goes on and on about how tough it is to fight the whole Government of the United States. As though every case in all our federal courts isn't just the same.

'And then he has the temerity to tell this court that the only thing he has to fear is that you officers of this court could be influenced by command. Never in all my years have I heard a court and the commander so insulted.

'Well, gentlemen, the accused,' he said, turning and shaking a finger in Paul's direction, 'is guilty as charged. We have proven that. And no amount of implied threats or slick maneuvers can change that fact. Paul R. Kelly is a rapist and a murderer. We have an eyewitness to murder.

'I ask you to find true each specification of each charge and when the time for sentencing comes, I will ask the ultimate punishment. Thank you.' He turned to glare at me and then turned his back and sat down.

Major Mills said, 'Has the prosecution anything further to offer?'

'It has not.'

'Has the defense anything further to offer?'

'No, sir.'

'Very well, I will now charge the court as to the law. And although unusual in a military trial, I shall honor Individual Counsel's request and charge you with the elements of what constitutes reasonable doubt. This is not usual in a military trial since members of the courts are not civilians picked off the street from motor-vehicle records, but generally well-educated officers.'

Ouch.

He continued in some detail outlining the charges and specifications as though he were talking to a bunch of ignorant people off the street, picked from MVB files for jury duty. He then went on to the charge on which I had stolen the march and the rest of the instructions which were given in all American courts of law. Lastly he read the definition of what constitutes reasonable doubt, as I had requested.

In essence, that charge merely says that to convict, a jury need not be convinced beyond "all doubt". To acquit, a juror must find a reason to have doubt. Whatever all that means. Except for a fanatic, one can never remove *all* doubt.

'The court will be closed,' Major Mills said and the members of the court filed out to begin deliberating. It was only 1030 hours; Major Mills must be pleased, I thought.

'It's Miller time,' Paul said softly, standing up. 'Knute, you did a helluva job, win, lose, draw, win, place, show. I appreciate everything. Sorry you got whacked on my account.' He sauntered to the back of the room for his AP escort back to the stockade to await his fate.

'CD?'

'I think you blew it all in summation. I also agree with Major Sully: you insulted every man in this room.'

He turned without shaking hands and walked out of the building.

Major Mills climbed down from his honorific position, attaché-case in hand. 'Could I see you, Captain?'

'Sure.'

'The base has a nice gym and a steam room. I want to loosen up and relax. Join me?'

'Why not?'

The major had been assigned a Plymouth and we drove to the other end of the field without speaking, changed into towels and after a shower, entered the wet heat. As soon as I stretched out on the wooden bench I realized that Major Mills had taught me something just great. I had never before gone into a steam room after a trial. I was always wound up like an overwound clock and tried always to ease back down with booze. This was the right way to do it.

After maybe half an hour, the steam room was all ours. I was sleepy. I was relaxed.

'Why?'

'Why what, Major?'

'You know my given name. The trial's over. But why? You blew the case wide open. Why fuck it up in summation? The court loved you. They love Paul. Everybody came to know it was a frame. Why?'

'Major, sorry, Hank. The wing commander/base commander called in the members of the court. Except for Leone, he's a pinch hitter. He told them he wanted Paul's ass. That's like an order to convict.'

'They wouldn't do that.' Honest indignation.

'These guys are all good men. But they need the military as much as the military needs them. They need the job. And the job says find this miserable fuck guilty. He has their life, their future, their wives and kids in his hands.'

'I can't believe you.'

'Hank, you remember in the old Bible . . . God tells one of the guys to slay his son, his only son. That's God talking. The guy's prepared to do it. Well, man, God talked to the court. You don't fuck-over God.'

'I don't believe they'd do it.'

'The toughest jump in the military is from Lieutenant Colonel to Bird Colonel. Colonel Smith is up for brigadier general. Lieutenant Colonel John Hawkins is up for the Bird Colonel. All the Pentagon can really rely on is his latest efficiency report. Colonel Smith will make that report. It puts the best man in the world between a rock and a very hard place. He's got four kids. He has a great combat record, lots of decorations. Laid his ass on the line in two wars. It can all come crashing down in one day. 'The day he votes against the man who can make him or break him.

'I can't blame him. That's why I gave him an out. It's risky, I know, but one of those guys might very well pick up on it.'

'Counselor, I'll admit you lost me.'

'Hopefully, one of them will say that I know they met with the commander. NCOs stick together, so they'll know, maybe, I know about the meeting. Fact is, I do. That meet might even be on tape. They'll never know that until after a verdict. My best guess is that at least one of them will contact the CO. If they vote to convict, the record will allow me to prove the CO's order to convict. Once I got command influence into the record, the reviewing authorities can't sweep it under a rug. It's there now.

'That does not look good for a guy who has his name before Congress to become a brigadier general. Kiss of death. Also that line about the Jew-boy lawyer. Won't sit well.'

'You're some devious fuck, Helbig.'

'That's another word for lawyer.'

'Helbig, you're one of the rare, almost extinct three-prong bastards. I love it. Come back on active duty.'

'Sure, and you'll assign me to Major Sully and Colonel Smith. Thanks for nothing.'

'Tell me one more thing, Helbig: did the colonel really call you a New York City shyster or was that also just for the record?'

'I got it on tape, Judge. Want to hear it? It's clear as a bell. We use the best recording equipment in the world. Jap stuff.'

'Jesus, you are a devious bastard.'

'Another name for lawyer,' I said.

38

Court Martial, Day Seven, p.m.

Major Mills and I had finished our lunch in the officers' club and were drinking coffee when a telephone call advised us to return to court. He had packed the night before but his shuttle to Heathrow was not leaving until 1600 hours. It was now just 1300. Also, the court might have questions of law, rather than a verdict.

The members of the court were in their places when we returned to the courtroom; CD was at the defense table; Paul was not. Assistant Trial Counsel was at the prosecution table. Major Sully was not. The stenographer was behind her machine, one leg under her, the other on the floor. She was buffing her nails.

'Everybody's been notified, Stenographer?' Colonel Hawkins asked.

'Yes, sir.'

Just then, Major Sully hurried into the courtroom. His face was flushed as though he'd just tossed off a couple of stiff ones.

Colonel Hawkins said, 'The court will come to order.'

Major Sully replied, 'All parties to the trial who were present when the court closed are now present except the accused, Paul R. Kelly, sir.'

'Major, don't you think it would be appropriate to have the accused present? This does concern him, don't you think?' The colonel sounded his usual gruff self, but it struck me that he was almost making an attempt at a funny.

COMMAND INFLUENCE

'Yes, sir. The stockade was the first notified, sir. I don't know what's holding him up, but I can make another call, sir.'

'We'll give it a few more minutes. I know how busy our air police are.' We waited. The spectator section was filled with NCOs and I could hear the murmur of whispered voices behind me.

'I'm sorry I mouthed off, Knute,' CD whispered.

'Nerves, CD, it's been a hectic couple of weeks.' I looked at the unlined face and had to grin. These had undoubtedly been the most stressful weeks of his short, happy life. I hoped for him that he'd never have any more like them. He was a good kid and he would be a good man who would never, back in Michigan, milk either his cows or his clients beyond their ability to produce.

Paul came in with his AP escorts and slid into the chair between CD and me. I wanted to give him a keep-your-apples-up grin, but I could not. He was ashen and his entire six foot two was trembling. He purposefully kept his hands under the table.

I had never before defended anyone. I had no idea of the trauma of these moments of knowing your fate had been sealed and yet not knowing what that fate was to be. Now, for the first time, I learned what it was like to know you have an innocent sitting next to you whom you may have failed. There are not many innocent people brought to trial anymore. Maybe over charged, but not innocent. Not even in Alabama or Mississippi.

Not *many* people.

But it happens.

God.

Colonel Hawkins said, 'I would ask the accused to rise and face the court.' I nudged Paul and he got to his feet, very slowly. CD and I rose with him. 'I, Lieutenant Colonel John M. Hawkins, as president of this Court will now advise you as follows:' He pulled the *Manual for Court Martial* toward him. It is my duty as president of this court to advise you that the court in closed session and upon secret written ballot. . . .'

I didn't have to listen any further. I had read the manual. The president of the court follows one of two sentencing guidlines. In the first of the guidelines, he uses the words 'advise you'. In the second set of instructions he reads 'to inform you'.

Colonel Hawkins read from the first set of instructions. The footnote says: 'If the accused is found not guilty of all specifications, the president announces: it is my duty as President of this Court to *advise* you'.

'Further,' Colonel Hawkins said, now no longer reading from the manual, 'the court directs Trial Counsel to inform Personnel that Paul is to be transferred from this base forthwith.

'The court stands adjourned.' Colonel Hawkins, followed by the members of the court trooped out in silence. Asshole that I am, I had to wipe some budding tears that were beginning to form. Paul stared at me for the moment and then he leaned over and hugged me. Behind us, the spectator section erupted like a long dormant volcano. Paul had tears in his eyes also. He kept hugging me and pushing me away so he could look at me.

"Jaysus," he finally said, hugging me and rubbing his palm across the top of my head. And then we were surrounded by uniforms, blue uniforms, fatigue uniforms. Above the hubbub, Major Mills said, 'Congratulations. You were right. Think about coming back to active duty. I promise you won't be sent back here.'

'I hope you get to enjoy some of Spain, Major.'

Sergeant Major Hamilton pumped my hand. 'This here party is going to be on the NCO Club. Starting about right now.' There were a lot of cheers and shouting. Free booze draws a crowd.

'Knute, thanks for everything. I promise you I'll never try cases back in Michigan. Good luck and God bless.' That's the last time I ever saw CD. I hope I was more help than hindrance.

Suddenly, Colonel Hawkins was there, shaking my hand. 'I respect what you did, the chance you took. I just wanted to tell you that you could be my RO anytime.'

'Colonel, that's the best thing anyone ever said to me.'

'Be well, Captain,' he said, and ducked out.

A moment later, *sans* Churchill, Inspector Anthony 'Ruff' Lane was at my elbow. 'There were times I had my doubts about you, laddie. But now, I say you be good enough for my niece. What plans have you, lad?'

'Tonight, to get wiped. Tomorrow, to go home.'

'There's some lads from New Scotland Yard who wish to speak with you.'

'I'll be in London, waiting for the first flight out.'

'The jolliest haven't arrested the constable yet. He's a mean sort so I'll be sticking to you like glue, me and Churchill. When you sober up, I'll be driving you to London. We'll muddle through your flight plans all right. And your intended will fly you home, Yank. I mean she'll be there for you to fetch your cocktails.'

'Great. But I think right about now, I need a drink.' I got my drink. I had a lot of drinks. All I remember is waking up in the dark, thirsty as hell. And stumbling over Churchill and Ruff, on the floor by the draughty door. Ruff didn't stir, nor touch his double-barrelled shotgun. Churchill didn't growl. Drunk as I was, I knew that I was not only very well protected, I was also a prisoner.

39

The heavy ground fog matched my mood, the taste in my mouth and pounding in my skull, particularly behind my eyes. We bounced along in the mini pick-up truck without a heater, the inspector cheerful and talkative. He had packed a thermos of strong, black tea, no sugar or lemon or milk, and meat loaf sandwiches. I sipped at the tea and nibbled a bit, but it took some time for my Alka-Selzer to settle my stomach and stop the pounding in my head.

Inspector Lane was going on enthusiastically about the countryside we were coming into, the Cotswolds. I began to feel better. A thin few rays of sunshine, my first in England, swept up the fog, and here and there a bit of blue sky peeked enticingly through the high cloud cover. Unlike the area around the base, we were now coming into rolling, wooded country with streams and little lakes. We went slowly through small villages that looked like John Ford had designed them for his movie, *The Quiet Man*. Little stone villages with slate or thatched roofs, little shops and inns, cobblestone streets. One village in particular, Broadway, really turned me on and I wanted very much to stop and look around. This is what I had expected of the English countryside, not the bleakness of the past days.

Ruff Lane and his niece had worked out all the details. My very comfortable and warm London hotel room near Piccadilly, the Warwick – no charge. A dinner of Dover sole with asparagus in browned butter at the Savoy Grill – no charge. Several bottles of wine tasted very good to my untrained palette and my first order of crêpes Suzette, literally, between the taste and the alcohol, put me on cloud nine.

The inspector even had the clout to have two inspectors from New Scotland Yard come to the hotel instead of my going to the Yard. We met in the bar. That room divided the customers who came in off the street from those who came from the hotel lobby by a partial partition. Same long bar, same bartenders, but the tables and booths and the bar itself separated.

The inspectors were both young and in apparent awe of Ruff. I don't think, based on my limited experience, that the British are ever obsequious, but these two came close. They spent about twenty minutes going over the matter of Constable John J. O'Brien. The next two hours or so, we talked about 'the job'.

The inspector had a room next to mine with an open connecting door. Churchill, however, was assigned to the foot of my bed. The constable was not yet in custody.

I slept the sleep of the just and the drunk, dreamless for nine and a half hours. I awoke to the smell of strong coffee and bacon coming from the connecting room. The hotel supplied bathrobes and I slipped one on and went to what Ruff said was a typical English breakfast, which is undoubtedly why cholesterol is a number one killer in the British Isles. But good.

And now, after an escort through Heathrow, no passport check, no luggage check, I boarded for my return flight. The inspector and his niece had it all worked out. She was on the flight. She would have a two-day layover at Kennedy. She was, however, assigned to first class, and poor me, I was in tourist on a crowded flight. The inspector took me aboard and seated me next to a window seat. He leaned over me, oblivious to the hoard of noisy, shoving passengers.

'Farewell and God's speed, lad.'

I tried to get up but he pushed me back into my seat. 'I will never know how to thank you.'

'You have, laddie you have. You brought down O'Brien. I've fought his type my whole damn life.' And he was gone.

Epilogue

The jury returned to the courtroom at 2.30 in the afternoon, six men, one of them a black history teacher, six women, three of them black. Our county has a small minority population. It had taken some effort to assure a jury that could not be labeled racist. White cop, black killer. That was a card I did not want played if there was a conviction.

From their faces as they filed into the jury box, I could read nothing. They did not look at me, at Defense Counsel or at the defendant. Four and a half hours was not a long deliberation in a first-degree murder trial. They had worked through their lunch hour, but it had been a three-week trial. In a criminal case all twelve jurors have to agree on conviction or acquittal. If they cannot, then they report to the judge that they are "hung". The judge can then instruct them to go back to their deliberations and keep trying, or he declares a mistrial and discharges the jury. The prosecution must then decide whether to try the defendant again.

The jurors knew from the onset of the case, from jury selection, that this was a capital case, that they would have to decide guilt or innocence and, if they convicted, then would still have to hear evidence for and against the death penalty and decide between life and death. No one could say how long that phase of the trial would take and all had been away from their normal life for three weeks. A heavy burden on the prosecution, I thought. It had been easier for prosecutors under Mario Cuomo. As governor, every year he vetoed the death penalty law passed by the legislature. But with the advent of Governor Potaki, the bill was signed into law and we prosecutors could no longer bitch about how we needed the death penalty while in reality hating the extra burden it placed on us.

Asking a juror to decide guilt or innocence is a heavy enough burden. But within reason, because the juror knew that a judge, not he, would decide what penalty fitted the crime. A juror could tell himself there might be no penalty or a slight one. But now in a first-degree murder case, the juror knew he would also have to decide life or death. That, perhaps, is asking too much. Judges get paid for that: jurors hardly get carfare.

If this jury acquits, they could be home within an hour and not face jury duty again for three years. If they convict, they are stuck in this courthouse for more days. All of these thoughts came to me as the jury was seated, all staring blankly at nothing as the bailiff yelled.

All through this trial my mind went back constantly to the trial of Paul R. Kelly, the ex-brother-in-law from whom I had not heard since his court martial.... For some perverse reason, I had asked my overly efficient secretary, Jenny, not only to find out what had happened to Paul, but also all the characters I had been involved with during the days I had spent at RAF Singlebury as though I planned a thirty-year reunion. Of course, Mary and I were in quite close touch with her uncle, Ex-Inspector Anthony 'Ruff' Lane of New Scotland Yard. Ruff had given Mary away at our wedding in Rumford. He was still a consultant to the Yard. His child-mistress was married, a doctor with three children in Manchester. I had met her husband, also a doctor.

'All rise, the Honorable Alfred C. Keegan.'

County Court Judge Keegan swept into his seat, his robes swishing. 'Please be seated.' He waited as we all took our seats. This used to be the most adrenalin moment in my young life. Now it seemed like coronary time.

'Has the jury reached a verdict?'

'We have, Your Honor,' the history teacher, foreman of the jury, said, rising.

'What is your verdict?'

'In the case of the People of the State of New York versus Tyrone Jackson, charged with murder in the first degree, we the jury find the defendant guilty as charged.' The jury foreman sat down and there was total silence in the courtroom.

Defense Attorney Ken Jason Jones was the first to recover. He jumped up. 'Poll the jury,' he said huskily, 'I don't believe this.' If there was a racist in this courtroom, it was Ken Jason Jones. He could not believe four black people would vote a black man guilty of killing a white man.

The bailiff polled the jury. Each stood as they were called and answered the question: 'Is this your verdict?' with the answer 'Yes.'

'Ladies and gentlemen of the jury, I want to thank you for your attention to this case, for your careful deliberations and your patience with attorneys for both sides and the many delays. As you know from the *voir dire, you* not I, now in 1999 must decide whether the defendant spends the rest of his natural life incarcerated, or be put to death under our laws. I regret the changes in our laws that place the burden upon you instead of the judge. Be that as it may, I shall now, thanking you again, allow you a two days' respite while we prepare for the second phase of the case.'

Judge Keegan banged his gavel and swished off the bench. Bailiffs manacled and removed Tyrone Jackson. Ken Jason Jones gathered up his papers and glowered at me. The press, all but artists and journalists who had been barred, came leaping in with their television machines. It was a sort of circus affair, and I got out of it, into the elevator and up to the top floor. I knew that shortly I would have to meet the madness, make a statement and answer questions. But right now, I did what I had learned years ago, I took the service elevator to my car and went for a steam bath.

After the mandatory press conference, it was well after five in the afternoon by then, Jim Walsh and I were among the few still in the office building. He would be handling the second phase of the trial, the death-sentence hearing. I was not a big advocate of the death sentence. It took about seven years for a death sentence to go through the appeals process, at an astronomical cost of millions of dollars. Incarceration costs about $40,000 a year versus about $20,000 to send a youngster through a good college. All of this did not and does not make much sense to me.

'Boss, you don't give a flying fuck do you, about how it comes out? I mean if Tyrone goes to Hell sooner or later?'

'Jim, just so he's off the streets. Either way, it's too damn expensive. Our legal system has problems; it costs too damn much either way.'

"Yeah, well, I brought you a little of the twelve-year-old Jamieson. Will you have a nip?'

'Sure. Mary's uncle got me started on Jamieson. He's still doing some kind of cops and robbers work. Sure, I'll have a snort. Then, I'm going home. I guess after this, I won't have to campaign too much.'

At this point, overly efficient Jenny came into the office. 'I'm about to leave, boss. But I got your nostalgia package together. With no little effort. The military does not like giving out any information, and your Paul Kelly was a bitch to track down. Anyway, here's what you wanted.' She made a slight curtsy and sashayed out.

As always with Jenny, it was letter perfect.

Paul R. Kelly. Discharged, Master Sergeant, honorable, full benefits, June 7, 1976. Last assignment, instructor, Wiesbaden, Germany. Divorced, July 19, 1976, married Karen Schneider, German National, August 14, 1976. Motel operator, Marietta, Georgia, January, 1977 through 1988; convicted for fraud and sentenced to one year, Marietta County Prison. Divorced, March 17, 1999. Croupier, Mississippi Riverboat, Biloxi, Mississippi, January 15, 1990 to the present. Arrested for sexual abuse of a fifteen year old. Charges not prosecuted. Married to same.

In red ink Jenny wrote under the typewritten report, 'Gee, your bro-in-law is some dude. Introduce me sometime.'

Technical Sergeant Conyers is retired and back in Japan with his wife.
Sergeant Major Hamilton is retired, running a general store and doing a lot of hunting.
Technical Sergeant Quirk McQuirk is married, living in Canada and running a delivery service.
Captain C.D. Day is practicing law in his hometown in Michigan. He does not try cases.
Lieutenant Colonel John Hawkins is a brigadier general in charge of a South Asia command.
Colonel J.J. Smith was killed in a routine training flight over Norway. He was never promoted.
Constable John J. O'Brien spent thirteen years in prison and then disappeared.
Major Henry DeWitt Mills is now a full colonel, stationed at the Pentagon.

I shoved Jenny's notes across the desk. Jim read them quickly and grinned his disarming grin which the juries loved.

'I'm with Jenny. Your boy is something else. Getting three quarters of his base income tax free, free medical and making all that gambling money also damn near tax free. And a teeny-bopper wife. More fun than we ever had, Knute!'

'I think I'd like that drink, Jim. A big one.'

We had a drink. No, we had two drinks, straight. Good thing I had a driver to take me home. As they say in the military: RHIP – rank has its privileges.